Fury
of the Dragon
Goddess

SARWAT CHADDA

RICK RIORDAN PRESENTS

DISNEP • HYPERION

Los Angeles New York

First Edition, August 2023
1 3 5 7 9 10 8 6 4 2
FAC-004510-23167
Printed in the United States of America

This book is set in Palatino LT Std, Adorn Roman,
Stone Informal ITC Pro, Palatino LT Std/Fontspring
Designed by Jamie Alloy and Tyler Nevins

Library of Congress Cataloging-in-Publication Data
Names: Chadda, Sarwat, author.
Title: Fury of the dragon goddess / Sarwat Chadda.
Description: First edition. • Los Angeles : Disney Hyperion, 2023. •
"Rick Riordan Presents." • Audience: Ages 8–12. • Audience: Grades 4–6. •
Summary: "When the ancient Tablet of Destinies falls into the wrong hands,
it is up to Sikander Aziz and his friends to save humanity from having its
future erased by two fearsome Mesopotamian gods"—Provided by publisher.
Identifiers: LCCN 2022025099 • ISBN 9781368081825 (hardcover) •
ISBN 9781368081917 (ebk)
Subjects: CYAC: Mythology, Assyro-Babylonian—
Fiction. • Gods—Fiction. • Goddesses—Fiction.
Classification: LCC PZ7.C343 Fu 2023 • DDC [Fic]—dc22
LC record available at https://lccn.loc.gov/2022025099
Reinforced binding

Follow @ReadRiordan

Visit www.DisneyBooks.com

SUSTAINABLE FORESTRY INITIATIVE — Certified Sourcing
www.forests.org
SFI-01681

Logo Applies to Text Stock Only

To Sarah, for having faith

Then she gave him the Tablet of Destinies
and made him clasp it to his breast.
"Your utterance shall never be altered!
Your word shall be law!"

—*The Epic of Creation,* translated by Stephanie Dalley

ONE

"ASSALAMU ALAIKUM, SIK!"

"Waa alai— Ooof!"

Daoud grabbed me at the door of the hotel suite when I arrived and literally hugged me off my feet. Ya salam! The guy gave super-strength hugs. But just as I was starting to suffocate, he dropped me to give me a good once-over. He grinned as he rubbed my cheek with the back of his hand. "Mashallah! Is that stubble?"

"I *am* fourteen, Daoud," I muttered. That said, I was a little proud of the few hairs I was cultivating. My English teacher thought they gave me a "bad-boy intensity," and don't tell anyone, but I was also practicing the "slow squint," a total alpha-male move. When you get it right, your enemies tremble and the girls swoon.

I dropped my suitcase and took in the view. "A big change from the deli, isn't it?"

The ceiling had to be the height of our apartment building back home, and the chandeliers reflected a constellation of light over the enormous living room. Floor-to-ceiling windows looked out over Green Park, with golden sunlight streaming in and the ivory gauze curtains shifting in the warm breeze. The wall paintings sat in ornate gilt frames, and the Ming vase beside the door was overflowing with wild orchids. The scent off those flowers lifted me into a dream. It felt otherworldly, which, I suppose, it was. I was a long, long way from my home in Manhattan.

"You like? The agency insisted I stay at the Ritz." Daoud turned his head so I could get a good look at his profile. "*Cosmopolitan* called me 'the hottest thing to come out of the desert since the racehorse.'"

Weird as that comparison was, the more I thought about it, the more it fit. Daoud's mane—very black, very shiny—was wild and loose, and he had soft, light brown eyes. There was a long-limbed sleekness to him, coupled with a natural grace. Back when he worked for my parents, no one had chopped cabbage with as much elegance.

I tested out the armchair. *Very* comfortable. "Fame and fortune at last, eh?"

"The good times are to be shared, cuz! Just wait till you check out your room. The bathtub's so huge you could swim laps in it! And you can hear Big Ben chiming from your balcony!"

⚔️〰️

"I have a balcony?"

Hey, don't judge! All I had back home was a cracked windowsill with a few miserable-looking plants lined along it.

"Sorry I missed your birthday. Did you get my presents? Wait..." Daoud sniffed deeply. "Hugo Boss body lotion. Lancôme shampoo, and is that...the sandalwood underarm deodorant? Always keep that close. It's a teen boy's best friend."

"There's no way you can tell all that with a sniff," I replied, resisting the urge to check my armpits. "Can you?"

He tapped his nose. "This doesn't lie, Sik. How are your parents?"

"Good. They send their salaams."

"I sent tickets for them, too, y'know. They could have come with." He gestured to the rest of the suite. "Room for everyone."

I shrugged. "When was the last time Baba and Mama took a break from the deli? Summer's their busiest time."

"Yeah, poor workaholics." Daoud slung his arm over my shoulder. "Anyway, I'm gonna show you the sights, cuz. There's no place like London!"

Yeah!

London! In England! Land of kings and queens, afternoon tea, and driving on the wrong side of the street. I'd almost been run over twice, and I'd only been here an hour.

It was a shame Mama and Baba hadn't been able to make it, but I hadn't come alone. I looked over my shoulder. "She was just here."

Then I heard yapping down the hallway, and all my alarm bells went off. "Just a second, Daoud."

I ran back into the marble-clad corridor and found her by the elevator bank, next to an old woman and her poodle. Rabisu was squatting down and tickling the dog's ears. Her turban—pure 1940s Hollywood—was partially unraveled, revealing a pair of stubby horns. Fortunately, her floor-length kaftan covered the rest of her demon form.

"What a tasty little animal," said Rabisu.

The old woman tittered. "She is, isn't she? Say hello, Fifi."

The dog yapped, and Rabisu licked her lips. "She looks good enough to eat."

I reached them and looped my arm through Rabisu's. "Say good-bye to the sweet lady and her *pet*."

Rabisu huffed with indignation. "I wasn't going to eat it!"

The elevator door pinged open, and the woman hurried in with Fifi. Looking a little scared, she punched the buttons until the doors closed.

Phew. That was a close one. "You remember what I said about lying?"

"Fine. I *was* going to eat it," snapped Rabisu. "You have such strange rules about eating creatures. Chickens, good. People, bad. Cows, yes. Horses, no. Dogs . . . depending on if they have a name or not."

"And that dog has a name, so it's off the menu." I took her by the claw. "Come on. Daoud's waiting."

Rabisu tried to straighten her disheveled turban, and a moment later, we were back in Daoud's suite, where he was pouring out iced tea. "Rabisu, this is Daoud. Daoud, this is Rabisu."

Rabisu cleared her throat loudly.

"Really?" I asked her. "Fine. Daoud, this is Rabisu, the terror of Nimrud. The battlefield stalker whose very name makes . . ."

"Makes the udders of cows shrivel," Rabisu prompted.

"Yeah, the udder shriveler. And there was that thing about the camels losing their humps in fright, and something about how the Chaldeans built a mountain of skulls in your honor. That's all of it, right?"

Rabisu held out a claw to Daoud, just like I'd taught her. "Rabisu, the demon of deformities. Not that you have any. Unless you'd like some?"

To Daoud's total credit, he didn't bat an eye. His smile just switched to full charm as he shook her claw. "Assalamu alaikum, Rabisu. I love the horns."

⩗⧈⧈⧈⧈

Rabisu's tail twitched under her kaftan. "You are very perfect-looking. For a mortal."

You may ask what I was doing vacationing with a real spawn-of-the-netherworld demon. First, I hadn't exactly planned it this way. I'd sort of ended up with Rabisu after I'd killed her boss, Nergal, the ancient god of plagues. It had made things a little awkward between Rabisu and me at the beginning, but we were good now. Second, she wasn't quite as monstrous as Nergal's other minions. Everyone thought her claws were just very expensive snakeskin gloves, and her horns usually remained hidden under her turban. Her tail was easily covered by her kaftan, and though her tusks still drew attention, people were usually too polite to mention them. Not everyone can afford good dental work. She was barely five feet in height, but don't let that fool you. She still had a demon's strength and was as tough as a mountain.

So, here we all were. Me, the son of deli-owning Iraqi immigrants; one ancient Mesopotamian demon; and Daoud, longtime friend of my brother and currently the hottest face of the season, enjoying the most expensive suite in the Ritz. It was going to be a great vacation.

And I couldn't wait to get started. I pulled a brochure out of my pocket and waved it around. "I definitely want to go here first—the Tower of London. The most haunted place in Britain. Maybe we'll see Anne Boleyn wandering around with her head missing."

Gruesome, I know. But the Tower is a castle's castle. William the Conqueror had it built as soon as he became king, and there's nothing that tells the cowering population that you're here to stay more than a massive stone fortress in the heart of your capital. There was even a place nicknamed "the Bloody Keep."

Daoud peered over my shoulder. "Yeah, and we can check out the Crown Jewels—if they're still allowing that. Security must have been upped after the break-in at the Louvre last week."

I frowned. "That's the museum in Paris, right?"

Daoud nodded. "Did a shoot there. Me with the *Mona Lisa*. I think the theme was Beauty Through the Ages," he said. "Anyway, the Tower of London isn't far from here. And you never know, I might get invited to the next coronation. I'd look amazing in an ermine cape. And a crown or two."

"The king's still very much alive," I said. "And he's still got plenty of years ahead of him."

Daoud laughed. "Maybe. Or maybe not now that you're here."

"What's that supposed to mean?"

"It's just... you bring the party with you, don't you?"

I slapped him with the leaflet. "Nothing like Nergal is ever going to happen again. This is going to be a drama-free vacation. Got it?"

"If you say so, cuz." He caught his reflection in a nearby mirror. "Look at that. A wrinkle already. Thank Allah for Photoshop."

Rabisu leaned over the sofa, chin resting on her fists, and sighed. "You're so beautiful. I could eat you up."

I peered at her.

"What?" she exclaimed. "That was a figure of speech!"

"Just checking." With Rabisu, it was always worth making sure. "Should we buy tickets for tomorrow?" I asked Daoud.

He waved his hand. "I can charge it to the agency. I have a per diem allowance."

"For how much?"

He pointed at his face. "Excuse me? You're looking at the cover of this month's *Vogue*."

Typical Daoud. He went through life floating on a cloud of being idiotically handsome. I know we should value what's on the inside, but that doesn't sell, well, anything. Daoud was in the business of selling dreams, and people would give everything they had for their dreams. And why not? Sometimes they were the only things that kept us going.

⚑ ⚐ ⚑ ⚐

"Hogwarts!" shouted Rabisu. "Let's go to Hogwarts!"

"It's not a real place," I said.

Her eyes narrowed. "That's what they want you to think. Last year I found this camp off Long Island, along the North Shore. It had all these kids who—"

There was a loud knock at the door.

Daoud darted to answer it. "Got a surprise for you, Sik. She arrived this morning."

Who was he talking about? I didn't know anyone who traveled except...

Daoud swung the door open. "Ta-da!"

She hadn't changed a bit.

Her dark eyes were just as intense and brooding under her neat bangs. Her hair was wound in a neat crown braid— yes, I had learned the names of hairstyles from Daoud— and she wore a pair of sleek black pants and a T-shirt, an outfit that looked simple but probably cost a month's salary. Tucked under her arm was a wooden paddle with a big red ribbon around its handle. She saw me and smiled.

That smile stunned me. I stood there, staring. I'd probably still be there even now if Daoud hadn't nudged me. That was our secret code for *Don't just gawk like an idiot. Say something.*

I shook myself out of my stupor. "Assalamu alaikum, Belet."

Belet. The girl who'd saved New York from the plague god. Daughter of the goddess Ishtar. Belet, the baddest of badasses. And my best friend.

"Belet?" growled Rabisu, her beady red eyes glowing. "Demon killer!"

Uh-oh . . .

"Demon!" snarled Belet.

Aaaand there went my drama-free vacation.

TWO

RABISU VAULTED OVER THE SOFA, SCREAMING. I TRIED to catch her by the tail, but she was already across the room, her claws reaching for Belet's throat. Belet wrapped both hands around the paddle and smashed it into the side of Rabisu's head. The impact shattered the wooden paddle to splinters, leaving Belet with just the handle, but it hardly slowed the demon's momentum, and the two fighters collided and went tumbling across the floor.

"Stop them!" yelled Daoud. "Watch out for that—"

Belet flipped Rabisu over her head and straight onto the Ming vase. The next moment, Rabisu was covered in orchid petals and broken china.

Daoud pushed me forward. "Do something, Sik!"

"Like what?"

Rabisu hoisted the armchair over her head as if it were a plastic stool.

I stepped between them. "Listen! You don't need to do—"

I didn't get to finish, as I had to hurl myself out of the way of the flying furniture.

Belet neatly sidestepped it, but the demon brought her claws swinging in from both sides, determined to disembowel her sworn enemy. Belet blocked the onslaught with the handle.

"Enough, you two!" I grabbed the back of Rabisu's kaftan and hauled her away. I glared at Belet as she raised the handle. "Put that down."

Belet scowled and slapped it into my palm.

"Shukran," I said. It still had the ribbon on it. "This for me?"

"Welcome to England," said Belet with minimum joy as she gave Rabisu what I could only describe as a textbook slow squint. It was definitely an alpha move when *she* did it. "It's a...*was* a cricket bat."

"I've always wanted to learn that game," I said, trying hard to bring the atmosphere down from DEFCON 1.

"What's *she* doing here?" Belet asked with a sneer. "She was trying to kill you last fall."

"You killed Tirid," snarled Rabisu. "She was my friend!"

Belet waved her hand dismissively. "Impossible. You don't have any friends."

Ya Allah.

I stepped between them. "I know you've had your differences, but—"

"Differences?" snapped Rabisu. "She chopped Tirid's head off!"

Belet smiled. "It was a very special moment for me. For Tirid, maybe not so much."

I glowered at her. "You are not helping."

I owed my life to both of them, several times over. I wasn't going to pick sides, because both sides were wrong. "You're guests of Daoud's. What's the old desert law?" I asked him. "Your family's Bedouin."

Daoud looked up from collecting the broken pieces of the vase. "The law of hospitality? Three days. The host is obliged to keep the guest fed and protected for three days."

Rabisu crossed her arms but noisily scraped her claws. "I can wait three days."

Belet arched an eyebrow. "Suits me."

"That's not the point I'm trying to make. You just need to—"

At the sound of a polite cough from the doorway, we all turned. "Is everything to your...? Oh. Oh dear."

"Oh, Pierre." Daoud hopped over the remains of the armchair and joined the man, who, judging from his pristine tailored suit, must have been a hotel manager. "Let me explain. Somehow."

⟁⟆⟐⟊⟂

Pierre shook his head. "Mr. Hassan, this is the Ritz..."

One lifetime ban coming right up. This was bad. I hadn't even gotten around to pilfering the toiletries yet.

"...and we have catered to royalty, popes, and the world's greatest rock bands. Our job is to satisfy our guests' every whim. Nay, it's not only our job, but our solemn duty," said Pierre, his hands clasped together as if in prayer. "And this is certainly less damage than what was left by the Ladies' Choir of Cardiff last weekend. I shall have it cleared up immediately. Some complimentary champagne for the inconvenience? Alcohol-free, naturally."

"That would be... nice?" Daoud said cautiously. Then he realized the manager was serious, and he looked around. "Anyone else need anything?"

Pierre took our orders—Rabisu wanted everything on the appetizer menu—then left with a humble apology, closing the door gently behind him.

"Handsome mortal, where is your bathroom?" Rabisu asked Daoud. "I need to scream loudly and for a prolonged period, or else I might do something Sik might regret."

"Third door on the left," said Daoud.

Rabisu nodded and departed, but not before shooting daggers at Belet. Daggers? More like flaming scimitars, actually.

The scream that came out of the bathroom was long,

ear-piercing, and followed by what sounded like a person bashing their head—or horns—against a wall.

"When are you going to deal with her?" snapped Belet.

It must have been the jet lag, but I didn't quite get the euphemism. "*Deal* with her?"

Belet leaned closer. "Gilgamesh gave you the most powerful magical weapon in all existence. Abubu was forged for one purpose alone—for dispatching demons in a violent and permanent manner."

"Rabisu's not that bad! She just doesn't understand the . . . er, rules that well. So, I'm teaching her."

"She's a *demon*, Sik. The rule for demons is very simple and hasn't altered since the days of Hammurabi: Thou shalt slay the demon."

"I'm pretty sure you just made that up."

"It's in the appendix," she replied matter-of-factly. "It's not my fault you can't read Babylonian."

Classic Belet. Never missing an opportunity to remind everyone exactly how superior she was to us public-school-educated mortals.

"You just need to get to know her."

Belet crossed her arms tightly over her chest. "Never going to happen."

There were times, more often than I would have liked, when Belet's stubbornness and talent for concentrated violence were assets. They'd gotten us out of more than one certain-death scenario. She was rude, painfully blunt, and borderline arrogant, but she was the best friend I'd ever had, and I knew she would stand by me no matter what, without asking for anything in return. People like that don't come along often. What I'm saying is, I was willing to cut Belet a lot of slack, as long as she didn't do any actual cutting.

"You and I need to talk," I said. "Right now."

"Fine," Belet replied with a surliness that would have had her mother in tears. She got up. "My room's through there."

"You're staying here, too? But what about...? Never mind."

She led the way, but the moment we were inside, I slammed the door behind us. "What is wrong with you?"

"With *me*? You're the one who brought a demon. And how did she get here in the first place?"

"Ah, that was weird. Rabisu came to see me off at JFK, and it turned out that Lady Gaga was on the same flight. Someone mistook Rabisu for part of her entourage, and before I knew it, she was up in first class drinking champagne with the rest of them, singing 'Born This Way' in ancient Sumerian. I, of course, had to sit in coach. Still, we got backstage passes for Lady Gaga's London concert next Friday."

"That's the most ridiculous story I've ever heard, but knowing you, it's probably true."

"Cross my heart and hope to die."

"That's not likely to ever happen, is it?"

Have I mentioned my strange medical condition? No, it's not infectious or anything. The truth is going to come out sooner or later, so I might as well spill it now.

I'm immortal.

Totally unkillable, and believe me, people have tried.

Can I fill in the details later? I want to stay in the moment.

Belet huffed loudly as she did her best to avoid my gaze. "So, this Rabisu is your chum now?"

"I was trying to get her back home to the netherworld, but something, er, went a bit wrong with the barriers between realities, and it looked like existence was about to collapse. But it's all good now." I tapped the wall. "See? Solid, with every dimension present and correct."

I know, that also sounds utterly ridiculous. But it's also totally true. I'm not even including how Rabisu and I defeated a host of ancient anti-gods with a shovel or how there was a brief appearance of a kid on the back of a multi-colored unicorn. I'm still not sure I didn't hallucinate that last part.

"I should have been there, Sik. I could have helped."

𒀸 𒅆 𒄭 𒋛

"I know. But it all happened really fast. Rabisu is one of the good guys, Belet. You need to trust me on this one."

"Okay," she said reluctantly.

Wow. Just like that? I'd expected at least one sarcastic comment, probably in Latin. "What's wrong, Belet?"

She huffed again. "This isn't how I thought things would turn out, either. I wanted to surprise you."

"You definitely did."

"But it's more than that." Belet pushed her suitcase off the bed and plonked herself down. "You know how I was brought up. Mother recognized that there was something dark in my heart, Sik, and she tried her best to heal it. With her frivolous attitude, her attempts to get dolphins for our swimming pool, all those ballet lessons, ridiculous parties, and glamorous clothes. I thought they were stupid and pointless, but you know something?"

"You miss them. I get it. They were Ishtar."

"She was trying to show me there was another side to life," Belet went on. "All I've done is embrace conflict. I just want to fight, Sik, and it's getting worse now that she's gone. I'm full of anger." She gritted her teeth as she pressed her fist against her chest. "There's a bomb in here, just wanting to explode. I thought seeing you—"

"Would be fun?"

"Fun." She nodded slowly, as if trying to understand

the meaning of the strange word. "Mother *was* fun, wasn't she?"

"Time to tell me what's going on, Belet," I said. "My ego's not so big to think you came here just to see me."

"Before she . . . Mother had been planning to come over to London."

"Let me guess: London Fashion Week?"

"Shopping." She picked up a folder and drew out a photo and handed it to me. "She wanted to buy this."

I'd expected to see a pair of shoes or maybe a palace. What I didn't expect was a slab of clay. "A tablet? What's on it?"

She shuffled up beside me so we could both look at it. "No one's been able to translate the cuneiform. It's not Sumerian, Babylonian, Assyrian, or any period recorded in history that we know of. It's a protolanguage. Perhaps the original all the rest are descended from."

"It looks badly damaged. Maybe the markings have just faded? Iraq's deserts are littered with these."

That's how it all began, writing. Marks on clay that, over the centuries, became a system, became a language, and started history. And so many tablets had survived— entire libraries' worth. This one was chipped, had cracks running across it, and the wedge-shaped text was barely visible. "What's so important about this one?"

𒀀𒇽𒀸𒅆𒄠

Belet handed over another photo. "Recognize him?"

It was a statue, lying on its side and half-buried in the sand. A team of excavators was working around it, just enough to uncover some of the face and its left side.

"Alexander the Great?"

"Well done. We'll make a scholar of you yet. And look at what he's holding."

"A tablet. Strange. He's usually depicted with a scepter or a sword. It must have been important."

Belet opened the folder and revealed a stack of papers and photos. "Mother thought so. And she wasn't the only one. This is from the Ayyubid dynasty."

It was a xeroxed copy of a painting of a man sitting in a garden with a tablet on his lap. There was no mistaking him—the undisputed hero of the Islamic world.

"Saladin," I said.

"What's he doing with the tablet?" asked Belet. "No one had written on clay for a thousand years by his time. He should be sitting reading a scroll."

"It's the same tablet? Are you sure?"

"Why else would Mother have had it in this folder? There's a letter in here from Cleopatra. *The* Cleopatra. Apparently, she had the tablet for a while. Mother wanted it, but by the time she caught up with him, he'd been assassinated, and the tablet vanished in the chaos of the civil war that followed. The next time it turned up was with this guy Sultan Mehmet II." She picked out another facsimile. The hawkish gaze of a conqueror gazed back at me. In his palm rested the tablet.

"Ottoman, wasn't he? Not really my period."

Belet collected the sheets and put them back in the folder. "He conquered Constantinople and brought an end to the Roman Empire once and for all."

"Alexander. Saladin. Cleopatra and Mehmet. If you made a list of the most influential people in history, they'd be in the top ten."

"Mother traced the tablet to the museum of antiquities in Baghdad. But that was back in 2003, and you know what happened in 2003."

"The Iraq War," I said. "Mama and Baba told me all the stories."

"They tell you how the museums were looted? How priceless artifacts from the beginning of civilization were bundled into the backs of trucks and smuggled over borders and sold off to anyone with a shoebox of dollars?"

I heard the anger in Belet's voice. The girl was on a mission, and Allah help anyone who dared to stand in her way.

"Someone stole this tablet?"

"They emptied out the whole museum collection. But Mother tracked it down," she said. "The current possessor is Lady Fitzroy. She's an antiques dealer but has an interesting

ᴀ⟨ ⟨⟨⟩⟨ ⟩⟩ ⟨⟩

side business in the illegal sale of ancient artifacts. She's having a private auction tonight at her country home. The tablet's one of the items for sale."

"I guess invites are gonna be pretty hard to come by, it being so highly illegal and all. How are you going? Full ninja?"

"Better." She headed over to her closet and pulled out a dress. "Full Vivienne Westwood."

"Nice, but it's a little glitzy, isn't it? You can't climb up the battlements in that."

"I'm not going over the battlements, or crawling through the sewers, or swimming across the moat with a dagger clenched between my teeth. I'm going through the front door. You see, among the aristocracy, it's not about what you are; it's about who you know."

So, who did she know? "You can't be serious. Daoud?"

"He's on *everyone's* guest list."

"Won't there be, like, dangerous people in the place? Criminals and such?"

"Some of the worst in the world," Belet confirmed. "But I'll protect him."

Any hope for an ordinary, relaxing vacation had vanished far over the horizon. I hadn't even unpacked yet and we were already neck-deep in all sorts of danger. Belet could handle herself—she wasn't the one I was worried about. "If Daoud's going, I'm going."

"I know." Belet swung open the closet door, revealing one other item hanging within. "I got you this."

"A suit?"

"A *tuxedo*. Mother said every young man should have at least one."

I walked over to it and drew my fingertips along the sleeve's soft fabric. "How do you know it'll fit me?"

She smirked. "There's no mystery to you, Sikander Aziz."

"That makes me pretty boring, doesn't it?"

"It makes you honest." Belet unhooked the suit and held it out to me. "Put it on. We're going to a party."

THREE

"MAMA? BABA? CAN YOU SEE ME? I CAN'T SEE YOU."

"We can hear you, habibi!"

"Do you have your thumb over the camera?"

"Oh," said Baba. "How's this?"

Suddenly they both came into view on my phone screen. Baba was combing his hair quickly and Mama was adjusting her hijab, the silk one Daoud had sent her. They had the phone propped on the tabletop so I could see the rest of Mo's Deli behind them. It was early morning in Manhattan, and the sun streamed in from the windows, bathing the tables in gold. I could almost smell the coffee bubbling on the cooktop—Mama made it old-school Turkish—and I felt really homesick.

"Assalamu alaikum!" shouted Baba, as if he needed to be loud to be heard across the Atlantic. "Is that Daoud?"

Daoud budged up beside me so he could be in the shot. "Salaam, Uncle!"

"You're looking well, Daoud," said Mama. "A little thin, perhaps. Are you eating properly?"

"Of course not. I miss your cooking, Auntie. I thought Sik would have brought some of your baklava with him."

"I did." I looked over at Rabisu. "But someone ate it all on the flight over."

The demon gave a thumbs-up. "It was delicious."

"It was for sharing, Rabisu."

She rolled her eyes. We'd had this discussion before. "Demons do not share."

I turned back to the screen. "How is everything back home?"

Baba burst out laughing. "We're managing, son. Even without you."

"I wish you were here," I said.

Rabisu leaned over the sofa, pushing me aside. "I wish you were here, too! You need to add pigeon pie to the menu!"

Baba's eyes widened. "Did you say 'pigeon pie'?"

I pushed myself back. "No, she didn't. It's a bad connection."

"And eels! They're so yummy! They slither all the way down!" said Rabisu, smacking her lips. "And haggis! You can't get better than sheep guts stuffed with liver and lungs!"

I shoved her off the sofa. "Someone else is here with us—Belet."

Now Mama's eyes widened, and her mouth opened into a silent *ooh*.

"She came to London to see you?" asked Baba. "Mashallah!"

"Sik's girlfriend tried to kill me!" shouted Rabisu from the other side of the room.

"She is not my . . . and I'm starting to wish she'd tried a little harder!"

Rabisu snorted. "We'll know for sure in three days, won't we?" Then she promptly went to her room and slammed the door.

Phew. I turned back to the screen. "Sorry about that. Rabisu's jet-lagged."

Mama slid her hand into Baba's. "Mo talked about the city so much I feel I know it already. He had that list, remember? Of all the places he wanted to visit? The map's still on the wall, with all the sites marked. Too bad he didn't get to . . ." She paused to compose herself. "He'd be so happy that you're there. Tell him all about it, won't you?"

"He's here with me, Mama. He always is."

Mama's eyes glistened. "Have I ever told you how perfect you are?"

◁◁ ⧓⫯ ⧒▷ ⊣⊢

Rabisu guffawed, actually *guffawed*, from the other side of the door. Who knew demons had such great hearing?

Baba put his hand on Mama's shoulder. "You're embarrassing him. Doesn't mean you're wrong, though."

Daoud ruffled my hair. "I'll look after him, Uncle. Sik's going to have the best vacation ever."

"We need to start opening the deli, Sik. You have a great time and send us some photos," said Baba. "Ma'assalamah, son."

"Yalla bye." The screen turned dark, and I put the phone away. "Do you think the deli looked okay? I thought I saw—"

Daoud sprang up and stretched. "It's fine, Sik. You gotta switch off for a while. This is your big trip. We've got parties to go to, sights to see, food to eat. It's gonna be fantastic. Starting with tonight's soiree at Lady Fitzroy's."

"Tell me again how you know her?"

"A charity gig a few weeks ago with Bella Hadid. You must have heard about the drought in Iraq? Both the Tigris and Euphrates have run dry. Lady Fitzroy arranged a fundraiser, and you know how the rich are. Love nothing better than getting other people to give them money for their causes. My agent thought it would be a good idea to be seen there." He stood by the open window, looking out over Green Park. "Is it true? You still see Mo sometimes?"

"We have our little talks."

𒀀𒇷𒈾𒌗

Daoud didn't dare turn around, but I saw him stiffen. "He, er, ever mention me? At all?"

"He knows how you felt about him, Daoud. He felt the same way. He thought you were the best."

"Really? He told you that?"

I nodded.

Daoud turned back around, grinning. "We should call this the Mo Tour. Ask your parents to email a copy of his map, and we'll go see each place and tick them off."

My brother had been gone three years, killed in a motorbike accident out in Iraq. Yet I still expected him to walk into the room, or hear his laughter on the other side of the door. Ishtar had told me that love transcends all time and space, and she'd know better than anyone, wouldn't she?

Mo was living his best life, out under the supernova skies of Kurnugi, the netherworld. I'd visited him there, and we'd shared one last adventure, but that didn't mean I didn't miss him every single day. And, looking over at Daoud, I knew I wasn't the only one.

"Are we ready yet?" asked Belet as she entered the living room in her party dress.

Wow. I mean, ya salam.

"What's wrong with you?"

Daoud, once again, leaped to my rescue. He blew her a chef's kiss. "Absolutely nothing. Black diamonds suit you."

Belet blushed. Actually blushed. "They're just sequins, Daoud."

"Not on you they're not. Don't you agree, Sik?"

"Er, yeah. You look nice. *Really* nice." I admit it wasn't exactly the most poetic of compliments, but I did mean it. Then I noticed something else about her outfit. "Is that really necessary?"

"This? It's a fashion accessory."

"It's a sword, Belet."

She unsheathed the blade and turned it side to side. The edge sparkled in the light of the chandeliers. "I couldn't leave him behind."

The steel groaned, and an oil-like pattern spread over the blade as it spoke. "Is that Private Clown? What's he moaning about now?"

"Salaam, Kasusu," I said.

That was my life now. Demons, quests, and talking swords. Kasusu was a legendary blade, and over the ages had gained a personality, a life of his own. Needless to say, he had opinions, mainly about me.

"So, you're tagging along?" continued Kasusu. "Just make sure that when things kick off you stay well out of my way."

"When what things kick off?" I turned to Belet.

But before she could make up some excuse, Rabisu

barged in, wearing a heavily embroidered kaftan and waving a long strip of golden cloth. "Will someone fix this turban? I can't— By Ea! What's she doing with *that*?"

"I smell demon," snarled Kasusu. "I hate the smell of demon."

Why isn't anything in my life simple anymore? "Put the sword away, Belet."

She did so, reluctantly. "No one said anything about the demon coming."

Rabisu snapped her claws in front of my nose. "He doesn't trust me to be left alone."

"You're right—I don't," I said. "People bring their pets to the Ritz. I saw the way you drooled when we walked through the lobby. It was like you were at an all-you-can-eat buffet. Daoud, help Rabisu with her turban."

It took him mere moments to wrap it perfectly over her horns. Rabisu checked herself in the mirror. "I love it. The gold really brings out the red of my eyes."

We were ready to face the world. But was the world ready for us?

Daoud and Belet went to collect the car from the valet while Rabisu and I waited on the curb. It was a warm, musky evening. The West End buzzed with Saturday crowds heading off to theaters, clubs, and bars, and everything

⩓⫯ ⩊⫯⦂ ⫰⨪⨪

was a clash of bright neon and grand Georgian marble. I checked my reflection in the tinted windows of a waiting Rolls-Royce.

I'd never worn a tuxedo before. It even had a black silk cummerbund. The shoes were brand-new, but the leather was as soft as a pair of slippers. The cuff links were a pair of minute scimitars. If I say so myself, I looked *goooood*.

Rabisu looked up the street. "There it is again."

I followed her gaze. "What?"

"That van. The one with the painted signs and rainbow flag. I saw it earlier. It's been doing laps around the block. Here it comes."

A yellow VW camper slowly rolled up and stopped by the traffic lights. A rainbow flag hung limply from the antenna, and the van's exterior had been hand-painted with a peace sign, portraits of Gandhi and MLK Jr., and symbols from all the major religions and most of the minor ones. It was also covered with stickers. The WOODSTOCK 69 one caught my eye. The van looked that old.

The guy behind the steering wheel dangled his arm out the open window and smiled at me.

"Good evening," I said.

He nodded. "It's more than good—it's beautiful, man. You got to take time to savor the moment. Stop and salute the sun at dawn . . . Dance in the rain."

He looked harmless. I would have put him in his thirties, but the beard and long hair and bandanna made it hard to be sure, and his eyes were hidden behind a pair of rose-tinted sunglasses. He then held up his two fingers, shifted gears, and vanished around the corner. The license plate matched his sign: PEACE.

My attention shifted as a car honked and Daoud waved from inside a sleek panther-black Jaguar F-Type coupe. Belet rode shotgun with Kasusu across her lap.

"Nice ride, cuz," I said.

"Sponsors, Sik. I need to return it by the end of the weekend, valeted and with a full gas tank. Till then..." He pressed down on the gas pedal, and the beat of an engine roared.

"So, we ready?"

The van was gone. How had it slipped through the traffic, just like that?

Belet got out and tilted her seat forward to let me and Rabisu into the back. "What are you looking for?"

"A van. A big bright yellow one. It was right here."

It was subtle, but there was the brief flicker of something in her gaze. If I didn't know Belet better, I would've called it fear. "What's wrong?"

She caught herself. That emotion, whatever it was, vanished under her usual hard mask. "Nothing. We're running late."

I got in, squeezing beside Rabisu. We set off, but there was no sign of the van.

Why had it freaked Belet out so much?

I'll tell you this, I love castles! C'mon, is any other kind of building cooler? That'll be a no. The moats and draw-bridges, the turrets and battlements, the great dungeons . . . You can't go too over-the-top with them. Why settle for gutters when you can have gargoyles? When I was little, I used to make castles out of Legos, then smash them with my Star Wars figures. Even stormtroopers can hit something *that* big.

It's all about the Crusades—the centuries of war between Christians and Muslims over the Holy Land. Sure, plenty of bad things happened, but there'd been heroes. You had King Richard the Lionheart, and you had Salah al-Din Yusuf ibn Ayyub, better known as Saladin. He was Iraqi, too. See where I'm heading with this?

Saladin was simply the best. Warrior, peacemaker, and all-round decent dude. He sent his own doctor over when the English king fell ill. Even lent Richard a horse when he lost his in the middle of a battle. That didn't stop Saladin from kicking Richard's royal backside all the way back to England.

Fitzroy Castle rose out of the mists. This wasn't a driveway—it was a time tunnel. As we rolled underneath the arching boughs of the ancient oak trees, we seemed to be stepping back a thousand years. It had battlements and banners fluttering from the towers! I could almost hear the galloping hooves and war trumpets.

Daoud turned off the driveway and into a clearing where dozens of other vehicles were already parked. A valet approached as we slowed down. I was marginally disappointed that he wasn't wearing armor, and though he didn't have a halberd, he did have a shotgun. "This is a private function. The castle will reopen for visitors tomorrow."

Belet leaned across Daoud. "We're here to do some... shopping."

The valet poked the flashlight in to have a good look at us. "Any identification?"

Daoud held up this month's *Vogue*. "That's me."

The guy frowned. "I really don't think a photo of you as Tarzan counts as— Wait. You're Daoud Hassan?" His eyes widened. "Some of the boys said you'd been invited, but I didn't believe it. Big fan, by the way. You, er, couldn't sign something for me, could you?"

Daoud already had a Sharpie out. I guess this wasn't his first time. "Anything for a fan."

The valet rolled up his sleeve. "Here. On my forearm."

"Won't it wash off?" I asked.

The valet shook his head. "Not if I get it turned into a tattoo. I'm going to cherish it forever."

⚔ ⚒ ⚑ ⚔

Daoud signed with a flourish, and a moment later, we were parked and stretching ourselves out of the Jaguar. The valet was proudly displaying his autograph to the others.

And Daoud did look—there's no other word for it— fabulous. I swear the clouds literally parted as he straightened his cuffs and the moonlight shone *just so* on his chiseled features. If he did a hair flick, I wouldn't have been surprised if birds started singing.

Belet slammed the car door. "Rules don't apply to beautiful people, do they?"

"You must be used to it, having Ishtar as your mom," I said.

"And it was really annoying then, too. Dear Lord, the fawning that used to go on. The way people act just because someone's got clear skin and evenly proportioned features. That's all it is, you know." Belet shook her head wearily. "We get the tablet, and we leave. No hanging around for the after-party. Understood?"

Rabisu merely sighed. "Have you noticed how the light catches the waves of Daoud's hair?"

"Yeah, I have. So has everyone else," I said.

As we approached the castle, I was in for another medieval treat. "Look at that! It's got a moat."

A narrow stone bridge spanned the channel, which was sprinkled with floating lily pads. The bridge led to the gatehouse. Huge trails of ivy covered the outer wall and were wrapped around the crumbling towers. Belet hid Kasusu in a large geranium bush.

Rabisu tapped the head of a gargoyle statue on the bridge. "He really reminds me of my old boyfriend, Asag. We used to have picnics on the bone-strewn plains of Irkalla, where the spirits of woe howl throughout eternity." She sighed. "Good times."

Demons could have boyfriends? You learn a new thing every day. "What happened to him?"

"Run over in a chariot race."

"Wow. Sorry. That must have been pretty upsetting."

"Not really. I won." She looked around. "Are there swans in that lake? I'm just going to...have a look."

"Rabisu..."

"Yalla bye!" she declared, and ran off into the trees.

Belet grabbed my arm before I could chase after her. "Let the demon go. Better she cause trouble out here than in there."

"I feel kinda responsible for her. And she has a name. It's—"

"Whatever. Can we get a move on, please?"

We crossed the bridge and entered the large courtyard—or the bailey, if you want to use the proper ye olde term. The keep loomed ahead—a somber, squat gray toad of a building with banners bearing the family crest dangling on either side of the main doors.

〰〰〰〰〰

That crest. It was an argent wolf rampant upon a field of blood. You can't be a fan of knights without learning some heraldry. Below it was a motto in Latin. "Esurientem sicut lupus"?

Belet translated. "'Hungry like a wolf.'"

"Nice family."

A large tent had been erected for the caterers, and white-jacketed servants were crossing the bailey with trays and dishes. Half a cow turned on a spit over a huge log fire, fat sizzling as it dropped into the flames.

"So this is how the one percent like to party," I said, watching the cook carve a strip off the rump. "You think that cow is halal?"

"Nothing fatty," warned Daoud. "You'll never get the stains out. Which reminds me..." He caught my arm and looked me over. He tweaked my bow tie and checked my lapels before rewarding me with a megawatt grin. "Mashallah. You are ready to rock the—"

"Daoud! Darling!"

An old woman emerged from the tent. She strode up to Daoud and air-kissed him from two feet away with the loudest, wettest *mwah* ever. "So fabulous you could join us. Patricia! Patricia! Come and meet the young man I was telling you about!"

Daoud took her hand and kissed it lightly. "Lady Fitzroy."

She was tall and gaunt. There wasn't an ounce of fat on her, and her skin looked like it had been tightened and tightened over the years until it was almost transparent. She wore a sleek silver dress, and the necklace around her throat was a snake clasping its own tail. Her gray eyes matched the cold hardness of her ancestral home.

A moment later, another woman joined us. "Yes, m'dear?"

Lady Fitzroy gestured at Daoud with a talon-like forefinger. "This is the beautiful boy I was telling you about. Could you believe he's an actual Arab?"

"He doesn't look like an Arab, m'dear," muttered Patricia, and she finished off a pastry.

Lady Fitzroy laughed, and it was a harsh, broken-glass sound. "Not at all. You know what the Arabs are like. All swarthy and . . . Well, you know what I mean. No offense, of course."

Whoa. So polite and yet so . . . racist?

"Of course not," said Daoud through gritted teeth.

Lady Fitzroy's smile faded as she turned to me and Belet. "And these are . . . ? No, let me guess. Poor orphans! Yes, look at them both. Is this all part of the charity event from last week? It would be better if they looked a *little* more malnourished, but who knows? We might get a real humanitarian disaster with the drought. I'm hoping to reel in some A-list Hollywood celebrities then. Nothing trends higher than starving children."

"Nothing at all, m'dear," Patricia said cheerfully.

Lady Fitzroy gestured toward the great doors. "Make your way inside, Daoud. Eat, enjoy! Tonight promises to be most memorable!"

We watched her and Patricia go chasing after another new arrival—maybe a duke or some other royal, judging by the way they curtsied and fawned.

Daoud adjusted his shirt cuffs. "What do you think?"

"I think I speak for the two of us when I say she's an evil, narcissistic witch."

"Welcome to my world, cuz."

We entered the main hall, and it was like something out of Lord of the Rings. Suits of armor stood in the alcoves, and hanging on the stone walls were great tapestries and shields bearing the family's coat of arms: a pair of lions on either side of a sword. People mingled around the food tables, on the scattered sofas, and in the rooms branching off.

Daoud waved at someone. "Can you two manage by yourselves for a little while? That's the head of the Chaplin Films studio. How do I look?"

"Do you even need to ask?" I said. "Go. Belet's here to look after me."

𒀸 𒐊𒐊 𒂠𒈨𒐊

Belet stopped me as we reached the main hall. "Sik, I need you to remember that these are very, very bad people. If there is evil in the world, true evil, then the people in this place represent most of it. Do not speak to them, do not tell them who you are, do not ask what they do. They'll have their guard down, and they'll tell you things you do not want to hear."

"Seriously? What about that old guy, by the canapés? With that beard, he looks like he could play Santa at Macy's."

"Serbian war criminal. He's wanted for genocide."

Okay, okay, okay.

I pointed at the guy admiring the painting of a horse. "Him?"

"Mozambiquan warlord. Beside him is the CEO of the company that manufactures most of the world's cluster bombs."

I realized I wasn't at someone's quaint country castle. These weren't merely rich collectors. I was in Jahannam, and these were its greatest shayatin.

"Ya Allah, Belet. How do you know all this?"

There was a glimpse of pain in her face. "Mother tried to protect me from it, but you just hear things, don't you? She couldn't deny her nature, her purpose, no matter how hard she might have tried, and no matter her regrets. At one time, she was the goddess of heroes, of noble warriors who worshipped her and showered her with tales of their glorious victories, but then that changed, and war became all about maximizing cruelty, a kind of madness."

"That's what Baba says. War's a madness, a sickness we have."

"Your father's a wise man."

Then a gong sounded. Canapés were put down, and drinks were finished off.

"What's going on?" I asked as everyone headed toward one of the rooms off to the side.

"The auction," said Belet. "Come on. Let's go reclaim our heritage."

FOUR

"LOT FIFTEEN," SAID THE AUCTIONEER FROM THE PODIUM at the far end of the study. "And this piece of art requires no introduction. Recently acquired from the Louvre, it's my privilege to present *Lisa del Giocondo*."

The servant to the side lifted the white cotton sheet from the painting on the easel. The audience gasped.

I stared. "The *Mona Lisa*?"

"There was that break-in at the Louvre, remember?" Belet said. "The government covered it up, but a gang got away with the painting. I wondered when it might turn up."

"But...the *Mona Lisa*, Belet! We need to call the police!"

She tilted her head. "The head of MI5 is sitting right over there."

"But...the *Mona Lisa*."

Belet shrugged. "It's not the original."

"But you just said that painting was stolen from the Louvre...."

"Yes, but the real *Lisa del Giocondo* is hanging on a wall in Mother's Venice apartment. It's been there since Napoleon gave it to her as a thank-you gift for introducing him to Josephine."

"So, the one hanging in the Louvre...has always been a fake?" I said. "But that's terrible!"

"Why? Whoever did the forgery improved her smile. The original has her grinning, and let's put it this way, dental hygiene has come a long way since the sixteenth century."

"You must be joking."

She looked over at me, her eyes darkening.

"No, you're not. At all." I rocked back in my chair. "Ya salam. That guy just bid fifty million on a fake."

One of the servants carried away the painting when the bidding eventually ended at seventy million. But not everyone was happy with the result. The old Serbian started yelling at the buyer, a drug lord. A chair was thrown and tempers flared, all until Lady Fitzroy motioned for her guards to drag the Serbian away. She looked around the assembled room. "Poor Josif. I believe he would have won, but he's going through a very expensive divorce right now. Wife number six, I believe."

It was a feeble joke, but people laughed politely.

Still, tension continued to build. Audience members shoved and scowled, tempers simmered, and more than one bidder swore out loud when they lost. Lady Fitzroy paced the edge of the study, watching the crowd like a teacher with a particularly difficult class.

Belet nudged me as one of the servants approached the podium carrying a small book-size object covered by a cloth. He put it on the gilt display stand beside the auctioneer, who tapped his gavel for attention. "Ladies and gentlemen, lot seventeen will be of particular interest for any scholar of ancient history. This item has been authenticated—"

"Which is more than can be said for the *Mona Lisa*," I quipped.

"—as being over four and a half thousand years old. It originates from the earliest Sumerian period and is as fine an example of early cuneiform as can be found in any of the world's museums. And of course, it makes a wonderful paperweight."

The cloth came off, and all I could say was...

"Is that it?"

"Shall we begin the bidding at half a million?"

Belet raised her hand.

"Young lady in the Westwood. Now do I hear six hundred?"

Others joined in, and the price escalated rapidly over

the million mark. Two of the bidders turned on each other, snarling and making whispered threats. Lady Fitzroy was nowhere to be seen.

"One-point-three. Do I hear one-point-four?"

Belet raised her hand.

I nudged her. "That's one-point-four *million* dollars, Belet. You really want to blow it on a clay tablet?"

"A clay tablet Mother spent centuries chasing. So that'd be a yes, wouldn't it? Anyway, what else should I spend my millions on?"

How many fourteen-year-olds appear on the World's Richest list? Ishtar had been the goddess of love and war, two of humanity's great obsessions. It was no surprise she'd accumulated a vast, *vast* fortune from them. Now it was all in the hands of the girl next to me.

"Thank you," said the auctioneer. "Now one-point-five? Come on, ladies and gentlemen, this is a unique part of Middle Eastern history—nay, of *human* history. Any true historian would be delighted to make this the centerpiece of their collection. One-point-five? No? Going once…"

Ya Allah. One-point-four million for a clay brick.

"Going twice…"

Lady Fitzroy suddenly rushed in. Heads turned as she hurried down the center of the study, climbed onto the podium, and whispered to the bemused auctioneer. He stiffened slightly but nodded. Lady Fitzroy glanced around, her smile frozen on the wrong side of scared, then dashed out of the room.

"Ladies and gentlemen, this is most irregular, but lot seventeen has been unexpectedly withdrawn." He motioned to the servant, who covered up the tablet and retreated through a side door.

The auctioneer cleared his throat as another object, a gold-leaf crown displayed on a marble bust, was carried to the adjacent table. "Now, shall we proceed to lot eighteen? From the Schliemann private collection, we have this beautiful Bronze Age crown...."

Belet got up from her seat. "We need to find out—"

"Leave that to me," I said, and I was out and running down the hallway before Belet could say a word.

I caught Lady Fitzroy at the bottom of the grand staircase. She looked flustered, but the moment she saw me, a veil of calm fell over her brittle face.

You know what's the most essential skill in running a deli? Nope, not cooking. Not even giving the correct change. It's psychology. Seriously. You need to be able to read your customers, know what they want even before they know it themselves. Lady Fitzroy was frightened. Something in her carefully planned evening had gone very wrong and she needed someone to sort things out. Anyone involved in catering would recognize that.

"Too bad about that last item. My friend was very eager to buy that tablet."

"Your friend? Oh, you came with Daoud. Of course. The bid was getting rather high for such a young woman."

"Oh, she had the cash. Her mother's a big name in the war business. The biggest."

Lady Fitzroy's rigid smile faltered uncomfortably. "I'm afraid another offer came in quite suddenly."

"And it was one you couldn't refuse?"

"I . . . That's right."

Now, who could have spooked someone like Lady Fitzroy? She had some of the world's most nefarious war criminals under her roof, but this mysterious buyer had her quaking in her Jimmy Choos.

"Perhaps we could make an arrangement?" I continued. "I'm sure he doesn't want it that much."

"He's not here yet. Now, if you'll excuse me, the . . . canapés need my attention." And with that feeble excuse, she hurried off.

Belet came around the corner. "You won't believe what's happening. The auctioneer threw his gavel at one of the bidders. Everyone's losing their heads. What did you find out from the old witch?"

"Someone else bought your tablet and is coming to collect it."

𒀀 𒄴 𒁕 𒄭

"Who?"

"No idea, but whoever it is, Lady Fitzroy is terrified of them." I looked around at the entrance hall with its suits of armor and weapons display. "We need to move fast."

"You thinking what I think you're thinking?"

"How badly do you want that tablet, Belet?"

"Are you familiar with the phrase *I'll stop at nothing*?"

No one did intense like Belet.

I took a deep breath. "Then let's go get it."

FIVE

I DON'T KNOW HOW JAMES BOND DOES IT. IT'S impossible to creep around in a tuxedo. The brand-new leather of my shoes squeaked, and there wasn't much give in the bow tie—Daoud had tugged it pretty tight. But when I caught my reflection in one of the gilt-framed hall mirrors, I had to admit Ishtar had been right—every boy needs at least one tux in his life.

Ya Allah. Me, talking about clothes and fashion. Maybe I was spending too much time with Daoud. The sooner I got back to the deli and smelling of Cologne de Kebab, the better. If I wasn't careful, I might even end up using . . . hair products. I wondered how I'd look if I parted my hair on the right instead of the left. . . .

"Will you stop checking your hair?" snapped Belet.

I blushed brightly enough to light up the entire hall. "Where, er, do you think they took the tablet?"

"I saw the auctioneer go up those." Belet pointed at the dark oak staircase at the end of the corridor. "Let's start there. And stop squeaking."

"Me? What about you? You're literally sparkling. Ninjas don't sparkle."

She threw me one of her dagger glares, and if looks could kill—and I wasn't immortal—I would have expired right there and then.

I followed Belet up under the imperious gaze of the Fitzroy patriarchs. The wall was lined with portraits going back centuries. What you really noticed were the eyes, watching you from all those times past, following you. The family had found fame, wealth, and glory on the battlefield. They were generations of killers, and the portrait painters had seen a hint of that ruthlessness in each and every Fitzroy. One grandfatherly figure in a blood-red uniform had his ivory-skinned granddaughters standing on either side of his armchair, and the two girls in their silk gowns bore the same deathly gaze, their eyes as cold and gray as the winter sea.

We reached the top floor, passing no one along the way. A row of doors ran down both sides of the corridor.

"You check the doors on the left," said Belet.

"What if someone's there?" I asked.

"Didn't you watch any of those training videos I sent you?"

𒀀𒁹 𒈨𒌋 𒅖𒉈 𒌋𒈨

"I was planning to, honest, but the deli's been busier than ever. And remember, I'm not one for all the hero she-nanigans. That's your department."

"Not even one video?"

And now I felt bad. But it wasn't like she'd sent me funny cat videos. They'd been things like "How to Cripple an Attacker in Three Easy Steps" and "Secret Fighting Techniques of the Royal Marines." Oh, and the classic "Punching Someone's Teeth into Their Brain," which had totally ruined my appetite that one morning when I'd tried to watch it.

Belet picked a spiked mace off the wall and handed it to me. "Remember, plant your feet firmly and use your core to increase power. A little twist in the hips would help, but I don't want to complicate things."

So, with a twelfth-century mace in one hand, I tried the first door. The handle turned. Not locked. Good or bad? Only one way to find out . . .

A study. The moon shone through the far window onto a small desk and shelves tightly packed with old leather-bound books. A magpie sat on a branch just outside and looked at me. I shut the door and tried the next. Linen closet.

The third was locked.

"Belet?"

She came over and gave the handle a sharp twist.

"Promising. The three on my side were all just servants' bedrooms."

"So, you gonna pick the lock?"

She frowned. "What makes you think I can pick locks?"

"I assumed it was all part of your extracurricular activities. My bad." Then, after I'd mentally reviewed everything I knew about her: "But you can, can't you?"

"No. I don't need to steal. I am insanely rich."

"But we are stealing right now."

"We're reclaiming our heritage. There's a huge difference."

"There are men with guns here who would disagree with you. So, if you can't pick the lock, how are we gonna get in?"

"Hmm...if only we had something big and heavy we could use to smash the lock."

"Yeah, if we just...Oh." I raised my mace. "You were hinting, weren't you?"

"Just hit the lock, Sik. As hard as you can."

The noise from below was rising, becoming almost boisterous with people shouting at one another. The auction was heating up. "Now what are they bidding on? Van Gogh's *Sunflowers*?"

"I doubt it. Mother has that in her bedroom in Caracas." Then Belet winced. "Get a move on, Sik."

"You okay? You look pale."

"Just smash in the door before I smash in your face," she snarled. "I don't know why I burden myself with you. You're so useless."

Whoa. Where had that come from? I'd let a lot slide with Belet. She was abrupt, borderline rude at times, but she was never . . . nasty. And I wasn't going to let this pass. "No. Not until you apologize."

"For what? Telling the truth?" She held her fists by her sides, but they were shaking with the need to punch me. "You know I could hurt you? So easily?"

"Why would you want to do that?"

That stopped her. She stepped back, shaking her head. When she raised her gaze to meet mine, she looked bewildered. "I'm . . . sorry, Sik. That was uncalled for."

"Yes, it was, but I forgive you. You're under a lot of stress." I tightened my grip on the mace. "Now, firm stance. Power from the core. Use your hips. Right?"

Belet nodded. "You can do it."

"Bismillah." Then I unleashed my inner barbarian. The mace head slammed into the heavy iron lock, taking off the doorknob and buckling the entire mechanism. The jarring impact sent a shock wave up through my palms to my teeth, and a *thud* echoed back and forth between the stone walls. Then I gave it a second swing, taking out the lock and the wood around it in a burst of splinters.

"Nicely done," Belet said sincerely. "Shall we?"

𒀀 𒈨 𒂗 𒊑

"We shall." I gave the door a push and flicked on the light.

It wasn't exactly Aladdin's cave, but it was close. The Fitzroys had been looting other countries for centuries, and the treasures in here were just the tip of the iceberg. It was all methodically laid out by continent. To the left were artifacts from Egypt and Africa. Statues of animal-headed gods stood covered in plastic sheets, ready to be packed off to their buyers, along with face masks from the Ivory Coast. Wooden carvings taken from Buddhist temples were lined up alongside silver Tibetan jewelry, and the shelves were covered with jade talismans and statuettes taken from the palaces of China. There were also bureaus and locked cabinets. What were in those?

Belet nudged me toward the corner. "There. The Middle Eastern collection."

The glass cabinet displayed three beautiful Yemeni jambiyas, their hilts covered in silver filigree and scabbards studded with gems. We opened the drawers beneath and found antique jewelry laid out on padded silk. But the bottom drawer wasn't for gold or silver. It was for clay.

There were three tablets in Bubble Wrap. I unsheathed one of the daggers and cut off the wrapping. "You recognize the one we want?"

The noise coming from downstairs was turning even angrier. Shouts were joined by the sound of furniture being shoved and knocked over. Something had gone wrong. Belet felt it, too. "We need to be quick."

She drew out the photo of the tablet we were after, compared it to the first, and shook her head. Then she tried the second, and that didn't match, either.

Heavy footsteps pounded the stairs, heading our way.

Was there another exit? The castle walls were covered in thick ivy, easy to climb if we could get out there. Did the windows open? I looked and—

Saw something staring straight at me.

Oh. It was a just a bird, a magpie, hopping along the windowsill. Was it the same one I'd seen before? Maybe it had been attracted by the shiny things laid out in the room. It peered between the window bars. Then, with a tiny shrug of its wings, it flew off.

"This is the one," said Belet, holding the photo beside the third tablet. "I'm sure of it."

I grabbed the hunk of clay and shoved it into my tux jacket pocket. "Something very weird just happened."

"Tell me later," said Belet. "We're leaving."

Whatever was going on downstairs had turned into a riot. People were screaming, and I heard things being crashed into and breaking...and gunshots.

"Someone didn't get what they wanted," said Belet. "Stay behind me and protect that tablet."

A man stumbled into us before we could reach the

doorway. He was one of the buyers—a big guy with massive diamond-encrusted gold rings on each of his thick fingers. He stood there, blocking our way out, his teeth gritted and his bloodshot eyes wild with rage, intent on inflicting excessive bodily harm.

So you know what I did?

Yup. I left him to Belet.

She leaped across the room and grabbed his lapels. He staggered back as she hung off him and then headbutted him. He tottered on his heels, so she headbutted him again. No nose can withstand the impact of Belet's forehead twice. He fell backward into the corridor, lay there unconscious, and Belet neatly rolled onto her feet.

I followed her out. "You really do need to teach me how to—"

The castle echoed with the sounds of fighting, perhaps for the first time in eight hundred years. And I mean old-school fighting. We looked over the staircase banister to see people tearing at one another. They used pieces of furniture, weapons they'd grabbed off the walls and armor, and assorted cutlery. And if they didn't have weapons, they were pummeling, clawing, and biting. The Ming vases that had been lined up along the main hall were just shards on the carpet now.

We turned at the scream. A woman, her silk suit bloodied and tattered, charged at us, swinging her battle-ax wildly. Belet dodged left, dodged right, then flipped the woman over her shoulder, slamming her hard into the oak floor. How did she make it all look so graceful? Intense ballet classes?

"We're going to have to fight our way out," said Belet as she took two medieval longswords off the wall and inspected their blades. "Blunt, unfortunately."

I held out my hand for one. Belet looked at me with a frown. "These are mine."

"Both of them?"

She gave them a twirl and grinned. "Oh, yes."

Sometimes Belet could be pretty scary.

I collected a shield and the woman's now-discarded battle-ax. "That's another thing I've checked off my bucket list."

Belet stood at the top of the stairs. "Fighting with medieval weapons was on your list?"

"Yeah, like everyone else who plays Dungeons and Dragons. We're fifteenth level now—no more just roughing up goblins. We're taking on the boss monsters. Can't wait to fight my first dragon." I joined her and watched the fighting below. "They've gone berserk, rabid. This is just like last year in Manhattan. You think he's back? Nergal, I mean?"

"They're not showing any signs of disease, but there's something in the air. Don't you feel it?" Belet ground her teeth. "A building rage. I want to hurt people, Sik. Badly."

𒀀𒈾𒁺𒋡

"Was that what you felt earlier? At the door?"

She looked around sharply. "You don't feel it? Why not?"

I shrugged. "I'm a natural-born coward?"

"You're no warrior, but you're anything but a coward." Belet tightened her grip on her two swords. "The only way is down and through the melee."

She sounded waaay too eager; I had to make sure she and I were on the same page. "We have what we came for, so let's just find Daoud and Rabisu and get out of here."

"You're no fun at all."

"We're not here to have fun, we're here to— Look out!"

Belet blocked a descending halberd by crossing her swords, catching the massive blade a few inches from her head. The man attacking her growled like a rabid beast, but Belet kicked him square in the chest and sent him tumbling back down the stairs, taking out two elderly ladies who were tearing at each other with their fingernails.

It was total chaos, worse than the last half hour at the deli on Fridays, when it felt like all of Manhattan wanted their falafel wraps with all the toppings *right now* and *first*. People were getting medieval—literally—on one another's butts.

Belet worked her way down, me a few steps behind. She fought like it was a dance, each move exact, perfectly timed, perfectly placed. Step-by-step she battered and chopped down anyone coming at us, leaving groaning, bruised, and unconscious foes in her wake. Her swords were heavy lumps of solid steel, but she wielded them as if they were willow wands, adding in a few kicks, headbutts, and throws just to make it a full-body workout.

Me? I was keeping Belet out of trouble. I blocked the attacks she couldn't. I jammed my shield between her and a spear hurled from the hallway. When a guy came at her with a flail, I caught it on the rim of my shield . . . and my back. Immortal or not, that *hurt.*

They kept on coming. Not just at us, but at one another. Lady Fitzroy was whacking a servant with his own shotgun. She screamed so wildly her dentures flew out of her mouth. Sure, she was an evil witch, but I wasn't going to let her get beaten to a pulp by some frenzied warlord. "Step this way, Lady Fitzroy." I grabbed hold of her and swung her into the linen closet. I then wedged a chair under the door handle and left her beating her fists against the door. "No offense intended, of course."

Furniture had been smashed and paintings torn down. Smoke was pouring out of the auction room. But no one cared. Everyone just wanted to kill someone.

"Daoud! Daoud!" Where had I last seen him? "Time to go!"

"There! On the ceiling!" yelled Belet.

On the ceiling? What did . . . ?

"Get away from me!" Daoud yelled. He was dangling

from the chandelier as a mob below him frothed and screamed, trying to grab his ankles and tear him down. "Help!"

Then Rabisu came to the rescue.

Head down she charged, turban unraveled and streaming behind her, and rammed her stubby horns into the screaming masses, sending them flying. She skidded to a halt beneath Daoud and held out her arms. "I'll catch you, Handsome One!"

The rest happened so fast. Daoud fell into her arms, and Rabisu ran for the front door, carrying him as he sobbed into her shoulder. I threw my shield at the nearest madman, clearing enough space for Belet and me to follow, but not before we tore one of the centuries-old tapestries down over the heads of the screaming rioters, tangling them up to allow our escape.

Things weren't any better outside. I flinched as a shotgun blast took the head off a nearby gargoyle. The guard reloaded and turned the gun toward Belet. At that range, he couldn't miss.

Panic can sometimes help. If I'd taken a second to think about what I was doing, I wouldn't have done it. Charging a guy with a shotgun is pretty near the bottom of my list of good ideas. I slammed into him, and we both went over the edge of the bridge, hitting the water and sinking straight down into the weeds. We wrestled for the gun, stirring up

𒀸 𒄴 𒀭 𒅗

the mud, so everything went black. The guard clawed at my face, and I bit his fingers. I pushed my knees against his chest, forcing the air out of his lungs. He may have been bigger, and an ex-soldier, but he needed to breathe and I didn't.

He was getting desperate. He wasn't fighting now, only struggling. And growing weaker. I wrenched the shotgun out of his hands and threw it away. He gave me one last, feeble punch, and then that was it. His body went limp.

But I couldn't leave him there to die. I hooked my fingers around the back of his collar and started dragging him up, sinking deeper into the mud with each step. Then someone came splashing into the water, took firm hold of my jacket, and the guard and I were pulled out and unceremoniously dumped onto the lawn.

Daoud wiped sludge off my face. "*Never* do that again, Sik. You've ruined your tux."

The guard started sputtering, and Daoud hauled me back onto my feet so I could cough up all that stagnant water I'd just swallowed. "Get the car, Daoud. We need to— Hey, Belet!"

She'd grabbed Kasusu out of the geraniums and drew it from its scabbard. Lit by the flames pouring from the castle, Belet looked like something from Kurnugi. I approached, and she swung around, the sword an inch from my throat.

"We're leaving, Belet."

༄ ༅ ༆ ༇

Had she even heard me? Her neck muscles looked strained, like she was holding back a battle cry. The sword tip had neatly sliced my bow tie, and two black ribbons fell away, but I didn't dare shift my gaze from Belet's eyes. "Come on."

Then, suddenly, she slumped. I caught her before she fell, and she shivered in my arms. "I don't know what just happened."

Smoke billowed out of the smashed windows. The roof was burning. People fought on, seemingly oblivious to the carnage all around them. A pair of guys wrestled on the battlements before plummeting into the moat, their hands still locked around each other's throats.

Rabisu picked a water lily off my head and ate it. "That was the best party ever. Can we go back?"

I swung open the car door. "Get in, Rabisu."

"You never let me do anything fun." But she did climb in, with a loud, petulant huff.

I checked my jacket pocket. The tablet was still in there. "This had better be worth it."

Daoud revved the engine as I pushed Belet into the backseat with Rabisu. I kept Kasusu with me, because Belet's expression made it clear she was still burning to fight. What was wrong with her?

A sudden gust of heat made me turn around. Flames filled the entrance to the keep as great clouds of black smoke unfurled into the night and flaming motes drifted in the breeze like fireflies. Then, through the inferno, a man emerged.

He was on fire, but that didn't bother him.

I couldn't see him clearly—the blaze was too blinding—but he stood at the doorway with a battle-ax in one hand and an eight-foot-long great sword in the other. The flames licked his hulking, blood-drenched body, and smoke swirled around him like a cloak.

Somewhere in the woods, dogs howled. The trees shook as birds launched into the night sky, cawing in panic. The smoke covered the sky, but it felt—I can't explain it any other way—like the moon and stars were hiding in fear.

Daoud honked the horn. "Come on, Sik!"

It was hard turning away from this man in the fire. Despite the flames, our eyes met.

I never fight, not unless all other options have long gone. It's my nature to talk my way out of trouble or, if that fails, run away. But right then, holding Kasusu, I wanted to charge at this guy with it and unleash all my rage, all my fear, every emotion I'd ever held back in my life. All my pent-up desire for violence. He understood that terrible, destructive urge, this burning man. He was almost beckoning me, and I was *desperate* to destroy him.

"Get in!" screamed Belet.

I wiped my face, as if that could erase my fury, and took

a deep breath. I looked toward my friends, the people I was supposed to protect. I leaped into the passenger seat as Daoud shifted into reverse. In his rush to get out of there, he took a side mirror off a Lamborghini and scratched the paint on a Silver Ghost Rolls-Royce, but he kept going, churning up gravel as he slammed his way through the gears.

Belet grabbed my shoulder. "What happened, Sik?"

I sat there shaking. "I don't know."

I saw the smoldering man in our rearview mirror. His skin seemed to glow in the moonlight as the last wisps of smoke drifted off his shoulders. He raised his sword and pointed it straight at me. The message was clear.

I'm coming for you.

SIX

NO ONE SAID ANYTHING ON THE DRIVE BACK, NOT EVEN Rabisu. She squirmed and fidgeted, no doubt longing to revel in the chaos, but she could read the room well enough to see that the rest of us were in shock.

We'd gone about three miles before we were almost driven off the highway by a convoy of police cars and two fire trucks, their sirens screaming at the night.

The tablet felt heavy in my jacket. I took it out and brushed my fingers across its chipped, cracked surface. The faded cuneiform was compressed, as if the author had struggled to fit everything onto the single slab of clay. The text kept going onto the back and went around and around in a seemingly never-ending tale. That was ridiculous. There were only two sides. Nothing went on forever. "What's next, Belet?"

There was something wrong with her. It wasn't only that

she and Rabisu were in the back together, determined to stay as far away from each other as possible in the cramped quarters. She gripped Kasusu so tightly she was shaking, straining to keep cool. Rabisu watched her closely, warily drumming her claws on the armrest.

"Want to swap seats?" I asked Belet, even though I doubted that would be enough.

She blinked as if just waking up. "I'll get the tablet translated. Find out exactly why Mother wanted it so badly."

"I thought you said it wasn't in any language you knew."

"But I know people. Have you heard of the apkallus? The seven sages? If they can't translate it, then no one can. I'll put the word out and see if any are available. One of them works at NASA."

Rabisu scoffed. "The apkallus? Those fools?"

Belet's jaw stiffened. "They are the wisest people in history. They brought crafts, and knowledge itself, to the people of the world."

But Rabisu wasn't going to let this one go. "You know what you call a group of very, *very* clever people? A bunch of idiots. Last time I saw the apkallus, they were arguing over the best way to boil an egg."

"How about some music?" said Daoud, taking the temperature of the situation down from boiling point.

I turned on the radio and scanned for something soft

and calming. There had to be an easy-listening station somewhere. . . .

Daoud's hand shot up. "Hold on, cuz. Go back to the news."

"The news?"

"There was something about the California fires."

Another summer, another heat wave, another conflagration across California. Global warming, barbecue grill got out of control, someone tossed a cigarette butt from their car window . . . all of the above? Who knew?

I found BBC News, and we listened to how the wildfires were raging and were expected to get worse. Temperatures were skyrocketing and would continue to climb for at least another week.

Belet suddenly leaned forward. "Turn it up."

". . . breaking news. We have reports of a major fire at Fitzroy Castle, home of Lady Eleanor Fitzroy. No details confirmed yet, but there appear to have been numerous casualties. We'll report more as soon as we can. In the meanwhile, we have an interesting story about some very important ravens. . . ."

I switched it off. Listening to this wasn't going to lift anyone's mood.

"I hope Lady Fitzroy got out okay," I said, remembering with a jolt that I'd locked her in a closet. "She didn't deserve to die. Nobody does." Had that big man caused all the mayhem and destruction? I couldn't get him out of my head.

Belet shrugged. "Caedite eos. Novit enim Dominus qui sunt eius."

"What?" asked Daoud.

"'Kill them all,'" I translated. "'God will know His own.' That's pretty harsh, Belet."

"Since when do you speak Latin?" she asked.

Yeah, since when? But somehow, I just knew what she'd said. "Must have read it on the internet. It's a famous saying from the Crusades, isn't it?"

"Infamous." She peered at me curiously. "Still..."

"It's not like you to be so cold, Belet. People are dead."

"You don't think they deserved it? Those warlords, arms dealers, and crime lords? They've escaped justice long enough, and now it's caught up with them. Their victims will finally know peace."

That was callous, but this wasn't the time to argue.

I settled back into my seat as we turned off the A2 highway toward London.

"It's trending," I said, checking my phone after we returned to Daoud's suite late that night—or early the next morning, depending on your sleeping habits. "Hashtag FitzroyMassacre."

⸱⟨⟩⟨ ⟩⟨⟩⟨ ⟨⟩⟨⟩ ⟩⟨⟩⟨⟩

Daoud threw his ripped-up tux jacket across the floor. "Like I said before, you bring the party with you."

"How is this my fault?"

"Did you see Pierre's face when I returned the Jaguar, the bodywork peppered with shotgun pellets? He raised an eyebrow!"

"That's not so bad. Belet does it all the time."

"Not so bad? If the king raises an eyebrow at you, they send you straight to the Tower of London! Even now!"

I hadn't seen him this angry since he got a pimple on the morning of the *FHM* photo shoot. "Ya Allah," he declared. "There's only one answer to this. A full mani-pedi."

"At this time of night?"

"Hey! The salon has a twenty-four-hour emergency number, and this is an emergency!" He stormed into his room, slamming the door behind him.

"Well?" said Rabisu, glaring at me. "Go say you're sorry! You've upset the Handsome One! What if he gets a wrinkle now? It'll be your fault!" She gasped. "By Ea, what if he goes ... gray?"

"Come on, Rabisu! There's more to life than just looking good!"

"Of course *you'd* say that," she replied. "It's the only way you can justify ... well, your face."

"Says the creature with two uneven horns sticking out of her head."

𒀸𒄿𒄡𒀹

"They are not uneven! I just walk with a tilt!" She snapped her claws and pointed at Daoud's door. "Go apologize. Now."

I looked to Belet for support, but she'd already vanished into her own room. Just great. "Fine. Not because you told me to, but because Daoud's my friend." I then gestured to Rabisu and me. "Which is something we are not."

"Ha!"

At times Rabisu's direct approach to life, relationships, and what she considered edible was refreshing. This was not one of those times.

I found Daoud sitting on the floor in the dark, staring out through the open window at the oak trees. In the moonlight, he looked like a marble statue, or a ghost.

He didn't turn around. "A view like this proves I've made it, doesn't it?"

I sat down beside him. "Isn't this everything you ever wanted?"

Daoud frowned slightly. "I always thought I'd share it with him."

He meant Mo, of course. My brother had been as much a part of Daoud's life as he'd been mine, maybe even more.

"He'd go to the museums, and I'd go shopping. Then it would be dinner in Soho and walks along the Embankment at night. Coming to London was his dream, right?"

I pulled out the tablet and held it under the moonbeam. "What do you think he would've made of this?"

"I wish he were here to tell us."

"Me too, Daoud." The low light emphasized the shadows created by the wedges on the clay, making the symbols appear to move. "He'd force us to go to the British Museum. It has more artifacts than there are back in Iraq." I grinned, remembering what Mo used to say when he looked through the museum's catalog. "You know why the pyramids are in Egypt?"

"Why?"

"Because they were too big for the British to steal."

Daoud didn't laugh. "He'd wanted to go to Kew Gardens," he said. "Had it all planned out, right down to what we'd take on our picnic."

"Including a bottle of the Baghdad sauce?"

Daoud smirked. "You have to ask? The guy used to put it on his cornflakes. I think his taste buds must have burned out when he was little. There's no other explanation for it."

"*We* could go to Kew," I suggested. "It's not far, is it?"

"It won't be the same without him, Sik. He would have bored us with the Latin names of all the plants and wanted to spend hours taking photos of every single flower."

"He applied for a job there once. A three-month contract

just cataloging seeds. Can you imagine anything duller? Still, I wish he'd gotten it. Things would have turned out differently."

If he'd gotten that job, he wouldn't have ended up in Iraq. Ended up there and never come back.

It still hurt and it always would, Mo being gone. He was happy where he was, exploring the wonders of Kurnugi, but that wasn't the same as having him sitting with us right now, gazing out across the trees. The gauze curtains rustled in the cool night breeze, and for a moment, it felt like there *was* another presence with us. But it was just me, wishing.

SEVEN

THE SMELLS WOKE ME UP. IT'S ALWAYS THE FIRST OF MY
senses that kicks into gear, all part of living above a deli.
I lay there, eyes closed, slowly filtering out the mélange of
odors. They were all very yummy, and my stomach agreed
loudly.

Not even bothering with the hotel slippers, I shuffled
out into the living room. Four carts were lined up in a neat
silver row, all bathed in the sunlight of another glorious
English summer's day. Not too cold, not too hot, just right.

Daoud was doing his morning push-ups—one-handed,
because he was holding his phone in the other. The guy
knew how to multitask. "Hello? Can I speak to the person in charge? What do you mean 'in charge of what'? Of
everything!" He looked at me. "Salaam, cuz. Just arranging our visit to Kew Gardens. Go try the waffles. They're
gluten-, dairy-, and fat-free, cooked in ionized olive oil. And

before you roll your eyes at me, yes, ionized olive oil is a thing."

Ionized or not, the waffles looked delicious. I sat down and helped myself to . . . all of them. What can I say? I'm a stress eater, and last night had been, well, just this side of apocalyptic. "Where are the others?"

He swapped hands in mid–push-up. "Belet's gone out. Rabisu's in the kitchenette."

"Do I want to know what she's having for breakfast?"

"Probably not. You should— Hold on. Who's this? Dr. Sarah Anderson? Chief botanist? Great. I'm looking for a pair of VIP passes. You know, so we don't have to mix with regular people when we visit."

I put down my waffle. "Daoud, we can just get tickets from the website. Like everyone else."

"But we're not like everyone else, Sik! We're special!"

Honestly, it wasn't worth the effort fighting him over this. We were stuck in the orbit around planet Daoud. The gravitational pull of his ego was irresistible.

The one-handed push-ups became one-finger push-ups. "Do you know who I am? This is Daoud Hassan you're talking to! I'm on a first-name basis with Anna Wintour! Me and my very good friend Sikander Aziz, the savior of Manhattan, wish to . . . What's that? Really?" Daoud held out the phone. "She wants to talk to you."

"Me? Why?"

"Because my beauty intimidates her? I don't know. Just...just talk to her."

I took the phone and let Daoud get on with his thousand-a-day push-up routine. "Hello? This is Sikander Aziz."

"Hi, Sik. I'm Dr. Sarah Anderson, the chief botanist at Kew Gardens. This is quite a remarkable coincidence. Your name came up at this morning's staff meeting."

"That's...nice?" Also, creepy. Had word of my chance encounter with the flower of immortality somehow made it across the pond?

"Could you come here today? A member of staff knows you and is quite anxious to speak with you."

"Who is it? Can you put them on?"

Dr. Anderson hesitated. "It would be easier if you saw him in person."

Gilgamesh? It had to be! He'd been working as a gardener at Central Park when I'd met him, in a seven-tiered magical ziggurat that, somehow, nobody had noticed sitting smack-bang in the middle of Manhattan. But after the drama with Nergal, he'd packed up and moved on...to Kew? It made total sense! Having the most "main man" *ever* watching my back—and hopefully eager to explain what was going on—could only be a good thing.

Gilgamesh had given up being the world's most legendary hero. He was a pacifist nowadays, but that didn't mean he'd relinquished any of his power. He'd be exactly the right person to help us figure out who that burning guy was last night.

"What time?" I asked.

"We're open now. Just come to the reception desk and ask for me."

"I'm on my way." I hung up. "We're off, Daoud."

"Now? But I'm only halfway through my morning routine!" He switched to doing crunches. "Only another couple of hours and I'll be ready."

"I'll go on my own, then," I said. "Somebody wants to meet me—I think I know who." I grinned, but he didn't take the bait. He only grunted like the gym rat he was.

Rabisu stood in the kitchenette with a half-eaten sandwich. I noticed feathers stuck between her teeth but decided not to comment. London had plenty of pigeons to spare.

"I'm heading out for a while. Can I trust you to stay out of trouble?"

"No."

At least she was honest. "Fine. Just stay with Daoud and, I don't know, count how many sit-ups he does."

"The Handsome One exercises very often. It's something you should consider, too. Consider quite seriously."

"Thank you for your concern. No sign of Belet?"

Rabisu handed me an envelope. "She left you this."

"It's been opened."

Rabisu finished off her sandwich. "Yes. That was the only way I could read it."

Honestly, there was no point arguing with her over this—or anything else.

Belet's message was brief. She was off to track down one of the seven sages she'd mentioned last night. For once it was good news—the guy was working at the Royal Observatory in Greenwich, not far from here. I was to sit tight, not do anything, and wait for her to come back with the translation in a day or two. Could it be that simple? I hoped so. I really did. Then we could do the sightseeing we had planned and stop meddling with ancient artifacts and burning men and such. This trip could actually turn out to be *fun*.

Rabisu looked at me suspiciously. "You're smiling. It's weird."

"Am I? I'm about to see someone who can help solve a mystery, just like that." I snapped my fingers.

"It's never 'just like that.' So, who is it?"

Best not to mention Gilgamesh to a demon. He'd made life very difficult for a lot of her friends back in Mesopotamia, back when Gilgamesh was old-school— actually, the original school—and heroism came down to slaughtering your enemies in a great multitude. Rivers-of-blood-and-neck-deep-in-corpses kind of thing.

I finished lacing up my boots and gave them a stomp

to settle my toes in. "You might need a toothpick for those feathers," I said in parting.

They call the subway "the tube" or "the underground" here, and the map is impossible to decipher. How did anyone ever find their destination? I imagined commuters getting trapped on the Circle line for years, growing progressively paler from lack of sunlight and feeding on other passengers for sustenance. Also, why the ultra-bright colors? Gazing at the map gave me a headache, but I eventually figured out where I was heading and, thankfully, managed to find myself at Kew Gardens while it was still daylight.

I reached the reception desk. "Hi. I'm here to see Dr. Anderson. She's expecting me."

The receptionist directed me to one of the greenhouses. I peered around for Gilgamesh. You couldn't miss him— he's about seven feet tall with a physique that looks like it was hammered from granite. There were a few people at work, digging, pruning, and cataloging. I headed toward the one who appeared to be the supervisor. She had a clipboard at least.

"Dr. Anderson?"

She looked up. "Sikander Aziz?"

I nodded, still searching for the big guy. "So where is he?"

𒀸𒃻𒌋𒁕𒄩

She pointed past my shoulder. "Right there."

A man was on his knees, pruning a flowery bush. Not Gilgamesh, but . . . still familiar. He stood up, brushed the dirt off his pants, and wandered over, taking off his sun hat. "Assalamu alaikum, Yakhi."

More than familiar. Much, much more.

He grinned at me. "You've grown."

I just stared. It wasn't possible. But there he stood. Right there in front of me.

It was my brother.

Mo.

EIGHT

MO. WAS. DEAD.

He'd been killed three years ago, in a motorcycle accident in a village outside Mosul. Mama and Baba had received that middle-of-the-night phone call all parents dread, and our hearts had broken into a million pieces.

"Mashallah, you're as tall as me." He held out his arms. "How about a hug?"

It had taken years, but I'd finally come to accept that he was gone. I'd forced myself to move on, realizing that there were those among the living who needed me, and I owed it to myself to be happy without him.

He *couldn't* be alive.

This had to be a trick. Some demon in disguise was trying to exploit me, to use my feelings for my brother against me.

He wasn't the same Mo I remembered. He was older, more weathered and beaten up. His cheekbone was lopsided, and scars crisscrossed his face like a jigsaw puzzle. Half his hair had been reduced to patchy clumps growing beside trenches in his scalp.

Mo caught me staring and drew his hands self-consciously over his wounds. "The doctors did their best after the accident, but there was only so much a small refugee hospital could do. I was pretty mangled in the crash."

Yet this person was acting just like Mo. My heart was telling me, *This is your brother.* Why couldn't I be happy? Euphoric? Why was I so . . . scared?

I should have been jumping up and down. I should have been squeezing all the breath out of him with the biggest hug ever. Instead, I couldn't bear to touch him. What sort of brother was I?

Was it fear? Wariness? Or was I just being petty?

The first time Mo went off to Iraq, I was eight. Everyone had made such a huge deal of him leaving. I'd cried, begging him to stay, heartbroken that my big brother was going away for six months, which seemed like an eternity. I'd spoiled his farewell dinner with my sniffling. Mama and Baba had taken him to the airport without me. The first few weeks with him gone had been miserable. But then things changed. I got up and got it together. I started helping out at the deli. Everyone asked about Mo—of course they would—but they also gave me their orders and left me tips. I was special, too. I started being somebody.

Then he came home and it was all about Mo again. The local hero, the family celebrity. I was nobody once more. But at least I had a brother...until the second time he went to Iraq.

Now, apparently, Mo wasn't just back from a trip—he was back from the dead. He was standing right in front of me. The wish I'd wanted more than anything had been granted.

But it wasn't right. This wasn't how the world was supposed to work!

I was afraid to touch him—afraid that if I did, he'd vanish, like last time.

So, Mo just stepped forward and took me in his arms. Like an older brother would.

Ya Allah. It *was* him. I could never forget the smell of sweat and soil he'd always worn like a perfume. It didn't matter how many aftershaves or lotions Daoud loaned him—Mo always smelled this way. You couldn't fake it. He tightened his arms around me, and I knew he was real. All those times when I'd been little and scared—by the thunder, or some bully at school—he'd held me and I'd known, truer than anything, that everything was going to be okay.

Dr. Anderson cleared her throat. "Mohammed, take your brother to the café. You two have plenty of catching up to do."

Mo looked at me. "Come on. My treat. You ever had cream tea? It's the one thing the Brits have gotten right."

Dr. Anderson laughed and waved us off.

I couldn't help staring. At how he'd changed, and how he seemed exactly the same. He limped slightly and seemed embarrassed when I rushed ahead to open the door for him. The café wasn't big—just a half dozen plastic tables—but the glass walls looked out onto the dense foliage of one of the greenhouses. Mo showed the girl behind the counter his staff badge and placed the order.

He sat down opposite me and let out a deep, happy sigh. "Look at that beard. You planning on becoming an imam?"

"It's been three years, Mo. We all thought you were... weren't coming back."

He scratched at the scar running down his deformed cheekbone. "I'll give you the short version. I was traveling along the road back to the camp on my bike when this truck swerved around a corner. It was packed with sheep for the local souk. The road wasn't more than a track in the sand. . . . There was nothing I could do. All I remember before the accident were all these sheep just staring at me." He laughed. That barking, abrupt laugh of his, summing up all that was ridiculous in the world. "Can you imagine that being the last thing you see?"

"Then what?"

"Then everything got all messed up. I was in a coma, and the doctor didn't think I'd come out of it. Info was mis-reported to the NGO I was working for. They called Mama and Baba without double-checking. I'm so sorry, Sik."

"But that was three years ago, Mo. What have you been doing all this time? Why didn't you contact us?"

"I was transferred to another hospital. My skull had been shattered into a dozen pieces, as you can tell. It was a US military hospital used to dealing with this kind of injury. But I was recorded as a John Doe. They were in such a rush to get me there, no one bothered with the paperwork, and I got lost in the system. When I eventually woke up from my coma, I couldn't remember who I was. My memories were all jumbled. The doctors said memory loss is common after a serious head injury and my brain would eventually repair itself—they just didn't know when. So, I found work at the local school as the gardener. Then, over time, I made my way here. Kew Gardens is running a project out in Iraq. I applied for a position and got the job—I've been here for about a month now. Then, last night, a big piece of the puzzle fell right into place. I could finally remember what happened to me. I don't know how. I spoke to Dr. Anderson this morning, but we

⩜⧼⧧⧼⧠⧽⧬⊦

had no way of tracking you down. And then came the phone call. Can you believe it? It was all kismet."

"We've gotta call home right now." I checked my watch. Twelve o'clock here made it . . . seven there. "They'll be up."

"Who's 'they'?"

"Mama and Baba! Who else?" I pulled up FaceTime on my phone, but then switched to the regular deli number instead. I didn't want to freak them out too much at first.

Mo was frowning, though. "I . . . Okay, Sik. If you say so."

"What's wrong? Don't you want to speak to them?"

Mo began rubbing his old head wounds. "It's still pretty scrambled in here. Things don't make total sense yet. Sometimes I can't tell if my memories are real or just fantasies. Like, I have this weird memory of you and me swimming in the sea. And finding a cave with a flower in it. But that's not possible, right?"

No, it wasn't possible. And yet it had all happened—in Kurnugi. When he'd been *dead*.

The phone was ringing. It clicked. "Benny's Bagels. Can I take your order?"

Weird. I thought I'd punched in the right number. Maybe I'd used the wrong country code or something. I hung up without saying anything. I'd try again from the hotel.

The hotel . . . Daoud.

"Daoud's gonna lose it when he sees you."

"Who's Daoud?" asked Mo.

"Ya salam, Mo! He's, like, your . . . best friend ever? Come on, Mo. You two were always together. Like *really* close."

That was one way of putting it.

But Mo looked genuinely blank. Then he smiled. "I'm sure it'll come back when I see him. Ya Allah, Sik. I feel like I've been reborn. Like my whole life just started yesterday."

You know what? *That* creeped me out. Here I was, sitting with my brother who'd been dead. Mix-up at the hospital? Memory loss? I could almost accept all that except for one thing—I had gone to the land of the dead and *found him there*. Erishkigal, the queen of the netherworld, had name-checked him. Yet how could I deny what was right in front of me, and everything I felt?

I stood up when the cream tea arrived. "Come on. We're all staying at the Ritz. They make an even better cream tea, and there are some people I need you to meet."

Mo looked up at me, smirking. "Taking charge now, are we? You've changed a lot. Grown up a lot, Sik. I guess we do have plenty of catching up to do."

Now I laughed. It *was* him. It was *him*. A part of me had been broken off three years ago, but now I was whole again. "You have no idea, Yakhi. No idea at all."

It was Mo.

It was a miracle.

NINE

"HE'S ALIVE? ALHAMDULILLAH, SIK! ALHAMDULILLAH! Where is he?"

I'd sat Daoud down to tell him the news, but now he was jumping around the suite, yelling at the top of his lungs.

"No questions?" I asked him as he darted past where I was sitting on the sofa.

He slid to a stop. "What sort of questions?"

"I dunno, like 'How come he's alive? Where's he been for the last three years?' Those sorts of questions."

Daoud genuinely looked confused. "Why question a miracle?"

"It just seems ... too good to be true." It felt like I was betraying Mo by saying it, as if I was still, secretly, wishing it wasn't true.

Daoud grabbed my arm. "Last year I was frying onions at your parents' deli. Now look where I am."

"I wouldn't put this in quite the same category, Daoud."

"Then which category would you put it in? The same one as 'thirteen-year-old Arab kid drives a chariot pulled by winged cats, takes on the god of disease, and saves the world'? That category?" He pulled me up and spun me around. "We have a demon living in the apartment, cuz. Your girlfriend owns a palace."

"She's not my . . . Okay. When you put it like that, maybe Mo coming back isn't quite so strange. After all, I went to Kurnugi and came back. Why not him?"

"Where is he?"

"Downstairs. I just wanted to speak to you first. I know how you feel about him. But he's changed—inside and out. Mo suffered some major head injuries, and his memory's all scrambled. He doesn't remember huge chunks of his life. It was only yesterday that he remembered me."

Daoud stopped dancing. "What . . . what about me?"

"Give him time, Daoud. It'll all come back."

"You saying he doesn't remember me at all?" The disappointment in his voice was painful.

"We'll spend time with him—that'll help. And speaking to Mama and Baba will, too. I tried calling home but got some bagel store."

Daoud frowned. "Benny's Bagels?"

"Yeah. How d'you know?"

"Your parents took over Benny's. The owner was

retiring and he liked the idea of selling it to another family. The city has enough McDonald's."

"You sure Benny didn't set up somewhere else? Keep the name, and maybe his phone number is similar to Mo's? That could explain the mix-up. Maybe I did use the wrong country code. I'm still not sure about calling from abroad."

But Daoud wasn't interested in talking about bagels. He was checking his reflection. "I need to exfoliate! And look at my hair—it's a mess!"

If I were as crazy handsome as Daoud, I would thank Allah every time I looked in the mirror. Yet all he saw were flaws. And the weird thing was, the more successful he became, the more flaws he spotted. He'd once spent a weekend obsessing over the size of his earlobes—the right was ever so slightly longer than the left—and he'd refused to go out one time after he'd eaten a doughnut, weeping about how it was going to take his percentage of body fat into the double digits. I didn't get it, but Daoud was a mystery to everyone, including himself.

"You look great, Daoud. You always do."

He shook his head. "I thought I was over him, Sik. Now what's going to happen?"

"We got a second chance. How many people ever get that?"

There was a knock at the door. Daoud stood there, rigid with terror.

"It's just Mo," I said. "The same guy he's always been. Relax."

Daoud nodded, then quickly kicked off his flip-flops and draped himself over the sofa by the open window so the wind blew through his hair *just so*. "How's this?"

"Maybe a bit too much? Or possibly perfect?" I crossed the room and let Mo in.

Seeing him in the flesh—the real, living flesh—still hit like a punch in the chest.

Mo laughed at my expression. "You look like you've seen a ghost. Again."

He saw the world differently from everyone else, as if he knew some great, wonderful secret and needed just to recall it, which he could do easily, to bring up that laugh. It had echoed through our deli, through my entire life, and was like an extra heartbeat. Like the possessor of such a laugh had twice as much life as everyone else. Which was literally true. This *was* Mo's second time around.

Daoud sprang from the sofa. The guy could move, that's for sure. "Salaam, Mo. I'm—"

"Daoud Hassan," said Mo, his eyes widening. "Ya salam. I'm a big fan."

"Really?" asked Daoud.

Mo took his hand and gave it a fantastic shake. "Big, big fan. I hear that you're on the short list for the next...you know, that spy character. Mabrook! You'd be amazing!"

"Er, shukran."

I could see how awkward Daoud felt. Mo wasn't supposed to be a fan—he was a friend. More than that.

Daoud had put his life on hold for Mo, back when they were in Manhattan together. And after Mo's death, Daoud had tried, in his own odd, narcissistic way, to be the older-brother replacement. He'd worked at the deli and hung around the family to look after me because he'd promised Mo. That was next-level loyalty.

Now his life was, to anyone looking from the outside, a glamorous fantasy. But there were drawbacks. Like the one person he could be his true self with was just another fan, blinded by stardust.

They stood facing each other, neither one knowing what to do. They both turned to me for help. After all, I did have some experience coming back from the dead myself.

Mo stepped closer to Daoud, nodding as he walked around him. "Is that shirt an Antonius? The stitching looks like his work."

Daoud gazed back, looking more than a little surprised. "You can tell?"

Since when had Mo ever been into fashion? He'd been a patched-jeans kind of guy. But Mo wasn't done. "Look at these seams. A work of art. Don't you think so, Sik?"

"Er...yeah. Doing a great job holding up his sleeves. I love that."

𒀀𒈾𒊑𒌓

Just then I heard some singing in Rabisu's room. What she lacked in tone, harmony, and rhythm, she made up for in volume and enthusiasm. The door swung open as she declared, "...caught in a bad romance!"

She stopped in the threshold, and her gaze narrowed as she saw Mo standing beside Daoud. "Who is this, and why should I not kill him?"

That wasn't exactly the best start. I took a discreet step between my brother and the demon. "Rabisu, play nice. This is my brother, Mohammed."

"Is it?" she asked.

"Yes, it is." Then I turned to Mo. "This is Rabisu. She's, er..."

What? I didn't know why, but she had tinsel wrapped around her horns, and her tail was swishing happily from side to side. *Best to just get this out in the open and deal with it right here, right now.* "She's a demon from Kurnugi."

Mo looked at me, then at Rabisu. Eventually he shrugged. "My life's been pretty weird for a while, so sure. A demon. Salaam, Rabisu."

She did not reply but glared at him, her claws folded across her chest. "This isn't right."

"Does this have to do with what happened in New York last year?" said Mo. "I read about all sorts of riots. Some said it was a demonic invasion; others said it was aliens... something about seeing a UFO flying down Broadway?"

People need to reframe catastrophic events into a story they can understand. Which is why last year's infestation by Nergal and his plague demons had been named the Alien Variant in the press and social media, and the hordes of since-cured mutant poxies had become mere anti-vaxxers. It didn't come close to the truth, but most people can't handle the truth.

"That's one way of putting it. The UFO was actually a chariot drawn by winged big cats. *I* was driving it." I looked over at him, realizing how bonkers that sounded. "You do believe me, don't you?"

He shook his head. "Okay. We *really* have a lot of catching up to do."

Rabisu walked around my brother. "What's he doing here? He's supposed to be dead! Queen Erishkigal won't like this *at all*. She hates it when people leave her kingdom."

"He's not dead. There was a mistake."

Rabisu poked her own belly. "I have a bad feeling in my gut, right here."

"It's probably indigestion from that pigeon you had for breakfast."

She and I needed to talk privately, so I turned to Daoud and my brother. "Look, why spend today all cooped up in here? We're in London! Mo, you've always wanted to visit the British Museum—why not head there now for a couple of hours before dinner?"

Mo smiled. "I'd like that."

"Great. Why don't you and Daoud go down to the lobby to order a cab? We'll join you in a couple of minutes."

It was obvious I was trying to get rid of them, but Daoud and Mo didn't find it too hard to go along with my plan. Mo gazed around the suite. "Can I freshen up first? I'm still covered in dirt."

Daoud gestured down the hallway. "The door at the end. Use the shower if you like. And pick anything you want out of the closet. There are some samples from Stella McCartney's new collection."

"Not her Equinox line...?" asked Mo, trying not to sound too keen.

The moment he vanished, Daoud spun around. "He's definitely not the same Mo. We were friends for years, and in all that time, he never showed any interest in fashion. But now? He recognized my shirt's designer by the stitching!"

"Isn't that good? Maybe it's his memory coming back, but in a weird way."

"It's more than that, Sik."

What was bothering Daoud so much? "You're making a bigger deal than it is. So what if he recognizes a shirtmaker?"

Daoud prodded his chest. "A 'shirtmaker'? It's easier to get into Area 51 than to get invited to Antonius's store! Something's not right. Mo's not the same."

𒀀 𒑐 𒀯 𒈾

"Just give him time, that's all. We'll meet you down-stairs in a little bit."

He knew I was trying to shoo him off, but he left none-theless. We all needed more time to get used to Mo having come back from the dead. A *lot* more time.

Rabisu clicked her claws together. She did not look happy. "Yesterday he was dead, and now he's sightseeing with the Handsome One. Something is very wrong."

"You're just jealous." I tried to act as casual as possible, as if the whole world being turned upside down wasn't that big a deal. "There was a mistake at the hospital, and he lost his memory."

"He died and went to Kurnugi, where you found him. Your immortality gave you a free exit pass from the land of the dead, but your brother stayed there, where he belonged," she said. "Something has changed. What?"

"Maybe good things happen to good people? That's not a concept you'd be particularly familiar with."

"Good? You'd have to be a wali a thousand times over for this to happen!" snapped Rabisu. "We need to find out...."

Her gaze shifted to the open window and the balcony beyond. A bird was perched on the railing, its head moving from side to side as if following our conversation.

"It's a magpie..." said Rabisu. I'm not sure whether she was talking to me or herself. "What's it doing here?"

⚔ ⚔ ⚔ ⚔

She was right. It was just like the one I'd seen last night at Fitzroy's. Coincidence?

It fluttered into the room, perched itself on the sofa, and looked around. There were plenty of shiny objects in the suite. But its attention didn't go to the silver teaspoons or the glittering chandeliers—it looked straight at the clay tablet I'd left lying on the coffee table.

"Lunch is finally served," said Rabisu as she crept toward it. "How about it? I could stick you in the oven with a clove of garlic shoved up your—"

The bird flew off. Clearly magpies were a lot smarter than London's pigeons.

I held out her turban. "C'mon, Rabisu, take a day off. We're winning for once—why not enjoy it?"

While she was busy covering her horns, I tried contacting Mama and Baba again, but the call wouldn't go through. I couldn't pull up emails or access the website for Mo's Deli, either. Even WhatsApp was down. It was so frustrating when I had the greatest news ever to share! Maybe my settings were all messed up? It was a cheap phone after all.

Rabisu didn't seem too worried. "So you'll tell them face-to-face. Won't that be better?"

"Getting sound advice from a demon. That's how insane my life is."

"I'm the best thing that's ever happened to you," said

Rabisu as she tucked the end of her turban into place. "Few mortals have ever had the honor of calling Rabisu, the terror of the Chaldeans, their friend. And don't think I haven't noticed that you still haven't put up my photo as your screen saver."

"My phone crashes whenever I try. I don't think the facial-recognition algorithms can handle your ... unique look."

"Then how about a tattoo?" She really wasn't going to let this go. "My face emblazoned upon your forehead. It will make you much more popular than you are right now. Which is not very."

I picked up the tablet and tucked it into my day pack. Better not leave it lying around while we were all out. "We'll circle back to this conversation another time. Maybe in a century or two."

TEN

THE BRITISH MUSEUM WAS ONLY A FEW MILES AWAY—
just a ten-minute drive—but a lot can change in ten minutes. Like the weather.

The cabbie pulled over on Great Russell Street. I opened the car door and held out my palm to feel great fat raindrops coming down. "The sky was clear when we left the hotel."

"Welcome to England," said Rabisu as she stepped out. The slate-gray sky rumbled, and the rain pelted us hard. I held the day pack over my head as we stood at the tall black railings outside the British Museum. The building was colossal, like some ancient Greek temple on steroids. It had to be colossal—it held the treasures of the whole world within its walls.

Coming from the smart hotels and boutique shops of Piccadilly to here was like being transported back in time, to the grandeur of the British Empire. The museum's entrance was lined with immense columns, with a classical-style pediment decorated with a marble frieze showing the rise of Western civilization.

As if none of the others counted.

"Is that it?" said Rabisu. "But it's so dull! If you really want to impress people, you build a ziggurat. Everyone knows that!"

"Ziggurats haven't been a thing for a while, Rabisu."

She sighed.

I looked around for Mo and Daoud. They'd wisely taken another taxi but were nowhere to be seen.

"They must already be inside," I said to Rabisu. We went up the steps of the museum and through the massive bronze doors into the main lobby.

"Why didn't they wait for us?"

"Don't worry. I think I know where to find them."

I grabbed a map and waved it at Rabisu. "Room Seven. That's where they'll be."

"What's in Room Seven?"

"Mesopotamia—what else?"

The place was packed! Crowds swept back and forth across the Great Court. The roof dome was all glass, the sky above a somber, damp gray. Straight ahead was the Reading Room, but we turned left.

Two great stone scorpion-folk statues stood on either

side of the entrance to Room Seven. The upper torsos were human, and the lower were segmented with six legs and a giant curved tail bearing its deadly stinger. Their arms ended not with hands but with cumbersome, way-too-big pincers. I passed between them to my destination: the friezes of King Ashurbanipal's royal lion hunt.

"Rubbish!" declared Rabisu. She pointed a claw at Ashurbanipal galloping majestically upon a plumed steed. "He looked nothing like that! Had a massive wart right on his nose! Why did they leave that out? It was his second-best feature!"

"I know I'm gonna regret asking . . . but what was his best?"

"His hump!"

"Of course it was."

She tapped her shoulder. "Right there, and as big as a melon."

A couple of senior citizens on scooters glared at the disguised demon as she added a few more personal details about the ancient king that weren't in any of the history books. One of the staff members tutted loudly. I took Rabisu aside. "Look, why don't you go check out what's in the café? See if they do a fatoush salad, or just falafel."

"But I was at Nineveh, Sik. And believe me, those lions were not that big!"

"The *café*, Rabisu. Maybe they have pigeon pie?"

𒀀 𒈦 𒂊 𒉡 𒄿

That got her attention. "You think?"

I handed her a ten-pound note. "That's worth about fifteen dollars, so don't spend it all."

So where were Mo and Daoud? The gallery was so swollen with people you could barely see the displays. It was as if the whole world had congregated to see the treasures of Mesopotamia. It made me both proud and a little sad. There was more love for the people of ancient Iraq than there was for the current ones. Still, I was here, so I figured I might as well check out the other friezes. I saw more than lions prowling the walls. . . .

There was also a dragon.

And not just any old dragon, but the mother of all monsters herself.

Tiamat, the goddess of chaos.

Scaled, clawed, winged, and fanged, blazing with majestic horror. The frieze had sections missing, but that felt right, as if she was too much to be contained in a single image. She broke the boundaries, encompassing realms beyond any we could imagine or measure. In the brightly lit gallery, her capacity to terrorize was muted, but what must it have been like to see her bearing down on you in some dark temple full of incense and shadow? This was a scene from the *Enuma Elish*—the *Epic of Creation*—the tale of how the Mesopotamian gods fought and defeated the great chaos goddess and her host of monstrous spawn, and then built the universe from her corpse. If only I could have a better look, but there were just too many ...

Everyone stopped. I mean froze. Then, in a neat and orderly fashion, with a minimum of fuss and barely any noise, they all filed out. They ignored me entirely, stepping around but not acknowledging me in any way. The elderly couple's scooters hummed softly as they wheeled past me and through the exit. In a matter of seconds, I was alone in the gallery.

No, not quite. There was one other man. I'd seen him before, the previous night, standing in the blazing doorway of Fitzroy Castle, drenched in blood.

"Beautiful, isn't she?" he asked as he gazed at Tiamat. "So beautiful."

Where's the exit? That was my first thought. It was also thoughts two through to ten, but there was only one way out and that was past this guy, who looked eager for me to stay.

"You've created quite a stir, Sikander Aziz," he said as he turned away from viewing the frieze.

"So, you know my name, but I don't know yours." I hoped my voice wasn't shaking too much.

"Call me Lugal. It's a shame we didn't get a chance to meet yesterday. The fun had just begun."

Fun? He called last night's massacre *fun*? Ya Allah, who was this guy? Lugal? I racked my brain for a memory of that name but couldn't find anything. "I have to get home. I'm due for, er, a manicure."

Not exactly the wittiest of replies, and pure Daoud. I promised myself I'd come up with something fresher the next time I was in mortal peril.

"You have something I want, Sikander. If you give it to me, you can go back to your friends and I will trouble you no more."

Trouble? This Lugal was to trouble what nukes are to firecrackers. I wanted to be away—far, far away—because you knew that when he blew, he'd take everyone down with him. It wasn't just because he was big—and he was very big—but there was also a frenzy, a rage threatening to erupt from him.

He was trying hard to keep it together and failing. A thick red vein pulsed in his forehead, and his features were tense. His beard was patchy, and his hair roughly shorn and unkempt—stringy locks dangled over his left cheek. His suit had frayed cuffs, and he'd buttoned his shirt wrong, so the collar button didn't meet the hole. But instead of fixing it, he'd knotted a tie around it anyway. He'd even made a mess of that, too, with one end dangling way too long. His shoes were held together by duct tape, and their laces had snapped and been reknotted. The guy could have the museum to himself but couldn't get a spare pair of laces? The clothes maketh the man, or at least that's what Daoud said. Lugal's clothes were falling apart at the seams.

I knew that look. I'd seen it a hundred times before, when we served at the masjid's kebab kitchen back home. New York might be the greatest city in the world, but for a lot of people, it is their personal Jahannam. Mama and Baba had always done what they could for others like themselves, refugees who'd had to abandon their homes and all their loved ones. For people who had witnessed horrors that would haunt them forever. Post-traumatic stress disorder affects all victims of war, not just the soldiers. So, while I was scared of Lugal, I also felt pity for him.

"What's so important about that tablet?" I asked. "Ishtar wanted it, too."

"It can't do her any good now, can it?" said Lugal, rubbing his temples with his knuckles. "I want it because it's *mine*. It was stolen from me. Look at all this. These friezes were stolen, too. Shouldn't they be back in Iraq, where they belong? This entire museum was built on loot. These historians are nothing but thieves."

You know when villains are the most dangerous? When they're right.

It wasn't just the Mesopotamian artifacts. The Rosetta Stone was in the gallery next door. Plenty of people thought it belonged back in Cairo. Great stone carvings had been taken from the temples of Mesoamerica. Jeweled statues shipped from the temples of India and beyond. The British Empire had ruled much of the world once, and the world had paid for that "privilege" by handing over its history. That was the way of empires.

Lugal winced. I could tell there was turmoil deep within him, and it had been there for a long time. "You know what history is? Just a long series of dates and battles. Nothing more. You pretend there's some great noble purpose to your existence, but there isn't. It's all just chaos, Sikander. Believe me, I know."

"If that's true, then what difference would me giving you the tablet make?"

Lugal looked at me with the saddest gaze I'd ever seen. "It would give me some small measure of peace."

Was he another Mesopotamian god? His eyes shone with the same starlight as Gilgamesh's and Ishtar's, and he had the same presence, as if he was far greater than what we could perceive in our limited sense of reality. But with Ishtar and Gilgamesh I'd felt safe, cared for. With Lugal, all I felt was the threat of annihilation.

I shook my head. "I don't believe that."

"That's because you're young. If you'd seen what I've seen, lived merely a fraction of my lives, you'd feel only despair. That's why I'm speaking to you here. I want you to know my intentions are peaceful."

"They weren't so peaceful last night."

᯼ ᨑ ᨏ ᨔ

Lugal waved his hand dismissively. "Some people succumb to their dark side more easily than others."

"Are you saying I don't have a dark side? Wow, that makes me sound really boring."

He laughed. There was no joy in it at all, just weariness. "You really want to be like the daughter of Ishtar? She's so complicated, even she doesn't know who she is."

"You know Belet?"

"I know the type," he said. "Belet has more darkness in—"

He winced again, but this was an extra-big grimace. He screwed up his eyes really tight, and the veins on his thick neck stood out like steel cables. A feeble groan slipped through his clamped jaw. He pressed his palms against his head so hard I thought he'd crack his own skull. But he wasn't trying to break it—he was trying to hold it together.

I felt a pulse go straight from his mind into mine. I caught a glimpse of the turmoil inside him, the whirlpool of his thoughts and emotions.

What did I see? A swirling darkness. What did I hear? Only screams. Endless screams. But before I was compelled to add mine, it was over. Unsettling images—only half glimpsed and thankfully too faint to understand—flickered in my mind before they faded away like a nightmare in the morning sunlight.

How could anyone hold all that in their head and not

go insane? Answer? They couldn't. I stared at Lugal as he dragged great deep breaths into his huge chest, clawing back control, weak and temporary though it was. He slowly released his head and opened his eyes. The pain within them dimmed . . . a little.

Alarms sounded. From the other galley I heard shouts and . . . cheering? A few moments later, the floor shook as there was a thunderous crash. More alarms echoed from all directions. Then the sounds of stampeding feet and yelling.

"What's going on?" I asked.

"The people are reclaiming their heritage. Unless I'm very much mistaken, that school group from Athens is taking back the Elgin Marbles." Lugal paused as the sound of breaking glass came from above. "That'll be the mummies in Room Sixty-two."

"The mummies are escaping?"

"No, the Cairo tour group is smashing them out of their display cabinets."

"People can't do that! You can't let them!"

"Why not, Sikander?" He looked genuinely interested. "Weren't they stolen in the first place?"

"But . . . but there are rules." I didn't sound as convincing as I should have. "Otherwise, it's chaos."

"We understand each other perfectly," he said. "Ah, our meeting is about to end."

⟨꞊⟨ ⟨⟨꞊⟨ ⟨⟩ ⟩⟨⟩

I felt air moving behind me, and I ducked. Feathers brushed the top of my head, and when I looked up, a magpie had perched itself on Lugal's broad shoulders. The man cocked his head toward the bird, idly brushing its gullet with his knuckle. "So, loyal servant, what do you have for me?"

The magpie shook itself. Feathers fell from its wings and body—more and more as the bird grew and transformed. It dropped to the floor and shrieked, and that sound became a cry—a human one.

I know I should have turned and run, but the metamorphosis only took seconds, and in that short time, my mind wasn't on rational things. It was on this bird that was changing into...

...a young man. He stood up next to Lugal, straightened, and ran his slim, taloned fingers through the tuft of black and white feathers on top of his head. "He has it on his person, lord. In his backpack."

Lugal gestured toward me. "Then take it off him."

The young man adjusted his downy kirtle as if he had all the time in the world. "My pleasure."

The time to flee had arrived.

I spun on my heels and moved, but the magpie man was quicker. He may have lost his wings, yet he practically flew past me, blocking the exit. Beyond him, a riot was spreading through the Great Hall.

He tutted. "Just hand it over."

I really wished I'd watched at least one of Belet's how-to-fight videos. But I'd seen her in action plenty of times....

I double-darted, just like she'd done last night. Step left, leap right, then leap back left. Each move built up bounce, that springiness you get when everything's in sync, and...boom! I just touched the wall with my toe and then ricocheted straight into the magpie man's chest, kneefirst. He crumpled, and I slid past him.

How had that happened? It had been so...instinctive, like a routine I'd practiced so often my body just knew it. Had I really picked it up just from watching Belet? I didn't think kung fu worked like—

"Make way! Make way! Rosetta Stone coming through!"

I staggered back as a group of students ran past dragging the famous large, polished slab. The nearby elevator doors opened, and a family dragged out an ancient Egyptian sarcophagus. Across the Great Hall, another band of kids was lugging out a statue of Apollo. The British Museum, the greatest collection of the world's loot, was being looted. I didn't know whether to laugh or cry, applaud or condemn. Some guards were trying to stop the thieves, but one raider dashed out of the Japanese gallery dressed in full samurai gear, yelling "Banzai!" in an outrageous display of cultural appropriation.

Madness consumed everyone. And I felt it, like a pulsing, hot mass in my head. I wanted to join in, get swept up in the mob, let loose, be free. All those rules we follow, to keep society going? They hadn't just snapped—they'd been shattered.

But it wasn't total chaos, not yet. It turned into total chaos when the scorpion-folk came to life.

ELEVEN

THE TWO MASSIVE STATUES AT THE ENTRANCE TO THE Mesopotamian galleries began breaking apart. First there were just hairline cracks through the marble. The stone creaked. Then a loud grinding noise rose from the heads as they . . . swiveled.

My life had turned plenty weird since last year. I'd driven a flying chariot down Broadway and fought a demon who spoke in rhyming couplets. But this?

One of the statues, the male scorpion, flexed his arm. He opened and closed his pincers. The second, a female, wobbled on her plinth. Her body was half stone, half-studded, chitinous armor. Then, as the final shards of stone warped into flesh and the different segments scraped over one another, the scorpion-folk exercised their long-dormant limbs. The sound of their clicking pincers echoed throughout the Great Hall. Their tails jolted awkwardly, and they stumbled as their eight legs struggled to remember their original purpose.

The two scorpion-folk shivered from head to tail and turned toward Lugal.

Who pointed at me.

People screamed. The group carrying the Rosetta Stone dropped it on the limestone floor, and it broke. I know! I felt really bad—part of the world's heritage and all that—but my attention was overwhelmed by the two giant monsters scuttling toward me and, ya salam, with those eight legs they scuttled fast!

That's when the closest, the male, was hit in the face with a Victoria sponge cake.

Rabisu had found the café. She stood on one of the long tables in the northwest corner, a gang of schoolkids gathered around her. Some wore pieces of armor—Greek, Roman, and Anglo-Saxon—pilfered from various nearby galleries. One girl with a soufflé wore a solid-gold Aztec crown.

"Let them have it!" Rabisu yelled, unleashing the Great British Food Fight. Cakes, puddings, buckets of ice cream, and éclairs flew at the scorpion-folk. Some of the desserts splattered on the monsters' armor and faces; the rest fell short, smearing the floor with buttercream, jam, and crumbs. Rabisu was, naturally, loving every second of this.

𒀸 𒄄 𒁲 𒈨

And, in a world gone mad, she suddenly became the most logical thing in it. I wasn't in this alone. The two of us would handle it.

Rabisu leaped up and down on the table. "Ha! Is that the best you've got? Pathetic! Do you know who I am? I am Rabisu, the dreaded battlefield stalker who brought despair to the city of Eridu! She whose name was a curse to the people of Lagash for a thousand years!"

There was more, a *lot* more, but you get the idea.

Now, Rabisu was a demon, and she had, if not actual superstrength, then pretty amazing strength. I was sure she could handle two monstrous scorpions by herself, but sometimes logic and common sense don't win out. Sometimes you have to do something stupid to make a point. I scrambled to my feet. I needed a weapon, but the only thing nearby was a large brass vase stuffed with daffodils. I grabbed it and charged, scattering the yellow flowers in my wake.

The male scorpion monster spun around to face me. His stinger weaved back and forth over him, venom glistening on its needle-sharp point.

"Allahu Akbar!" I yelled, and swung the vase at the monster's head.

Clang!

Before he could recover, I swung again—a sweeping

and, even if I say so myself, majestic horizontal arc that caught him square on the side of his jaw.

How about that? I was fighting!

Maybe this hero lark wasn't so difficult after . . .

The scorpion-man caught the vase in his pincers and crushed it like it was a Coke can. I dived aside as his stinger swooped down. For something the size of an SUV, he spun around in an eyeblink. And I was all out of cake. He swung his pincer widely, smashing me from knee to shoulder and hurling me a dozen yards through the air to crash against the far wall.

I lay there in a pool of ice cream and frozen yogurt. Possibly some sorbet. Oh, and some blood. Some of my ribs were broken, and my knee had popped. My shoulder was torn and bleeding, and my T-shirt hung in shreds, red from the gashes across my chest. My inner organs had suffered massive trauma, and my heart fluttered, tripped, and stopped. Everything began to go dark. . . .

I was dead. And not for the first time.

Third? Possibly fourth?

Dying? I can't really describe it because it tends to happen fast. But the resurrection? Now, *that* I can tell you about. It *hurts*.

Wounds closed. Bones reset themselves, and I felt each one wriggle back into place. Three vertebrae rejoined my spine, and believe me, each nerve ending sent a fiery spike of pure electric agony right up from my tailbone into the back of my head. I blinked as I was refilled with life. Refilled to overflowing.

I buzzed, everything in the red zone, and my senses were supernaturally sharp, extraordinarily focused. I saw the battle in slow motion as my brain processed everything at ten times the usual speed. The scorpion-folk climbing over the café tables; Rabisu grappling with one of their tails while the schoolkids fled, stuffing cakes into their mouths as they ran. Looters struggled with some of the bigger treasures, like the huge iron statue of Shiva being rolled out on a trolley. Others had gone for more portable treasures— ancient jewelry, alabaster canopic jars, and statuettes.

I could hear their huffing, even the rushing of their blood. I saw beads of sweat flying on the other side of the hall. The smells of sweet syrup, cinnamon, sugar, and dust overwhelmed me as I got to my feet.

Everything felt... more. I was overflowing with life force, a strange side effect of coming back from the dead. It was like god surge, the power that allows supernatural beings to perform their inhuman feats. I couldn't match them, being still just mortal flesh and bone, but I was more than human, so much more. It wouldn't last long, so I had to get busy.

The male scorpion turned to stab Rabisu in the back while she dangled in the claw of the female. I grabbed a serving tray and threw it in my best impression of Captain America. The metal whined as it streaked through the air and struck the offending tail just under the stinger.

The scorpion-man screamed as gooey green blood frothed out of the severed joint and the stinger flew across the hall and embedded itself in the far wall.

But Rabisu was in trouble. She remained caught in the female's pincers, and if it wasn't for the demon's superhuman resilience, she would have already been snipped apart. And the scorpion-man, even without the stinger, could still tear me from limb to limb with its own pincers. It charged at me, and I drew on everything to stay out of his way. The trouble was, my strength was fading fast. It was as if my body was suddenly remembering its normal, tragically low limits.

And that's when Lugal made his move—and, I have to give him his due, what a move it was. He stalked toward the five-ton marble statue of the Lion of Knidos—look it up—and lifted it off its plinth as if it was papier-mâché.

Suddenly my immortality felt highly squashable.

I had nowhere left to run. Lugal didn't seem to care that he'd destroy the tablet, too. His eyes were filled with pure, incandescent rage.

Lugal hissed. He screwed his eyes tight and . . . faltered. He had me trapped, but there was another, greater conflict happening inside his head. He roared with fury and let the lion slip from his grasp. It shattered into a dozen pieces at his feet.

I was forgotten in his pain. He pummeled his fists against his head, blows that would have taken down a house, and their impact echoed horribly within the hall.

"My lord!" The magpie man ran to him as Lugal staggered, blinded by his torments.

"Hey, dudes!" someone said. "What's happening? This is heavy! Heav-eeee!"

Now what?

A guy stepped over the rubble of the Nero statue. It was the hippie I'd seen behind the steering wheel of that yellow VW. He picked up one of the daffodils that had dropped from the vase. "Seriously, why can't we all just get along?"

I stumbled to my feet as the scorpion-man swiveled around, snapping his pincers at everything. I waved frantically at the hippie. "Get out of here!"

He waved back with the daffodil. "Chill, Sik. Chill like an ice cube."

"How do we know each other, exactly?" I was turning out to be more famous than Daoud, and I didn't like it.

The scorpion-man charged. This was going to be bad. I stepped in front of the hippie, but he had other plans. He gently pushed me aside and faced the monster. With his flower. "Peace, man. Peace."

⟨꜀꜀ ꜀꜀꜀ ꜀꜀꜀ ꜀꜀⟩

He flicked the flower lightly, just tapping scorpion-man on the nose. A few petals fell off.

I held my breath, waiting for the monster to tear the guy apart.

But he didn't. He just stood there looking bemused. Then his shoulders slumped, and his head drooped. A moment later, he collapsed to the floor.

"How did you do that?" I asked the hippie.

"Flower power, man. Now, there's a young damsel in distress, and though I am firmly against all forms of gender stereotypes, I feel an intervention coming on."

Sometimes things change so fast all you can do is just hang on. "Er...okay?"

He bounded across the remains of the café, toward the scorpion-woman, who had Rabisu trapped in a corner. The guy must have had goat DNA, because I'd never seen anyone as light-footed. His sandals barely touched the floor, a table, and the rim of a teacup before he was aloft again, daffodil in hand.

"Eat petal!" yelled the dude, and he swung the daffodil with all his might at the scorpion-woman.

The impact of the blow shook the walls, caused the limestone floor to ripple, and blew out all the windows. Even the vast dome cracked, which I noticed as I flew backward into the ice cream counter and the world turned sweet and creamy.

𒀀𒐀𒀭𒁲𒐉

The scorpion-woman? She was gone, but now there was a slimy green smear on the wall and broken chitinous plates were scattered across the hall.

Rabisu helped me up. She wiped the Chunky Chip off my face. "Yuck. I think I must be lactose intolerant."

I stood there, or at least tried to—my legs were wobbly from the aftershock.

"Do you happen to know who that is?" I asked.

Rabisu barely looked over. "Him? Dumuzi. The god of flowers."

Dumuzi? I was pretty good on my Mesopotamian mythology, but that name didn't ring any bells. It did explain, however, how he'd been able to save us with a single daffodil.

"Sik! Sik!"

Belet ran toward us, Kasusu in hand. As she passed the stunned scorpion-man, she flicked her sword across his neck without pausing, and that was the end of the monster. Belet actually looked worried about me for a second, but once she saw that I was okay, she was all business. "What happened?"

Now that it was all over, I barely had enough strength to speak, but I squeezed out one word. "Lugal."

"You met him?" There was no mistaking the fear in her voice.

"He wanted the tablet." I scanned the hall, but he was

gone. The only sign of him was that foul magpie, perched high on one of the upper windows. Once our eyes met, it flew away. I was starting to hate that bird. But there were others here I needed to look out for. "We have to find my brother and Daoud. They're in the museum somewhere."

Belet shook her head. "I'm sorry. I thought you just said you needed to find your brother . . . ? But that's not possible, is it?"

"I . . . er, a lot has happened today. All of it strange and peculiar."

"Yes," said Belet. Funny how so much emotion can be squeezed into so small a word. She'd packed it with disappointment, a touch of anger, and a lot of *I can't leave you alone for a minute, can I?*

Best we move on swiftly. I pointed at Dumuzi. "What about him? He saved us, Belet."

"Which is as big a surprise to me as it must have been to you," she muttered. "But we don't get to choose our family, do we?"

Rabisu burst out laughing. "Of course. I forgot!"

Belet frowned. "Mother never should have married him."

I looked over at Dumuzi, who was drawing an invisible heart over his chest.

"*Married* him?" I asked. "Are you telling me that guy

is Ishtar's *husband*?" Then the realization hit like a ton of bricks. "But that then makes him . . ."

Belet's eyes narrowed to mean, unhappy slits. "Yes. My father."

TWELVE

PEOPLE WERE ALREADY GATHERING OUTSIDE THE
museum, recording the looting with their phones but
afraid to get too close.

"There's the Handsome One!" said Rabisu, pointing.
"He's safe, thank Ea."

Daoud was out front, busy taking selfies with a group
of Korean students.

Mo emerged from the crowd of hysterical teens, saw
me, and ran over. "Sik! Alhamdulillah! I was so...Look
at you! We need to get you to the hospital!"

"It's not as bad as it seems, Mo."

"You're covered in blood!"

"Some. Most of it is strawberry jam." I wiped my forefinger across my forehead and held it up. "See?"

"Still..." He held me by my shoulders. "I lost you once
already."

At one time, I would have batted him away, told him that I could take care of myself and I wasn't a little kid anymore. But now? He could fuss over me all he wanted.

Mo wiped my face with his sleeve. "This happen a lot when you go out?"

I ignored that and searched the nearby trees for a magpie. "Could you go and pull Daoud away from his fans? We need to get going."

Belet pointed across the street at the VW van parked up on the sidewalk. "There's our ride."

We heard approaching sirens and didn't waste any time bundling straight in. Dumuzi revved the engine the moment Belet slid the door shut. "Right on. Time to split before we're oppressed by the unthinking agents of the Man." A moment later, we were making our way up Tottenham Court Road just as a trio of police cars howled past. Fleeing the law was becoming a bad habit.

The VW's interior stank of cheap incense, and the seats were covered in tie-dyed cotton. I was wedged in between Belet and Rabisu, with Mo and Daoud opposite, while Dumuzi drove. "This is a beautiful moment," he said, wiping a tear from his eye as he looked at us in the rearview mirror. "My daughter has friends. Group hug?"

Belet drummed her fingers on Kasusu.

"Maybe later," said Dumuzi. "That was a heavy scene back there. So many really bad vibes. I think you each should take one of these." He pulled a small hemp bag from his glove compartment and handed it to us. "Hold these crystals. They'll cleanse your auras."

Daoud took one and laid it on his palm, gazing at it. "I'm feeling better already."

Belet flicked hers out the window. I guess she liked her aura just the way it was.

"Where we headed?" I asked the flower god. "Because Lugal knows we're staying at the Ritz..."

"Lugal?" asked Daoud.

"Yeah," I said. "The guy who set Fitzroy Castle on fire and who just tried to kill me in Gallery Seven. But you wouldn't know anything about that...because you were nowhere to be seen! Where were you two, anyway? If it weren't for Dumuzi and Belet, I—"

"Hey!" protested Rabisu. "I had everything under control."

"Uh-huh. When faced with deadly scorpion monsters, everyone knows the best course of action is to throw fancy cakes."

Rabisu crushed her crystal in her hands. "Saved you, didn't I? Not sure why I bothered!"

Even though we were safe now, I started shaking. I clutched my hands to keep them still, but that only made it worse. It must have been delayed shock, and hey, I *did* actually die, which, for most people, is a significant life event. Usually the last one.

How could everything be going so wrong so quickly?

Then Mo swapped seats so he was beside me and put his arm over my shoulder. "It'll be okay, Sik. I promise."

I believed him. Stupid, huh? I was immortal, I had a demon and the daughter of Ishtar backing me up, and yet it was Mo who made everything all right.

"That's so beautiful," said Dumuzi, sniffling. "And don't you worry, I know a place you'll be safe."

We turned north in Camden and wove through the winding streets into a residential area. I'd always thought of London like Rome, all clad in marble, majestic statues on every street corner, and lined with avenues of elegant houses straight from a Jane Austen movie. But this part? Most of the houses were boarded up, and their yards were overgrown with weeds. We passed the burned-out remains of a Porsche.

"Nice neighborhood," said Belet.

"Property is theft," said Dumuzi as he turned into a driveway. "The world was meant to be shared, not hoarded. Welcome to my commune."

It would have been glorious a hundred years ago, maybe two. But now? The mansion was cloaked in ivy— it had climbed all the way up to the chimneys. Most of the windows were covered with planks of wood, and the building itself slumped, as if worn out. The roof dipped and was missing lots of tiles. In front was a cracked old fountain, its bronze mermaid spout badly rusted and looking forlorn among the weeds and litter. But light shone through the spaces between the planks, and the patchwork curtains glowed warmly.

As we hopped out of the van, Dumuzi said, "I'll ask Heavenly to make some rooms ready for you. West-facing, of course, where the feng shui's strongest."

Chickens roamed freely in the overgrown front lawn. A few sheep nibbled at the weeds. One, a shaggy ram with the most curly-whirly horns ever, stared at us suspiciously. "Baaa?"

Dumuzi shook his head. "They're friends, Seg Sag," he told the ram.

Seg Sag wasn't convinced and took a threatening step forward. "Baaaaaaa..."

"Yes, that includes the demon. This is a house of peace, Seg Sag."

I sidled up to Belet. "What's the deal with the ram?"

"He's just a big softie. Aren't you?" she cooed to the creature.

"Baaa," he said, sounding a little less hostile.

Belet tickled his woolly chin. "There. Told you."

Softie or not, Rabisu gave him a wide berth.

The interior of the house was as ramshackle as the outside. The yellowed wallpaper hung in loose strips, the plaster behind it was moldy, and the floorboards were warped with age and damp. Apparently, there was no electricity because the hallway was lit by candles. Yet there were some cheery elements. Flowers grew through cracks in the floor, bunting and Tibetan prayer flags dangled overhead, and tie-dyed sheets and murals threw wild splashes of color across the aged interior. A half-painted dragon straight out of the Dungeons & Dragons rule book wound its way up the stairs.

"Welcome," said Dumuzi, solemnly handing each of us a flower. "Come in and meet the others."

He introduced his people. We met a Shining Brook, a Moon Flower, and two Rainbows. Sunshine over the Glade led us to a dining room that had no furniture but plenty of rugs and scattered cushions, and a guy named Silver Horizon handed us bowls of hot lentils. "This will hold you over until the main course," he said.

It smelled delicious, and the cook in me had to ask, "Where did you learn how to make this? Some Michelin restaurant?"

"Wormwood Scrubs," he replied proudly.

"That's an odd name for a restaurant."

Belet took her bowl. "It's a prison, Sik."

"Twenty years, at Her Majesty's pleasure," continued

Silver Horizon. "But I'm a changed man, thanks to Dumuzi. Here, have a bun."

"Shukran."

Dumuzi took the others—even Rabisu—to help in the kitchen, leaving me with Belet.

"You want to fill me in?"

"He's my father. Most people have one. What more is there to know?"

I tore open my roll, which had a perfect crust on the outside and was fluffy on the inside, just like Mama's. I dipped it into the lentils for a good soak. "He's just not who I would have imagined as Ishtar's actual husband. She was pretty high maintenance, and Dumuzi is . . . come as you are?"

Belet sighed as she started to eat. "Opposites attract, and I think Mother appreciated the change from all the suitors who lavished her with jewelry and conquered kingdoms in her name. When Dumuzi came along, wearing his homespun linen and carrying a bunch of wildflowers, he was a break from those macho warriors. He made her happy. Made her forget who she was for a while. People expected so much of her, wanted so much from her, but not Dumuzi."

"Then why do you look annoyed? I'd think you'd be happy to see him."

"Because while he demands nothing, he offers nothing,

either. When Ishtar adopted me, he was supposed to be my father, but he came and went whenever the mood took him. He was great company, provided you didn't ask anything of him. The guy can't handle responsibility. That's the minimum requirement of a parent, isn't it?"

"Looks like he's trying to make up for it now, and he seems to be running this commune. Why not give him a chance?"

"I *am* giving him a chance. Why do you think I went to him?" Belet paced the room. "I looked for the apkallus, the seven sages. But they've just vanished and there's no sign of them anywhere."

"Is that so strange? Those guys probably don't advertise their presence."

"But *all* of them, Sik? At the same time? That's never happened before, not that I know of. So, I turned to my father. What other choice did I have?"

There'd been so many times when I wanted to be like Belet. To be fearless, to know what to do in every situation, to spend a week in Beijing followed by a month in Tehran, to be ridiculously rich. But then I'd realize how lonely she is. That what she wanted was someone to tuck her into bed, to leave the light on in the corridor outside. She craved the sound of someone puttering around in the kitchen, the smells of home baking, and the feel of well-worn clothes. Things I didn't think were special at all.

⋈⟨ ⋈⟨ ⋈▷⊣ ⊢⊣

She could never forget she was an orphan, found in the rubble of her bombed-out home when she was only a week old. Ishtar had taken her in, raised her with all the luxuries money could buy. Ishtar had loved her—loved her deeply—but in her own way.

Belet had the *Mona Lisa* hanging in one of her apartments but would have swapped it in a second for a homemade pie baked just for her.

"You really know your way around the kitchen, Yakhi," Mo said to me.

Everyone had to do their part at the commune, so naturally I volunteered for kitchen duty. I decided to make a chopped salad. Mo joined me, much to Daoud's obvious disappointment.

I flicked the shredded lettuce in the salad bowl and started on the onions. "You worked in our deli as long as I have."

"Did I?" He tapped his head. "It's all so jumbled up."

"It'll come back. You remembered me, didn't you? Hey, it's easier to cut tomatoes with a serrated edge. Here, use this."

"But it's a bread knife, Sik."

"Trust me. It's a kitchen hack," I said. "And what's all this about you being into fashion? Daoud tried so many times to get you interested, but you didn't know your Pierre Cardin from your peri-peri."

"If you say so. But take a look outside, at the garden. What do you see? What colors catch your eye?"

Outside there were branches covered in leaves. Long grass. More leaves.

"Green?"

"Emerald. Turquoise. Lime. Olive. Seafoam. And those petals by the window aren't just any green; they're jade. You have to appreciate the beauty in the smallest differences."

Daoud was right—this wasn't the same old Mo. Where had he picked up all this passion for colors? He'd been interested in pressing flowers, an extension of his training as a botanist, but that had been for scientific reasons, not artistic.

In the backyard, I saw Daoud examining the vegetable plot while also keeping one eye on Mo and me. Dumuzi was trying to distract the ram from Rabisu, who was hiding up a tree.

"So, what's the story with Daoud?" asked Mo, trying so hard to sound super casual about it.

"He smuggled himself over from Iraq when he was just a kid," I explained. "Poor guy had no family and was just dropped into the system, not speaking a word of English. Maybe it was because your Arabic was way better than mine, but the two of you just hit it off from the beginning. Since then? He helped out in the deli when you . . . left."

"So, we've been friends a long time?"

"More than friends, Mo. Can't you tell?"

Mo chewed his lip. He never used to do that. "Look at me, Sik. Look at Daoud. The guy's just . . . you know. Me? I've been run over by a truck. Literally."

"Daoud's got a scar, too," I said. "Just under his left eye."

"Like a teardrop. He told me he got it when he lost someone and a single tear ate into his skin."

"Daoud said that? I never took him for a poet. He doesn't take much seriously, Mo. Except . . ."

"Fashion?" asked Mo.

"Nope. *You.*"

Mo shook his head. "Maybe the old me. Not this version."

"Some things never change. The best things." I watched him make a mess of those tomatoes. "Though remembering them may take some time, it'll be worth it."

He nodded, and we went about prepping the rest of the meal while making small talk, but I was getting a little weirded out.

"The smell of this food reminds me of the camp."

"Camp?" I asked. "What camp?"

"You know—the Markazi refugee camp? In the Al Anbar province? Where we grew up. That I remember all too well."

"No, that's wrong. Mama and Baba got out of there when you were little. You three came to America. I was born in New York."

"You sure? But it's all so clear. I can even remember the color of our tent. I can see the carpet we had, and the water bottles we lined up. Water was delivered every other day and rice on Wednesday and Fridays. Food packages from the NGOs. It's as clear as you standing right there."

Still, when he mentioned the water stand, I remembered it, too. I could picture us lining up with our plastic buckets. I remembered us making bedding from empty rice sacks.

But that wasn't possible.

Was it?

"Your room's ready," said the flower god after Belet and I had done the dishes. "Your friends are already getting settled. Follow Dreamweaver upstairs, but mind your head on the pyramids hanging from the ceiling. They're for channeling Earth's energies along the ley lines."

Belet stood up and collected Kasusu. "We need to talk about Lugal, Father."

"In the morning. I'll be up at dawn for the sun greeting. Nothing heals the soul more than the blessings of Shamash."

"That sounds perfect," I said, taking a step between the two of them and gently cradling Belet's arm. I looked over at the guy in the wolf's-head T-shirt. "Dreamweaver? Lead on."

The room was at the top of the house, among the eaves. Five thin mattresses had been laid on wooden pallets and covered in handmade quilts. Moonlight shone through a small window, and water from an earlier rain shower dripped down between the loose roof tiles. I kicked off my boots and crawled onto my bed between the puddles.

While Rabisu chewed on her midnight snack of raw rat, Belet set to work sharpening Kasusu with a whetstone. The blade's curved edge resembled a silver grin in the moonlight.

Daoud started his Face Pilates exercises, and Mo slid his bed over to my area. "Make some room, Yakhi."

I shuffled over as he scooched his pallet beside mine and settled down with his hands behind his head. "You lead an interesting life, that's for sure."

"You're taking all this weirdness very well. Most people would be freaked out by—"

Rabisu slurped wetly as the rat's tail slithered through her lips.

"—a lot of things."

She burped.

"You mean the demons and gods and magic?" Mo asked. "I don't know what to make of it all. We believe in the Shahadah, Sik, or have you forgotten?"

𒀸 𒄑 𒅂 𒀀

"'La ilaha illallah, Muhammad rasulu-llah,'" I recited. "'There is no god but Allah, and Muhammad is his messenger.' Of course I haven't forgotten."

"Then how do you make sense of it? Ishtar, Nergal, Gilgamesh, Dumuzi . . . Are they angels? Djinn? Shayatin? Something else?"

"Mama calls them djinn, and that works well enough. She sees them as spirits that decided to defy Allah and make mischief among humanity."

Mo nodded. "That makes sense. Djinn who have come to believe they are what the ancient Mesopotamians called them."

I shrugged. "I'm no imam. This is deep philosophy. I did ask Ishtar about it once."

"What'd she say?"

"She said she wasn't even sure what she was. The ancient people had called her a goddess because she was greater than they were. Then the term *djinn* was used in another culture. Nowadays she might be called . . . a superhero—Belet referred to it as the Thor Conundrum. Anyway, Ishtar admitted that there were mysteries far beyond her. Someone created her, after all. She mentioned a divine presence called Ea, but Allah works, for me."

"Did you believe her?" he asked. "I want to understand."

"Some things don't need to be understood, Mo, just appreciated. I think that's what she was trying to tell me.

Wonder at the world and enjoy it. That's the sort of thing the goddess—or djinn—of love would say."

"Love *and* war, if I remember my mythology," he said with a yawn. "It's been quite a day, hasn't it? It was only last night I had my first glimpse through the fog."

I took out my phone. "Let's call Mama and Baba right now and blow away some more of that fog." This time I looked up the country code and checked to make sure I had all the bars I needed.

The phone rang twice before it was picked up. "Benny's Bagels. What can I do for you, pal?"

"I'm looking for a deli called Mo's."

"None with that name here. Would you like today's special? We've got—"

"Listen to me. It's called Mo's, and it's on the corner of Fifteenth and Siegel. It's been there for years."

"That corner's *ours*. You've made a mistake, pal. Try googling." And then he hung up.

I stared at the screen. The number was right. I did try finding Mo's on Google, and there was nothing. Nothing. How could that be? How could it just be . . . gone?

"It's okay, Sik," said Mo.

"No. No, it's not."

I hated the way he was looking at me. Pitying, but not surprised. As if he was shrugging and saying, *What did you expect?*

᚛ᚐ᚜ᚔᚐᚋ

I expected Mama and Baba to pick up the phone. I expected them to be living on the corner of Fifteenth and Siegel just like they'd been *yesterday*.

But so much had changed since then, hadn't it?

I looked over at Mo. Alive, when he shouldn't have been. I'd gotten my brother back, but at what cost?

I dropped onto my mattress, physically and mentally exhausted. I'd have to find the answer in the morning.

Waves crash against the gray shore. A harsh, cold wind spits icy water against my bare skin, and freezing wet sand squelches between my toes. The clouds churn, and the horizon is broken by flashes of lightning.

It is desolate, but I am not alone.

Lugal stands knee-deep in the surf. His kirtle is made of golden material, and he wears heavy jeweled bands on his arms. He is not the broken man I met in the museum, but regal, noble, full of pride and arrogance. His attention is on the sea as he pleads, "Mother! Mother! Do you hear me?"

The sea answers. It speaks in a language older than the universe, a language not made of words but the rawest, most base emotions.

Rage. Misery. Despair. And a terrible, all-consuming loneliness.

Lugal wades deeper into the waves. "Mother, they killed him. His own children killed him! How could they be so cruel, so deceitful? It was Ea who murdered him. Ea put the great Apsu into a deep sleep and murdered him as he lay defenseless. Now Ea wears his crown, carries his scepter, and parades among the gods, declaring himself their king. The usurper wears the crown that should be mine. Mine! Come and aid me, Mother! Let us avenge ourselves on the treacherous gods! I beg of you!"

The world trembles as a cataclysmic thunderclap echoes across all existence. The roiling clouds hurl down torrential rain, and lightning sizzles across the tops of the waves. The ocean surface surges as giant things stir in the depths.

Lugal raises his hands. "Thank you, Mother."

The ground splits around my feet, bubbling as it spews out a host of scorpions that swell in size from moment to moment. Their shells crack as their upper torsos transform into humanoid bodies. Their stingers drip with black venom.

Leviathans crawl from the sea. Serpentine bodies as long as freight trains, encrusted in gigantic barnacles, and with spiny back ridges. Each of their footsteps shakes the ground. Their cavernous mouths are filled with fangs, and lightning crackles within their black maws. Other beasts, hideous hybrids with too many limbs, heads, and bodies, emerge from the water. More and more gather on this gray beach, a host of monsters born from the primordial sea. They are a mob—a mass of scales, tentacles, fangs, and claws, beasts made only for destruction.

Lugal bows his head. "Thank you for your blessing, Mother. With this host, I shall tear down the palaces of the rebel gods and drag them here to sacrifice them to you. It shall be as if they never existed, and you will have the peace you crave. This I swear."

He turns and wades back toward the shore. But when the waters are merely splashing against his ankles, he pauses and reaches down.

"Another gift, Mother?" He digs in the mud, pulling at something. "Ah. The greatest gift of all."

He pulls free a tablet. It's small in his hand. He wipes away the wet sand and runs his fingers over the neat, dense rows of cuneiform.

Then he turns slowly, and our eyes meet. His lips peel into an animalistic snarl. "You cannot defy kismet, Sikander."

THIRTEEN

I AWOKE IN A PANIC. STORM CLOUDS COVERED THE morning sky out the window, and there was a steady drip coming from the ceiling as raindrops rattled on the roof. The others were gone.

Had it happened to them, too? Whatever had happened to Mama and Baba? I stared into the empty shadows, and then I heard Rabisu downstairs. She was demanding third helpings. I'd never been so relieved.

I grabbed the tablet. I was expecting it to feel warm, to have some sort of power radiating from it, but the clay was as cool as ever, and there wasn't so much as a tingle in my palm. My last dream had set my heart racing. It wasn't just the host of monsters that had come crawling out of the sea, or Lugal staring straight at me. It was the fact that we had made a real connection. He knew that I knew what the tablet was.

I ran downstairs in my bare feet. Some things could not wait. "Belet!"

I burst into the breakfast room. Mo was pouring tea while Belet sat on an upturned bucket with a chipped plate on her lap, spreading honey on her bread. Rabisu was helping herself to the contents of the compost bin.

I looked around the room and out toward the garden. "Where's Daoud? He needs to hear this, too."

Mo handed me a cup. "You okay, Sik? You look rough."

Rabisu chewed a banana skin. "The Handsome One has gone for a run around Hyde Park."

What had I expected? The world might be falling apart around our ears, but he had to maintain his 9-percent-body-fat regime. "Never mind. We need to talk."

I sat down next to Belet. "What's that story about the creation of the world? Y'know, the Mesopotamian one? Quickly!"

"The *Enuma Elish*, you mean?"

"Yeah, yeah, yeah." I held the tablet tightly, as if I could squeeze out its secrets. "Ya Allah, we are in so much trouble."

"What's wrong, Sik?" asked Belet.

"How does it go? It's a war between the new gods and the old ones, right?"

"Yes. Apsu, the father of all creation, has been tormented by the younger gods, his offspring. They're totally out of control, rampaging and making mischief. He has no peace, so he decides to destroy them. He discusses it with his wife, Tiamat."

"Tiamat, the mother of all. The primordial sea..." I thought of the giant frieze I'd seen at the British Museum. "The goddess of chaos."

Belet nodded. "But the plan's overheard by one of the younger gods, Ea. He casts a spell over Apsu, making him fall into a deep sleep. Then he sneaks into Apsu's chamber, kills him, and becomes the ruler of the younger gods."

"But the story doesn't end there, does it?" I asked.

"No, that death kicks off the main event. Tiamat declares war on her offspring, the gods of Mesopotamia. They had killed her husband, and she wants revenge. So, she goes to her one loyal son, Kingu, and puts him in charge of the war."

"The Big Man," I said, reminding myself of the Mesopotamian word for war leader as it all clicked. "The *Lugal*."

"Of course," said Belet. "And to help him fight it, Tiamat gives birth to a multitude of monsters—dragons, giant serpents, scorpion-folk, and more."

I remember the rest. The younger gods were terrified— this was the goddess of chaos after all, and their mother. One of them, Marduk, was chosen to fight her and her army. So, he took his weapons and mounted his chariot pulled by four demonic horses and galloped off to battle, riding the storm clouds. He fought and destroyed Tiamat and captured Kingu. According to the myths, Tiamat's body was used to create the universe. Her scales were put in the sky as stars. Her tears became the rivers, her bones the mountains, and so on.

"Whatever happened to Kingu?" I asked. "I mean, after he lost to Marduk?"

"Mother told me he was captured alive," said Belet. "The gods were weary of waging battle, so they created their own servants to do it in their place, just as Tiamat had created them. They used Kingu's blood to make humans."

I picked up the rest of the story. "Tiamat gave Kingu more than a legion of monsters. She gave him ultimate power over everything that existed and would exist. She gave him the power to decide everyone's fate."

Belet's gaze fell on the chunk of clay in my hand. "How do you know?"

"I saw him pick up the tablet in a dream. And I started thinking of all the terrible things that have been happening lately. The wildfires in California, the drought in Iraq, the flash floods with whole towns washed away..."

"That's why Lugal's so desperate to have it back," said Belet. "His mother gave it to him before her war against the gods. The tablet would guarantee victory because if he lost a battle, he could merely use it to change the outcome, *change his fate*."

I looked over at Mo. "That's what's happened to you. I wished for you to be alive, and I was holding the tablet at the time. So fate took a different path."

"By Ea," whispered Rabisu. "You are in so much trouble."

I'd gotten my brother back but lost just as much. "What happened to our parents, Mo?"

Benny's Bagels. No website, no emails, no sign of them at all. It was as if Mama and Baba had never existed.

"Sik, you really want to discuss this now?" he said, sitting down. "You're upset."

"Upset? You have no idea, Yakhi. Just tell me."

"Okay. But you know as much as I do. It's the one piece of my memory the fog has never clouded, though I wish it had. They died, Sik. They died a long time ago in the refugee camp. From tuberculosis. It could have been cured with antibiotics you can get from any pharmacy, but not in a camp overflowing with people fleeing war. They died, and it's been us ever since. Just you and me." He knelt beside me. "Sik, tell me what's wrong."

"This." I put the tablet on the kitchen table for all to see. "It brought you back and took them away. Mama and

Baba *raised* us, Mo. We lived in Manhattan and ran a deli. And you died. But now you're back. All because of this."

Mo had turned pale. He was scared, and he had every reason to be. We all want the world to make sense, don't we? He was trying to hold on to his version of reality even as it crumbled in his fingers. "It's just a tablet. Iraq's deserts are littered with them."

"No. This one is unique, and Ishtar knew it," said Belet. "So did Alexander the Great, Cleopatra, Saladin, and Mehmet. People who were able to change the fate of the world . . . because they possessed this."

Mo stared, horrified, at the tablet. "What is this?"

My throat was so tight I could barely speak. "It's the greatest artifact in all creation. It's the tablet of destinies."

FOURTEEN

BELET GINGERLY TOOK THE TABLET FROM MO. "LOOK AT it. Chipped. Cracked. And the text is barely legible."

"Nimium ne crede colori." The phrase just rolled off my tongue.

Belet's brow was furrowed. "'Trust not in looks.' Very good. Where did you learn that?"

"I...I don't know. Google? Like everything else?"

"Really?" she replied, utterly unconvinced. "Any other strange talents arise since you got your hands on the tablet? Abilities you shouldn't have?"

So much had happened since we'd grabbed that lump of clay, I didn't know where to start. Wasn't I just the same old me? Nothing special. Just a kid who helped out at his parents' deli and could chop onions without crying and...

"At the British Museum when I was fighting that magpie

guy...I actually beat him. Not by luck, either. I dodged him twice in the same second—"

Belet raised her eyebrow. "Double-darted? That takes impeccable timing, Sik. You're more likely to trip over your own feet than escape. Anything else fighting-related?"

I shook my head. "If you asked me to do it now, I wouldn't know where to start. It was just an instinct, or trained muscle memory switching on for a second, then off just as fast. Is it all because of that clay tablet?"

"It's far, far more than that," said Belet. *"Everyone's* destiny—kismet—is written upon this. You could read your fate, know what would happen before it happened. But it got damaged over the centuries. Now it allows you to not merely read your destiny but also *alter* it."

"Is that why Ishtar wanted the tablet?" I asked.

Belet shook her head. "I think she wanted it taken off the market. Before it did more harm."

"So this is why you're back," I said to Mo. "But why did we lose our parents?"

Belet turned the tablet over, inspecting it from all angles. "You know anything about chaos theory?"

"Something to do with a butterfly, isn't it?"

She looked surprised. I guess she was revising her opinion about public-school education. "Well done. Yes. The butterfly effect. When a butterfly flaps its wings, that minute movement can lead to a tornado in the Midwest or hurricanes across the Pacific. The smallest changes can have profound, catastrophic repercussions. The trouble is, you can't predict them." She looked over at me and my brother. "You brought Mo back. But how many other destinies had to change to allow that? Both before and after the event, that moment should have been his death."

"Before and after? But Mo's accident was three years ago, and according to him, our parents died nine years ago!"

"If time's a river, you threw a huge rock into it, and the ripples spread in all directions, upstream and downstream. That change will affect *everyone*, Sik. The biggest changes will be those closest to the accident—nearest to where the rock landed, if we stick with my analogy—but even those people who seemingly had nothing to do with it will have felt minute tremors. Tell me, when did we first meet? Actually talk?"

"What's that got to do with anything?" I snapped. "Okay. At school, of course. You were in class upsetting the teacher."

"What was his name?"

"It was..." I frowned. I'd had him standing up front, glowering at me, every day for two years. "It was..."

I couldn't even picture him. The more I concentrated, the harder it became. "I can't remember. It's not important anyway."

⟡⟡⟡⟡⟡

"Fine. Maybe he's not. But who did you sit next to, Sik? The guy you'd known since kindergarten."

"That's easy. It's...It's..." I closed my eyes, trying to picture the classroom. He was right there, on my left. I could turn my head and see...nothing. "What's happening? Why can't I remember?"

"It's those ripples, Sik. Your past has changed, too. In one version, your brother is dead and you and your parents live in Manhattan and run Mo's. But in the other one, Mo is alive and your parents never made it out of the refugee camp. There are two versions of you now, existing simultaneously and fighting each other. Two versions with different pasts, memories, talents. As time goes on, one of those versions will fade away. You won't remember—no one will because it never existed."

I held out my hand. "Give me the tablet, Belet."

"Why?"

"Why do you think? If I changed destiny once, I can change it again. Give me the tablet right now!"

She stood up, clutching the tablet against her chest, and stepped away. "Think about it, Sik."

"I have. Give me the tablet."

"I'm sorry, but I can't. That rock's been thrown, Sik. Those ripples have already occurred. Now you want to throw another rock. But that's not going to flatten the effects of the first disturbance—it will only make them greater. You'll be multiplying the changes, making those ripples bigger and things more chaotic. We need to think this through and not get caught up in our emotions."

"That's easy for you to say—you don't have emotions like normal people."

Belet's gaze darkened. "You think I don't realize that I could use this to get my mother back? I could just make my wish and have Ishtar walk into this room this very minute."

Suddenly it all made total sense! "Then why don't you? Listen to me, Belet! Maybe that's what your mom wanted. She knew about the tablet and wanted you to use it in the event she died. This is a win-win! You get Ishtar back, and I save my parents."

"But what about—" Mo started.

I bulldozed over him. "We'll both have what we want. You go first. Do it right now! Bring your mom back!"

It was a brilliant idea, wasn't it? We could fix everything, and I mean *everything*. World hunger? Wish it away! Wars? Over! The Mets' recent losing streak? Fixed! Sure, we'd probably need to be careful with our wording, but how could we not use the tablet to fix all those injustices?

Why didn't everyone understand how much good we could do? Mo looked bewildered, Rabisu was frowning at me, and Belet? She watched me suspiciously. Why couldn't she see I was trying to help her? Why was she being so stupid?

Then the craziest idea came into my head. I know—another one.

There was no need to play nice. I could just take it from her. I'd get Ishtar back and show Belet she was wrong and I was right.

I know what you're thinking. Hey, Sik, do you want to keep your teeth? This is Belet you're talking about! The ultimate badass who could take on Shang-Chi with or without those ten rings. You're just going to embarrass yourself even trying.

But I was taller than her, heavier, and, thanks to a sudden growth spurt, getting pretty buff. You'd be surprised how many calories you burn off working in a deli all your spare hours. And, somehow, I knew how she'd fight and how I'd respond. I was already rocking on the balls of my feet. I could get the tablet from her.

Belet raised her hand. "Don't try it, Sik."

Mo stood up and put his hand on my shoulder. "Calm down, Sik. Let's talk this through some more. Make sense of what's going on and work out what our options are."

"Move your hand, Mo." I don't think I'd ever spoken to him like that, with that level of threat. He sensed it and stepped away. He was actually scared of me. I should have been ashamed. That wasn't how you treated those you loved.

"Just give me the tablet, Belet." Part of me didn't want her to. How good was she, really? Would she hold back when facing me? That would be her mistake. Something strange was going on, but I couldn't make sense of it even if I'd wanted to. Right there, right then, I wanted to *take her on*.

"By Ea, are you two really going to fight?" said Rabisu. "That's awesome. Sik, watch out for her—"

Just then the back door crashed open, and Dumuzi stumbled in carrying an armful of strawberries. "Look at these! Someone get the vegan cream out of the fridge, and we'll...Whoa. I'm feeling some very negative vibes radiating in here. Like, *exceedingly* negative. This is a house of peace, guys. How 'bout we form a circle and do some Tibetan chanting to fill our souls with love?"

"She has the tablet of destinies," I said. "Tell her to give it back to me."

"Hey, man, I am not about to lay the whole patriarchy thing down on my daughter. She's an independent young woman, and if she's holding on to the tablet of— Wait. The tablet of destinies?" He dropped the strawberries. "Heav-eee."

"He's already used it," said Belet. "Now he wants to use it even more." She didn't take her eyes off me in case

I tried something. That was wise of her because, yeah, the moment she shifted her attention, I was going for the tablet.

"Let's de-escalate this situation, guys," said Dumuzi. "I mean bring it waaay down. Belet, please go check on Silver Horizon. I can smell the muffins burning."

"What about the tablet?" I snapped.

"Whoa, Sik. Chill. I mean to subzero. Come with me—let's have a heart-to-heart." He opened the door to the yard.

I peered out. "But it's still raining."

"You worried about catching a cold?"

I looked over at Mo and Rabisu. Mo gave me a nod. After the way I'd snapped at him, I'd expected something sour, but Mo wasn't like that. The shame I'd ignored earlier now hit hard.

So Dumuzi and I headed out to the garden. Like the rest of the place, it was a ramshackle mess. The foliage was overgrown and pierced with thistles, and the grass was sprinkled with dandelions. It was chaotic and glorious at the same time. The air was dense with the smell of damp soil and decaying vegetation, and the various flower scents were dizzying. What earth I could see was almost black, and the plants were bursting, all in full, explosive bloom. The sunflowers towered over us, and the petals of the daffodils shimmered like pure gold. Honeysuckle climbed over the rotting furniture, and a hummingbird fed from the intensely blue and purple orchids that sprouted among the rich weeds. Dumuzi brushed his fingers along a row of pink roses, and each one swelled, erupting with perfume as he passed. I stared at a leaf, mesmerized by its many shades of green, the minute veins running through it, the raindrops pooling and then sliding off the tip, creating sparkling cascades all around me.

Rain beat on the glass roof of the greenhouse in a perfect rhythm. The surface of the small pool chimed with dancing splashes. I heard the tune within the downpour. The rumbling clouds created a base echo, and the pitter-patter of heavy drops on the foliage made it sound as if the plants were laughing.

Dumuzi plucked a tall thistle stem and turned to me. "What do you think, Sikander?"

"Are you making this happen? Is this some part of your god surge?"

"Me? Not at all. There is the divine all around us, Sikander. Every moment of every day. But here, in a garden, it's quiet enough to hear it. You just need to turn on, tune in, and get ready to drop out."

"My brother wants to know what you are. Truth is, so do I. I have so many questions about all this . . . god business."

Dumuzi walked to a chestnut tree that dominated the far corner of the garden. Its heavy boughs had spread out over the surrounding plants, and its roots had entwined with the mossy brick walls. "Look at this tree. All these branches are different, yet they spring from the same trunk. You can choose to sit under one branch to enjoy the shade or find shelter from the rain. But there are many other branches, too, many other shelters. Maybe religions are like that."

"So, are you really a god, Dumuzi?"

He shrugged in a most ungodlike manner. "That term is thrown about a lot nowadays. Maybe it would help if you defined yours."

"Define Allah? How can I define a being that is... everything?" I asked. "Not just everything there *is*, but everything there *was*, and ever will be." All those countless hours at the masjid, I thought I'd have a better answer... "All-powerful. All-knowing and all-loving. Y'know... Allah."

"Seems like a good definition to me." Dumuzi gazed up at the dripping canopy as he pondered. "But that *doesn't* sound like anyone I know. My kind—Ishtar, Nergal, and the rest—drift along the river of time. We had a beginning, and, sooner or later, we will have an end. We're certainly not omnipotent, omniscient, nor, sadly, omnibenevolent. Some of us are far from any of those."

"Then what *are* you, exactly?"

"A farmer. What I've always been. But isn't that special enough?"

◄⫟ ⫟⫟ ⫟▷ ⊢⊣

Not the answer I wanted, but maybe it *was* enough.

Dumuzi waved the thistle like a wand. "Do you trust me?"

Whenever anyone says that, there's only one right response.

I backed away. "No, not really."

He waved the thistle from side to side. "Bummer."

Was he trying to hypnotize me with a weed? "What are you—"

He tapped me on the forehead with the thistle, and I . . . dropped out.

Out of my head, my consciousness, out of the world around me and down into the grass. Into the soil, into the black depths of the earth. Into the forever darkness.

FIFTEEN

ACRID BLACK SOOT STUNG MY EYES. I CHOKED ON ASH.
The air swirled with thick smoke and carried with it a
stinking, putrid smell, like meat left out in the sun. My skin
felt slimy. Where was I? I heard distant cries, screams too,
and then a brief gust of wind revealed my surroundings.

It was a war zone. The buildings around me had been
destroyed. Rubble covered the streets and wrecked cars
smoldered. The buildings lining the wide boulevard were
nothing but burned-out shells. It was nighttime, but the
sky glowed with a thousand fires.

Baghdad? Fallujah?

Then I saw a street sign hanging off a crooked pole.

Broadway.

This was Manhattan.

I should have recognized it instantly, but all war zones
look the same in the end. In the aftermath of destruction,

cities can die, lose their identities and what made them unique. One ruin is just like any other, the world over.

What had happened?

I walked forward cautiously, peering at the looted storefronts and torched theaters. Who had done all this? Had there been an attack? But where were the scattered shells, the bullet holes in the walls, the bomb craters? Instead, I found crude homemade weapons abandoned in the gutters: spears made from sticks and kitchen knives, axes made with battered sheet metal, and spiked baseballs. Rats, big and diseased, scurried along the wreckage.

Then I heard a snort and a loud crunch nearby.

"Nothing better than to sup on raw pup! What more is there to tell? Now, what is that I smell?"

It couldn't be. It couldn't be.

I ducked behind a battered Ford Mustang as a pair of figures emerged from an alley.

The first was rat-faced, with a long, twitching snout covered in wiry black hairs and wearing a pair of pince-nez that magnified his beady crimson eyes. His companion was squat and barrel-chested with huge bulbous eyes and a wide, slime-dripping mouth.

I knew them both. Ratty went by the name of Sidana, and Toady was called Idiptu. They were demons I had met last year. And they were supposed to be dead. Sidana had been killed by Belet, and Idiptu had been torn apart by a bunch of lamassus, but only after I'd run him over in my chariot.

But not in this version.

I couldn't get hurt in my own dream, could I? This wasn't *real*.

Idiptu flicked his tongue in and out, his eyes glowing a sickly yellow. "Tastes kinda familiar, don't it?"

A swarm of ugly, bloated flies gathered around them, buzzing loudly. Sidana put his fingers between his crooked teeth and let out a sharp whistle. Moments later, a plague dog came scurrying to his side. It had been a human once, but disease had deformed it until it was bent over and unable to stand, so it moved on all fours. It wore the rags of a police uniform. Sidana rubbed its mangy scalp. "That's a good boy. Now find your new . . . toy."

The plague dog sniffed the air and growled, its gaze shifting in my direction.

I needed to get out of here, but somehow I didn't think clicking my heels three times was going to work.

The plague dog raced around the front of the car and howled when it saw me. I swung the car door open as it charged.

It slammed into the door—ouch—and I did feel bad for a second, but then Idiptu pounced onto the roof, whipped out his tongue, and wrapped it around both of my hands. With a jerk of his head, I was tossed across the street.

Sidana came running at me, his red eyes bright. "Oh, what a delight! Another juicy boy to tear and bite!"

I'd forgotten how terrible his rhymes were. I got to my feet, but this was only going one way. Badly.

"Am I interrupting?"

All three of us turned to the woman standing a dozen yards down the street. She wore a hodgepodge of outfits that shouldn't have worked thrown together like that, but as always, Ishtar looked fabulous. She swept her hair from her face and smiled at me. "It's been a while, Sikander."

The two demons forgot all about me and spread out to take on Ishtar. The scimitar in her hand, Kasusu, growled, "So what are we waiting for?"

What indeed?

You want me to tell you how the fight went? It hardly seems worth the trouble. Sidana and Idiptu were scum, bully boys who preyed on the weak. They were battlefield scavengers, picking over the bones alongside the jackals and carrion birds.

Ishtar? She was the freakin' goddess of love and war, and right then she went full war.

The demons should have run, but their problem was they were just plain stupid.

It ended as soon as it started. Sidana crumpled to his knees even as his head bounced down the street, and Idiptu fell to the left *and* right as his body was parted neatly down the middle from crown to crotch.

Despite the smoke and the stench of the dismembered demons, Ishtar smelled of warm lemons, but that was just me. The goddess's fragrance was always the scent you loved most. She'd chopped her hair short, and it looked like she'd used dull shears to do it, but like her ragtag outfit, the cut suited her perfectly. When I'd known her, she'd always worn designer outfits, delicate but outrageously expensive jewelry, and just a hint of makeup, probably to bring her *down* to mere human beauty. Now, even though she was smeared with soot, disheveled, and scarred, she was just as mesmerizing. She was bare-footed—that's how she always fought—and sported a dented bronze breastplate. She slid Kasusu back into his scabbard made from a Chanel handbag. Her smile was exaggerated by the scar running from the side of her lip to her ear. "I thought you were long gone."

"Manhattan's my home," I said.

"Not anymore. It's Nergal's capital now, inhabited by his demons and the poxies."

"But we beat him, Ishtar."

She arched her elegant eyebrow. Now I knew who Belet had learned it from. "Not in this life we didn't. Despite all our sacrifices, he won. Was there a moment when things could have turned out differently? I don't know."

"So, we're here to go after Nergal and finish the job?"

Ishtar shook her head. "He's long gone. Once America fell, he set sail for Europe. He unleashed the Black Death, the Spanish flu, a new coronavirus strain, and his own special supernatural illnesses. The whole place is one vast stew pot of mutation and corruption. There's no way to stop him, Sikander."

"There has to be. We can't just let him win. What about Belet? With the three of us, there has to be a chance. We'll find a way."

"I'm searching for her. That's why I'm still in Manhattan. My daughter's out there, somewhere." Ishtar wiped her face. She looked so tired and . . . Was that a tear? It couldn't be, could it?

"Let me help," I repeated. "I owe Belet that much. And I think I know where we might find her."

"You sure you want to go through with this?"

I got the feeling Ishtar didn't want me tagging along, and it wasn't just because I wasn't a warrior. There was something else she wasn't willing to share.

I just had to trust her. "Come on."

There were flies everywhere, so thick that they covered whole buildings, and when they swarmed, it was like the sky was screaming. Poxies and demons watched us from their lairs in the ruins, spitting and snarling. Some hooted and yelled mockingly, but that's all they did. They knew Ishtar. One glance from her and they would slither away, dragging their victims with them.

The city stank. Sewage streamed across the streets, and there were pools of filth covered with flies and decomposing bodies—animal, human, and something made from both. This wasn't just a war zone—it was Jahannam.

"I want you to leave the fighting to me," said Ishtar. "Don't interfere, no matter what. Understand?"

Why had she even brought that up? But I nodded. "There. Just ahead."

Mo's Deli was just a shell. I barely recognized it. The walls were blackened with soot, and the roof had collapsed as if something large had landed on it. Georgiou's pizzeria across the road was all boarded up, but there was no sign of life. Anyone who could have left had done so.

What had happened to my parents? "Ishtar, do you—"

Someone moved in the shadows. Ishtar pushed me behind her as she drew Kasusu. "Leave this to me, no matter what."

Who was lurking within Mo's? The figure shook itself and flies whined as they rose around them like a black mist from a grave. Then the person laughed. Or at least I think it was laughing—it was more a harsh rasping.

The person clambered nimbly over the rubble that had

once been my home and stepped up onto a broken wall. They carried a crude piece of metal that had been turned into a sword.

"So, you finally gathered your courage to face me," they said.

Ishtar stepped closer. "I don't want to do this."

The figure laughed again. Why did that sound make my blood run cold? Was this another demon? It looked like a human. Why was Ishtar so afraid? What could be so terrible that even the goddess would hesitate?

Then the person noticed me. "You came back, Sik. Why?"

It wasn't a demon. It was Belet.

SIXTEEN

SHE WAS JUST SKIN AND BONES, SICKLY AND WILD-EYED.
The Belet I knew was gone, leaving this feverish creature
in her place. She tightened her hand around her sword
hilt as her gaze darted maniacally from me to her mom,
and then she smiled. It was cruel and utterly without pity,
without humanity. "So, who wants to be first?"

I wasn't going to let this go the way it was headed. "Put
down the sword, Belet. Let's just talk this through. We're
on your side."

Belet drew the blade across her bare arm even as she
glared. "Talk, talk, talk. That's all you ever do. You're a
coward, you know that? If you'd fought like I'd wanted you
to, then . . . Never mind. It is what it is. Nergal showed me
that I was better off without either of you."

"Nergal? He's not your friend, Belet. Whatever he said,
it was just to hurt you."

"Really? Then how come I can do this?"

She leaped. Not just a yard or two, but across the whole street. It happened in an eyeblink. She hit the ground beside me and her sword came up and . . .

Ishtar rammed into her daughter, sending the two of them flying. They smashed into a wall, and through it. Yet an instant later Belet was stumbling out, dusty and bleeding but otherwise unharmed. How? A mortal would have been turned to paste by that collision.

She saw my bewilderment and laughed. "Poor, stupid Sik. You think you're the only one with divine gifts? Nergal gave me his blessing, and his power. You can't beat me."

"I'm not here to beat you, Belet. This isn't you."

"This *is* me, but better." She turned slowly as Ishtar climbed out of the rubble. "Ah, Mother. Did that hurt?"

Ishtar slowly raised Kasusu. I could see her heart wasn't in this. Every move was slow, reluctant. "I am sorry, Belet. I'm sorry I abandoned you on Venus Street. He was too strong. You should have run."

Oh no. That's why Ishtar was alive. Back in my *original* version of the world, she and Nergal had fought on Venus Street. The battle had been brutal, and Ishtar had been killed. But in this version, she had survived . . . because she'd run away, leaving Belet to face Nergal on her own.

Belet's eyes blazed. "I stayed to protect *you*. They say

you're the goddess of love, but now I know you love only yourself. You were never my mother."

For her entire life, Belet had craved Ishtar's love. There could be no greater betrayal. I saw then how the rest had played out. Nergal had infected Belet, twisting her already vulnerable mind and turning her against her own mother.

There was no going back for either of them.

Nergal had won . . . everything.

Mother and daughter circled each other, Ishtar hesitant, Belet searching for an opening. How could I stop it?

There was only one way.

"I've seen enough, Dumuzi." I turned my back on both of them. "You've made your point."

Ishtar sighed even as she tightened her grip on Kasusu. I watched her face become impassive, blank except for the tears falling. Belet growled. It was a bestial, monstrous noise that echoed with the sound of a heart, all but calcified with hate, breaking.

"Enough, Dumuzi! I don't need to see this!"

The stink of smoke and rot gave way to the smell of damp earth and blossoms. Instead of grit and broken glass under my feet I felt soft grass. My surroundings dispersed as I returned to the garden and to Dumuzi, sitting on a fallen log and weaving a daisy chain. He didn't meet my gaze. "How was your trip?"

𒀸 𒐊 𒂖 𒁉 𒄭

"Mind blown, and not in a good way." I understood. I was very familiar with Belet's coolness, the way she always tried to be in control. I'd only seen her cry once, and that was when she was practically dead. Even then she'd wanted me to turn my back so I wouldn't see her vulnerability. "Okay, I get it. We can't use the tablet."

"Not without making things worse. Kismet was meant to follow one path, Sikander."

I shook my head. "But I have to get my parents back. There must be a way."

"Sikander, do you not see—"

"I've seen plenty," I snapped. "I already know fate takes unexpected turns. You think I haven't had to pick up the pieces of my life and start all over again? Been there, done that. If there's a way to save the day—and the day is a long, long way from being lost—we'll find it. Me and Belet," I said. Then: "And Rabisu. Probably."

"Sikander, defender of humanity, eh?" said Dumuzi.

"Maybe not all of humanity, but I know how to look out for my friends."

"Belet has a dark streak in her. She may give in to it if she doesn't learn that she is valuable to others. Or, more simply put, that she is loved. Monsters are made when you rob people of love."

"Belet is not a monster, Dumuzi. She knows people care about her."

𒀸 𒈹 𒂍 𒌋

"But do you really dig where she's coming from?" he asked.

Nothing becomes dated quicker than slang, especially slang from fifty years ago. "Er...what's that in modern English?"

He sighed. "Do you love her?"

I was shocked by the frankness of his question. "How...how can you ask me that?" I spluttered. "I mean, I'd take a bullet for her, but that's not exactly a big ask for someone like me."

"Right," said Dumuzi, catching on. "Belet told me about your immortality. It does have its perks, doesn't it?"

I was still reeling from his other question. My feelings for Belet were...complicated. Sure, we'd had some major bonding moments, like that time we saved New York together, and the last few nights here in London had been pretty intense, but that didn't mean I was going to ask Mo to start making floral arrangements for my wedding. Those times with Belet when my palms had grown sweaty and my pulse started racing had much more to do with fighting demons than with being in love with her.

Okay, that was a strange comparison. Fighting demons is not the same as being in love. I think. I'll have to circle back to this one day.

I looked over at Dumuzi. "You don't think she's...

y'know, in love with me, do you? Can you detect that sort of thing?"

Before he could answer, the bush in the corner erupted with laughter. It shook wildly and, for a moment, I was afraid it would burst into flames in an Old Testament kind of way. But then out tumbled Rabisu, crying with laughter.

I hauled her out of the foliage. "How long have you been hiding in there?"

She wiped the tears from her eyes, peered at me, and burst into even more raucous laughter.

"Rabisu! Just shut up!"

She was literally doubled over. "I can see it now! Can I plan the engagement party? Please? Oh, by Ea, I think I'm going to die!"

"That's not funny! This was a private conversation. Spying on people is bad!"

"Spying on people is the best!" she replied. Then she slowly straightened, took a few breaths, and fanned herself. "There. Under control. Haven't laughed so hard since Pompeii. Everyone running around flapping their hands and screaming. Awesome light show."

"Remind me why I let you tag along?" I said to Rabisu as we followed Dumuzi back into the house.

"Because you're in love with me, too, and can't bear to be apart for a second?" she replied. "Romance is in the air. Or it could be the flu turning your cheeks red."

᯾ ᯾ ᯾ ᯾ ᯾

I raised my hand to my face without thinking. "This was supposed to be a relaxing two weeks seeing the sights, eating fish and chips, and hanging out backstage at Daoud's modeling gigs. It was supposed to be fun. Instead, it's turned out to be anything *but*."

"It *is* fun," said Rabisu, with a mischievous glint in her eye. "And somehow I think it's going to get even funner."

She turned out to be both right and so very, very wrong.

SEVENTEEN

———◆———

BELET WAS LAUGHING. SHE WAS LAUGHING AS MO SPUN her around the tiny breakfast room to salsa music coming from the old radio on the shelf. Daoud was back from his run, glowing with sweat, recording the action on Mo's phone. There wasn't much space, but they wove around it as lightly as feathers on a breeze.

Belet danced with her eyes half-closed, as if midway toward a dream. Her smile...What can anyone say about a smile, really? She smiled big, giving her unrestrained laughter plenty of space. Her loose locks swept her bright, rosy cheeks. Dancing made her happy.

She caught sight of me. "Your brother can dance!"

He really could. Mo was swirling, swaying his hips, and weaving Belet around him, spinning her with his fingertips.

The old Mo had plodded around the dance floor like his feet were trapped in mud. He couldn't even bob his head

◆⟨ ◈⟨ ◉⟩ ⊢◆

in time to "Bohemian Rhapsody." This new Mo was ready for *Arabs Got Talent*!

Mo dropped onto a chair, breathing hard, and gestured toward me. "Take over, Sik."

"Me?"

"Yeah, you. Why not? You're a great dancer. Belet, you should see him. Moves like a gazelle."

Belet flicked her hair away from her eyes like she just didn't care. "Come on, then. Show me what you've got."

"I can't dance with you! I mean...I can't dance with *anyone*!" I threw up my hands to protect myself. "I can't dance, period."

The mood didn't burst—that would have been exciting at least. Instead, it just deflated. Daoud turned the dial to another station, and Belet, bursting with life and joy a second ago, coughed and started collecting the dishes. Mo shot me a look that was so "disappointed older brother" that I almost wanted to cry for Mama. Daoud began gathering up the cups, but Mo stopped him. His eyes locked onto mine. "No, Sik will do it."

So, a few moments later, I joined Belet by the sink as she soaked the plates in a bucket of foamy water. She was still smiling while elbow-deep in suds. "Your brother can really move."

"First time I've ever seen him do that." I collected a dishcloth. "I'll take drying duty."

𒀸 𒐊 𒁹 𒈨

Belet squirted more dishwashing liquid into the bucket. It smelled of lemons. Funny coincidence, right? Suddenly it felt very much like Ishtar was nearby, just out of sight, but watching.

"There's a big investigation into what happened at the British Museum yesterday," Belet said. "The prime minister's personally taking charge."

"That was only yesterday? Of course it was. Wow. And, if I remember correctly, we left behind a beheaded scorpion-man."

"I wouldn't worry about them tracing anything back to us. The prime minister's a buffoon," said Belet. "The biggest suspect is the headmaster of a school where a hoard of Anglo-Saxon artifacts were found hidden in the gym."

"That's one way of making up for a lack of funding."

"By the way, what happened between you and my father outside?" asked Belet.

"He showed me that using the tablet would only lead to bigger trouble."

"Just like I told you," she said. "We need to stash it somewhere so no one is tempted to use it. Especially Lugal. What's his end goal, do you think?"

"He wants peace—or at least that's what he told me."

"It didn't look very peaceful at the British Museum."

"You know what they say"—I stacked up the dried cups—"si vis pacem, para bellum."

"Now you're showing off," said Belet. "But perhaps you're right. 'If you want peace, prepare for war.' And war is something Lugal knows better than anyone."

"Not that it's done him any good. He's . . . broken. All the things he's seen—all the suffering and destruction—have repercussions. He's tormented by them."

"Perhaps that's why he wants peace."

I remembered the frenzied look in Lugal's eyes when we'd fought at the museum. "Whatever his version of peace is, we don't want it."

We carried the dishwater out into the garden. It seemed pointless to pour it on the flowers when they were already being soaked by rain, but every bit helps, I guess.

I raised my face to the deluge. The raindrops actually stung. "It always this rainy here?"

"It is heavy for the season," she said. "And doesn't look like it's going to stop. They've activated the Thames Barrier."

"The what?"

"It's exactly what it sounds like. A giant mechanical wall across the Thames. It was built as a response to climate change and sea levels rising. It's gone up to prevent London getting flooded."

"And what will happen upriver?"

She frowned. "Some towns along the river will go underwater if this carries on much longer. All ships

᯽᯽᯽᯽᯽

crossing the Channel have been called into harbor. A fishing fleet vanished out there last night. Six ships just... gone."

"You think it's got anything to do with us? The tablet?"

"Who knows?" She met my gaze. "But the tablet's not safe in our hands. Or anyone's. It's a shame it was ever dug up."

I saw her point but couldn't agree with her. "I'm not giving up Mo. And I'm going to find a way to bring my parents back, too. You know that, right?"

"I know. We'll fix this, somehow."

When we returned to the kitchen, I could hear laughter coming from the other room. Mo was telling the story of when I'd fallen into the lake in Central Park the day after we'd watched *Jaws*. But his version was different from how I remembered it. In mine, Baba was the one who'd been forced to wade in, dressed in his best suit, to get me out. In my hysteria, I'd knocked him over. But in this new version, I was rescued by a passing cop. I'd made the officer fall, too, so the anecdote was somewhat similar. It was still funny the way Mo told it, and still cringeworthy hearing it.

Dumuzi walked in and joined us by the sink. "Groovy news, daughter," the flower god said. "I've found one of the apkallus. We'll hand him the tablet, and he'll know what to do with it."

Belet looked surprised, almost shocked. "You found one? I... Thank you, Father. I mean it."

The apkallus. The wisest, cleverest people in all of history. Surely they could find a way to bring my parents back?

Were my troubles almost over?

EIGHTEEN

"**WHAT ELSE CAN YOU TELL ME ABOUT THE APKALLUS?**"
I asked Belet.

We were all back in Dumuzi's VW and driving through London in the dead of night. I sat squeezed between Mo and Daoud, the backpack containing the tablet in my lap. Rabisu sat opposite, Dumuzi and Belet up front.

Belet was watching the road ahead through the rain-splattered windshield, her hand clasped around Kasusu. We were close to saving the day, and she was making sure we didn't run into any "surprises."

"According to the legends," she said, "the apkallus brought crafts to humanity. We were living in caves, frightened of everything, living lives no better than animals, and the apkallus showed us how to build, how to farm, how to make tools and weapons. Now they're helping us understand our place in the universe—the one we're meeting is helping NASA repair the Webb Space Telescope.

"But their greatest gift was writing. They invented it, and it's still a passion today. Last I heard, they were developing the world's first global language. It's a form of modern cuneiform." She pulled out her phone and showed me the screen. "Here it is."

We all leaned closer to look at this marvel. A global language? You'd have to be beyond a genius to... "Those are emojis, Belet."

She nodded. "Pictures to represent words or phrases, depending on the context."

Mo nudged me. "Just like cuneiform."

"But... emojis?" It wasn't worth asking Belet if she was joking, because she never was.

"Everyone understands them," said Daoud.

"Oh, come on. It's not as if you can translate the poetry of Omar Khayyam with emojis."

"First volume is being published next year. I'll see if I can get you invited to the launch party." Belet peered out the windshield. "What is going on? The traffic's not moving at all. Are you sure this is the right way?"

Dumuzi glanced over at her. "The apkallu is flying into Gatwick Airport, so we need to take Tower Bridge. Isn't it beautiful?"

If you've ever gotten a postcard from London, chances are that this bridge was on the front. I suspected Dumuzi had taken this route just to show it off. But I had to admit the sight was pretty cool, especially all lit up, even through the curtain of rain. Unfortunately, the drawbridges were up to allow ships with masts to come upriver. We should have guessed this would happen late at night, to minimize disruption to car traffic. We were lined up behind half a dozen other vehicles.

Daoud yawned and then checked himself in his pocket mirror. "Look. I'm getting bags under my eyes. My career's over."

"Your beauty is everlasting," said Rabisu. "I will dedicate a dozen heads to you by the next full moon."

"Er...shukran?"

Mo tapped the side window. "Since we're stuck here for a while, mind if I hop out and take some photos?"

I peered out, unimpressed. "It's raining, Mo."

"It's always raining here, Sik. Anyone want to join me?"

Daoud sat up. "You want to take some photos? Just give me a moment." He shook his locks loose. "There. Ready."

The pair of them jumped out, and Daoud set himself up with the Tower of London as a backdrop.

Belet sighed. "Go and keep an eye on them, will you?"

I already had a foot out the door. "It would be easier if there were two of us."

𒀸 𒐼𒐊 𒅎𒁽 𒅆

"Okay, why not."

"Rabisu? Want to come with?" I asked.

The demon nodded and wriggled along the seat. "Do they still stick the heads of traitors over the gates?"

Belet looked over at her. "If you feel peckish, remember not to eat any of the ravens."

"Even *I* know that," huffed Rabisu.

I wasn't sure what *that* was all about, but as long as the two of them were agreeing, I was happy to let it go.

I entered total tourist mode. Views from the river are the best—you don't have buildings in the way.

The Houses of Parliament were a mile upriver. The great amber face of Big Ben proclaimed it was a few minutes before two a.m. Beyond that lay the ivory dome of St. Paul's Cathedral. But over my shoulder on the northern bank stood the ominous Tower of London. The wind blew sheets of rain against the battlements, as if the elements were attacking the great keep where all the treasures of the kingdom lay.

I joined Belet at the railing and took out the tablet. "Once we hand this over, what are you going to do?"

"Carry on what I've been doing. Find a way to rescue Mother."

"I'll be by your side when you go save Ishtar. You'll do it."

"How can you be so sure?" she asked.

"Because you're you. That'll never change."

She pointed at the tablet. "Put it away before you accidentally drop it into the river."

"The bottom of the Thames might be the best place for it. It'll save us a trip, that's for sure. And then Daoud can get his beauty sleep."

"There are more important things in life than Daoud's puffy eyes."

"Don't let him hear you say that." I held out the tablet. "Well? Should I chuck it in?"

Belet peered over the side. "That's weird. It should be low tide."

"What?"

She looked back along the river. "Ships pass under here during low tide because it gives them the maximum clearance. Where are the boats?"

She was right. No vessels were sailing up or down the river. The other drivers were getting bored and irritated, and the one in the truck was honking his horn. Had someone fallen asleep in the control room?

I pointed downriver. "Wait . . . Something's coming."

It wasn't a ship. The water rose as a wave surged along the river. A big black shape was under there, and it was heading in this direction. I peered closer. A large, scaly back briefly broke the surface before sinking below. "That doesn't bode well."

"No, it doesn't," said Belet. "We need to get out of here."

I ran to the first car, the one nearest the barrier, and banged on the window. "Mister! Turn around!"

The water swelled, throwing ten-foot-tall waves over the bank. Towering geysers spurted into the night sky, and through the murky depths I glimpsed a pair of gigantic, glowing yellow eyes.

The roar started low but quickly grew in volume. It turned into a thunderous bellow that shook the bridge. The mist over the waters parted as that back rose out of the surface again, a few hundred yards downriver but getting closer fast.

The driver leaned out the window as he rubbed the sleep out of his eyes. "What's going on, mate?"

The bridge trembled, rattling the suspension chains. The road rippled like it was made of rubber. The asphalt cracked, and the towers swayed.

"Get out of the car!" I told him. "You need to run!"

"I am not leaving my car!"

The whole bridge was rocking and this guy was worried about his beat-up Ford? I opened the door for him. "Get out now!"

Belet was heading down the street, shouting for everyone to back up and get off the bridge. But instead of listening, the drivers were getting out to look. Mo was literally dragging people away. And there was something else going on. A large truck had parked at the end of the bridge, blocking the road.

I caught up with Belet. "It's a trap."

"It always is." We headed over to Dumuzi's van, and she popped the door open. A moment later, she had Kasusu unsheathed and ready. Dumuzi seemed oblivious, just bopping to a pop oldie on the radio.

"Let me guess," the blade said to Belet. "Private Clown has stumbled into a trap."

Belet twirled the sword in a sweeping figure eight. "This one's not entirely his fault."

Rabisu joined us. "I think we've fallen into a trap."

Ya salam. All three of us agreeing. Things had to be bad.

The bridge rocked again as the monster in the water slammed into its foundations. The north tower began cracking and chunks of stone tumbled down. One large section crashed into the hood of the car in front of us.

"Sik!"

Mo and Daoud ran over to me. "We need to get out of here. Yallah."

More chunks of tower plummeted. Sooner or later, one was going to hit and turn our party into a red smear.

The truck blocking the road was offloading its contents. Two scorpion-men were already clambering over the steel-work, and a fresh host of monsters had formed a barrier behind the truck to prevent any escape. In front of the truck, bathed in the red taillights of the last car in line, waited Lugal.

He looked even more frayed than before. The sleeves had come off his jacket, and his pants were torn at the knees. He pulled at his already-ragged beard as he yelled commands to his followers.

Dumuzi exited the van and went to face Lugal. "Maybe we could all talk this through?" he offered. "I've got some herbal tea in the glove box."

I heard what sounded like thunder. But it wasn't the clouds bursting—it was the south tower. A huge crack split it in half as the water creature attacked its foundation. The whole river rose, and waves crashed over the banks as glistening black scales rose from beneath the surface. The serpentine thing gathered its coils around the tower. Its giant scales rattled like a clash of ten thousand shields, and those eyes, huge yellow spotlights of pure malice, blinked slowly even as it slithered higher up the tower.

A basmu serpent. I'd fought one while swimming in the Sea of Tiamat. But that had been in Kurnugi. . . . How could one be here, in the real world? Was Lugal so powerful he could summon monsters from the netherworld? That news report about the lost fishing fleet was beginning to make horrible sense.

Hundreds of feet long and dozens of feet wide, it wrapped itself around the tower like a boa constrictor on a palm tree. It looked old, like prehistoric, with scales that were encrusted and scored. Its head could have been that of a crocodile, but it was large enough to swallow a city block in a single snap. Shipwrecks, ancient and recent, were wedged between its teeth. One vessel, a modern fishing boat, still had its emergency beacon flashing.

How could we hope to beat this creature? It wasn't even worth trying. Run? To where? There was no way to escape. We were nothing compared to the spawn of the goddess Tiamat. It was about to wipe us out without it even realizing because we were so far beneath its notice.

Then I saw Mo and Daoud standing hand in hand. When faced with death, they'd reached out and found each other. Rooted to the spot, they stared at the rising snake.

That shook me out of my stupor. You'll go the extra mile for others even if you won't do it for yourself. Whatever else happened tonight, I wasn't going to let Mo and Daoud get hurt.

More slabs of the tower fell from above, shattering windshields and pelting us with shards of jagged stone. I ducked and darted between the raining debris to reach the pair of them. "We need to get off this before one of those gargoyles falls on our heads."

Mo glanced up. "Gargoyles? The bridge doesn't have— Look out!"

I turned. But I didn't just turn. I twirled on the ball of

my left foot, bringing up my right, loose, fast, and high. I didn't even think—it was pure reaction.

My heel made contact with a body. The fight was over before I'd even known it had started. I lowered my right foot to the ground as a winged creature spun wildly to the side. He slammed onto the roof of the camper van, shaking his head, dazed from the kick I'd just landed on the side of his head.

Daoud gaped. "How'd you do that?"

I wasn't exactly sure myself, but right now I was very glad I had. Belet had explained that my past had changed and there were two versions of Sik now. One version apparently knew how to kick butt *very hard*.

The winged creature had a man's torso, a bird's head, and taloned feet. He shook his wings to reveal black and white feathers. Huge eyes glared from either side of a savage beak.

Magpie-man was back. But now I knew who he was. Memories from the other Sik, the one who sprang from the alternative fate, brought not only ass-kicking skills but also a whole library of mythology knowledge. "Anzud, I presume?"

"You know who I am?"

"The thief of the gods. You stole the tablet of destinies once before, didn't you? Is that why Lugal hired you?"

His eyes flashed with anger. "Give me the tablet, mortal,

and I'll make your death quick. Deny me my prize and you'll suffer an eternity of pain." His talons created sparks on the metal as he launched himself toward me.

No time for another spinning hook kick. No time to get help from Belet or Rabisu or Dumuzi, either—they were too busy dealing with Lugal and his minions. Drivers were screaming and fleeing around me as the bridge shook more and more violently as the basmu serpent tore huge chunks out of it. Daoud and Mo were doing their best to help people get away, guiding them through gaps in the melee.

Anzud was double trouble. His taloned feet were wicked enough, but his fingers ended in nails as curved and as sharp as sickles. On top of that, he moved in three dimensions compared to my two. He flicked his wings to attack from above, then darted away only to swoop in again a wingbeat later.

And yet . . . I dodged. I ducked. I hit back. Not with the usual flailing of my hands, but with real, solid punches, well-aimed kicks, and even a few sharp elbow strikes to his ribs and one to his jaw.

Anzud had expected an easy win, and I'd expected a quick and painful defeat, but as we dueled back and forth across the bridge, we were both in for a surprise. The end came suddenly. Anzud overreached, and I trapped his arm, twisting it behind him and forcing him to his knees. One snap kick to the side of the head and it would all be . . .

A piece of stone glanced off my head. I wobbled as my brain exploded with stars. The ground tilted violently as I stumbled to keep my balance, and I barely managed to brace myself against the side of the bridge. I had to keep fighting, but I felt separated from my body, and my senses and muscles were not interested in helping at all.

Anzud came over and pulled the tablet off me. I tried to bat his hand away, but I was reacting as if I was swimming in syrup. Anzud turned away and spread out his wings. He had his prize. Then, on second thought, he whirled around and stared at me.

Uh-oh.

He grabbed me by the collar and belt and, with a loud huff, lifted me up over his head. He carried me to the side of the swaying bridge.

Uh-oh.

No pithy one-liner. No gloating remark. No quip in ancient Sumerian. Anzud was all business. Through the spots crowding my vision, I gazed at the river below.

Then, with a grunt, Anzud heaved me off the bridge and into the black waters of the Thames.

NINETEEN

MY EYES TWITCHED AS RAIN SPLASHED ON MY FACE. A breeze blew across my sodden, mud-caked body. I reeked of foul, stagnant water. Why did my mouth taste so disgusting? What was that hideous squawking sound? I blinked and got the answer to the last question first.

Rabisu was running along the muddy bank, chasing a seagull. "Come here, breakfast!"

Breakfast?

It was a wet gray dawn. Seagulls hopped along the exposed low-tide bank, looking for breakfasts of their own.

A pair of boots came into view. Brand-new Burberry ones. "Daoud?"

"Let me help, Sik." He put his arms under me and pulled me up. The mud was reluctant to let me go. "I found him, Mo!"

My brother ran up and embraced me in a squelchy hug. He knew exactly what I needed.

"Come back!" yelled Rabisu to the fleeing bird. "Huh. I wasn't hungry anyway."

I coughed violently and spat out a wedge of gray-green river gunk. "We got away from the monsters?"

"Some of us did," said Mo.

I wiped the mud out of my eyes. It was then I saw Daoud had a dirt-splattered Kasusu in his hand. "Belet?"

Daoud shook his head. "We've searched this bank. Dumuzi and his pals are searching the other."

She'd be fine, I thought. Belet always came out on top. I didn't have to worry about her. She'd take care of herself. Then my guts surged and I vomited a bucket of river water.

Mo cleaned my face with his sleeve. Just like he used to when I was little and I'd made a mess with the tzatziki. "You had a rough night, Yakhi."

"Rough? More like apocalyptic."

We stood in the squelching mud of the Thames, four or five hundred yards downriver from Tower Bridge. Or what was left of it.

The southern tower had been crushed. There were giant claw marks on the stone walls, and the road itself had collapsed into the river, where it sat half-submerged, like an asphalt reef. The north tower leaned perilously to the side—one loud sneeze and the whole thing would tumble. Dumuzi's camper van bobbed in the greenish water. Police sirens cried louder than the seagulls, and the streets were closed off with blockade fences and flashing lights. Despite it only being dawn, a crowd had collected along the main barriers, and there were a few camera crews eager for the scoop. No one was paying attention to us wading in the mud.

Mo cupped my chin. "You okay?"

"I lost my shoe," I said. "I'm sorry."

"Can you walk?"

I shook my head. I couldn't say any more. It was taking all my strength not to cry.

Mo put his arms around me. "It'll be okay."

You try and hold it together. You face down gods, monsters, beasts out of nightmare; try to be strong because you don't want to let people down. I wasn't hurt—I was immortal! But standing there, wet, cold, and covered in mud as the sirens blared in the distance, I felt a total failure. I'd tried, and it hadn't been good enough. I'd always been told that if you just put in the effort, you will get what you want. If you don't, that means you're not trying hard enough, and you don't *deserve* success.

Belet was gone and so was the tablet, and it was all my fault.

Rabisu was standing there, watching the birds. "Look. The ravens are leaving."

𒀀𒈨𒁉𒌋

I was so busy being upset, I didn't pay enough attention to what she was saying. I should have. I really should have.

We returned to the commune. First thing, I took a shower while Heavenly found me some footwear. Second thing, we had some oatmeal with fresh blueberries.

At least most of us did. Dumuzi was too despondent to eat. His daughter was missing; most likely in the hands of Lugal. He curled up on the sofa, whimpering, and declared he was going to stay there until he died from grief sometime in the next one thousand years, possibly two.

Rabisu watched it all with a disdainful sneer. "What did Ishtar see in him?"

"He's in touch with his emotions, all of them, all of the time," I said as I furiously rubbed my hair with a towel. It had taken ages to get the mud off. Some of it had gotten into deep and awkward places. "But I've heard that girls like sensitive guys."

She snorted. "Not this girl."

"Let me guess—no flowers for you? Just...a mountain of skulls?"

She sighed. "One day, Sik. One day I will find someone willing to conquer nations in my name and make the rivers flow red with blood. There will be feasting for the crows and jackals, and the sky will echo with the lamentation of the women."

"That's almost poetic. Gruesome and slightly stomach-churning, but still poetic."

"Shukran. So, what are you going to do now, Sik? You've got to save Belet."

Now, that was unexpected. "You care what happens to her?"

"Not at all. But if anyone is going to kill her, it's going to be me. The three-day truce is almost up."

That was more like the Rabisu I knew and was strangely fond of. "Tell me again what happened after Anzud threw me in the river," I said.

"Belet charged Lugal. Went straight for him. She didn't have a chance, but after that? The basmu serpent tore up the bridge some more, and they all fled, taking Belet with them."

"If they took her, they want her alive. There's that." Not much to be relieved about, but better than the alternative. "What can you tell me about Lugal? Maybe there's some detail that might help us find her."

"How?" she asked.

I wasn't the clever one. That was Belet's department. I didn't know any of the mysteries of the Mesopotamian gods. I'd only talked to Lugal that once. "He said he wants peace. He's got a funny way of going about getting it."

Rabisu shook her head. "There's no place more peaceful than a graveyard."

That was the thing about Rabisu. She went straight for the truth, even if it was horrific. *Especially* if it was horrific. "Do you know London at all?"

"I've known it since before it was bunch of huts along the river," said Rabisu. "This area here used to be a swamp where the druids carried out their human sacrifices. Those guys knew how to party."

"I'm sure they did. Since you're so well versed in the place, you must have some idea where Lugal might be."

"London's not exactly as I remember it," said Rabisu. "But some things never change. There's a place where everyone gathers to gossip, swap news, and give away secrets. And, though they don't know it, to engage in worship of Mesopotamia's greatest invention."

"Writing? We're going to a library?" I asked. "Is it some secret occult library that contains the mysteries of the cosmos? Because that would be pretty cool."

"Beer," stated Rabisu. "The Mesopotamians invented beer. We're going to a pub."

"What about me being Muslim do you not understand?"

She smirked. "Oh, leave the drinking to me."

"I'm going to regret this a whole lot, aren't I?"

Despite all the modern developments and renovations, the East End of the city remained a labyrinth of dark alleys and cobbled streets. It clung to the loop of the Thames, and the waterfront was dominated by converted warehouses. Sandbags lined the streets closest the river.

We spent several hours just wandering around in circles. I stopped Rabisu when we passed Karachi Kebabs for the third time. "Admit it, you're lost."

"I told you London's changed since I was here last!" She scowled at me and then pointed to the right. "That way. For sure."

"That way's the river."

"Ah, it's all coming back to me now," said Rabisu as she turned down a waterlogged alley that ended with steps going straight down into the water.

A rowboat bobbed on the surface, and a guy sat on the steps, hand-rolling a cigarette. He squinted as he saw us approach. "Rabisu?"

"Salaam, Urshanabi. Still working?" said Rabisu. She beckoned me closer. "I need passage for me and this one."

"I don't take mortals," said the ferryman. "You know the rules."

"He's different," said Rabisu. "Give him your hand, Sik."

I did, reluctantly, and his grip was cold and clammy. He peered deep into my eyes and I tried to meet his gaze, but all I got was a spinning sensation, like I was staring into a whirlpool heading into the darkest depths of the ocean. Urshanabi let go. "All right. But he's your responsibility, Rabisu."

She glanced back at me. "Don't I know it."

We climbed into the rowboat, and Rabisu nestled beside me on the bench as Urshanabi pushed off.

"I've never been in a pub before," I said. "Who runs it?"

Rabisu dipped her claws in the water, slicing the surface into so many ripples. "The owner is Siduri, always has been. She was the one who poured a drink for Gilgamesh before he went on his quest for immortality, and she pops up in a lot of other tales from all over the world, whenever a hero needs a jug of something to refresh himself before going off to fight the dragon or whatever it is. She has just a few, simple rules."

"What are they?"

Rabisu licked her lips. "First, no drinking the blood of other patrons. But that really only applies to the vampires, I suppose. Then there's the rule about—"

"Wait. Did you say vampires?"

"Did I? Anyway, moving on. Rule two: No credit. Doesn't matter who you are. You wouldn't believe how many come barging in, declaring they're the god of wealth and have entire palaces made of solid gold but they're just a bit light right now and dying for a drink. Nope. None of that. Coin on the table. Keeps everything honest."

"Anything else I should know?"

"Pleasure before business. That's Siduri's way." She clicked her claws. "Ah, there it is."

An aged leviathan of warped driftwood, draped in rope and nautical flags, loomed out of the curtain of rain. Was it a barge? A boat? A raft that had grown with the flotsam and jetsam collected over the ages? I couldn't tell. It creaked, and smoke wafted from a few rusty tin chimneys. We drew up beside a rope ladder hanging over the side.

"Up you go, Sik." Rabisu turned to Urshanabi. "Wait here."

"For how long?"

"You got somewhere else to be? You wait till we come back."

"*If* you come back," he muttered as he settled onto his bench and started rolling his next cigarette.

I helped Rabisu onto the deck. "What did he mean by that?"

"Stop fretting, Sik." She clapped her hands. "By Ea, I am parched. Let's get inside. Maybe Siduri's still doing karaoke Mondays."

We descended narrow steps toward an ebony door engraved with monsters. Serpents devoured hapless souls, winged nightmares carried off poor villagers, and long-fanged wolves tore apart cowering warriors. Not exactly encouraging. "What's this pub called?"

"This?" Rabisu pushed the door open. "This is the World's End."

TWENTY

MY FIRST EVER PUB. TOTALLY HARAM, BUT SOMETIMES you have to do what you have to do. You know how it looked barely held together on the outside? Same on the inside. The floor undulated with uneven boards, and the ceiling was ribbed with beams that were large, small, straight, and crooked. Smoke gathered in pockets between the deeper beams that were thick with grease and fat. And the place seemed to stretch out a long way. A really long way. "It's bigger inside than out. How is that possible?"

Rabisu shrugged. "Do I look like an architect? Come on and wipe your feet."

The customers barely gave us a glance. I followed Rabisu across the pub while she greeted a couple of Indian demons and dapped a Japanese goblin. A djinn nodded at us as flames rolled across his bare shoulders. He blew off the top of his drink, setting it alight. A werewolf wearing a silver collar chewed on a leg of cow. He growled as we passed by, and I shuffled a little closer to Rabisu and took her hand. In case she was scared or something.

I scanned the room, looking for someone in charge. "So where is she, this Siduri? We need to ask her—"

"Easy does it. We can't just go barging up to her demanding she help us on our quest. The rules, remember?"

"I stopped listening after the one about drinking blood. Sorry."

Rabisu smacked her lips. "No business is gonna happen until we've bought a drink or two."

I frowned. "Rabisu, we're here to find Belet."

"You asked for my help, remember that. So, we do it my way or not at all. And we're getting a drink. Only a small one, if that makes you happier."

It didn't, but we settled at a table between the ribs of the hull and sat on the adjacent bench. Rabisu peered at some runes carved into the wood. "Eric Bloodax was here."

"Anyone you knew?"

"Maybe. You'd be surprised how many Vikings called themselves Eric Bloodax." She turned back to watch the other patrons. "Not that it matters. Siduri banned all Vikings from here after Thor and Medb got into a fierce drinking contest."

"Did you just say Thor drank here?"

⚔ ⚒ ⚑ ⚔

"Everyone has at one time or another. Now wait here while I order a drink and ask if Siduri's free for a chat."

"What about me? What should I do?"

"Stay right here and don't talk to anyone."

I got a strong feeling I was cramping Rabisu's style, so she was ditching me to hang out with her demon chums. I was starting to think this was a huge waste of time, but what other leads did we have?

"Can I sit with you? Please?"

I turned around and found a girl standing right behind me. Somehow I'd missed her approach.

"Please?" she asked again.

Rabisu had told me to not to talk to anyone, but this girl looked lonely and scared. "Yeah, sure." I slid over to make room. "I'm Sik, by the way."

"I'm Lily." She sat down and smiled. "Thanks. You're my hero."

She laughed as I blushed. "What are you doing here, Sik?"

"I'm wondering that myself. What about you?"

She shrugged her pale shoulders. You know, she was really pretty. I mean, not just her blue-gray eyes and pure black hair, but also the way she looked at me. She wanted to be my friend. Some people just have the knack of putting you at ease. They make you feel special. She rested her head on her dainty little fist. "You must be very brave to come here, Sik."

You know something? She was *totally* right. Why did I always think of myself as the sidekick? This was my story, and I should be the hero for once.

Her fingers touched the back of my hand ever so lightly, but I got a little electric charge from them. "There aren't enough heroes in the world. Not real ones like you."

Finally, someone who really gets me.

I needed to play it casual. I'm sure I'd read that in my copy of *Dating for Dummies*, which had been an Eid present from Daoud. This looked like it was straight out of chapter twelve.

Take it easy. Don't overdo it.

"I defeated Nergal, the god of disease, last year. And I'm really good friends with Gilgamesh. You know him? I'm thinking about getting a tattoo when I'm old enough."

Tattoos were cool, right?

"What sort of tattoo?" she asked.

See? I told you!

"Maybe a cat."

"A . . . cat?" she asked.

"Oh, not just any cat. I mean a huge, winged lion. I have one—a real one, I mean. His name's Sargon, and when he's in cat form he spends his days lying on table four in our deli because it catches the morning sun. He likes that."

"A lamassu?" She sounded a little ... perturbed? "You have one?"

"Yeah, back in Manhattan. He belonged to Ishtar, but he moved in with me and—you know what cats are like— just settled in. He keeps the place demon-free." Then I remembered who I'd arrived with. "Mostly."

Lily shifted uneasily on her side of the bench. Maybe she was more of a dog lover? Not that being a dog lover was bad or anything, but when you own a deli, you need anti-rodent measures. Lily leaned closer and wrapped her fingers around my hand. Wow, she was stronger than she looked. "Do you like me, Sik? Say that you do. I like you very much. You're much to my ... taste."

"Er. Shukran?"

Ya salam. What big eyes she had. You might even call them hypnotic.

"Yeah, I like you, Lily."

"Would you do anything for me?" she asked, smiling.

Ya ... what big teeth she had. You might even call them fangs.

A distant part of my brain was waving red warning flags to get my ... She had the most amazing eyes. They were scintillating. "Yeah," I mumbled. "Anything at all."

A shadow fell across the table. "Hey, Sik. Who's your friend?"

Lily's eyes flashed as she turned. "Can't you see that—"

𒀀𒈾 𒂗 𒀭𒁷 𒄭

Rabisu grabbed Lily by the hair and slammed her head against the table. The girl snarled as she tried to wriggle out of her grasp. Instead, Rabisu whacked Lily against the table another three times before hoisting her off the bench. "I am really enjoying this. We can carry on, or you could leave. Which would you prefer?"

Lily glared back at her, but only for a moment. Then her gaze, and voice, fell. "Leave?"

Lily sulked off, and Rabisu took her place at the bench. "What did I tell you about not speaking to anyone?"

I shook my head. Now that Lily was gone, I felt . . . different. "What just happened? Who was that?"

"Lillitu. A blood drinker."

"A vampire?" I searched the crowded bar for another glimpse of her, but she was gone. "She was going to drink my blood?"

"And you were going to let her. Let me guess. Did she find everything about you utterly *fascinating*? Didn't that raise your suspicions almost immediately?"

I didn't like that Rabisu was stifling a laugh. "She expressed an interest in me. What's wrong with that?"

"By Ea, you are so naive." She took my arm. "Let's get this over and done with before you sell your soul to that shaytan over there."

"There's a shaytan in—"

"Come on." She pulled me off the bench and across

the pub. We climbed a wrought-iron spiral staircase to a kind of mezzanine that overlooked the main floor. It was covered in plush rugs and silken cushions—Persian and Egyptian, mainly—and to our left were three guys in dark kaftans, puffing away at ornate shishas that filled the room with rose-scented smoke. Each man had a bare scimitar laid across his lap and watched us like a hawk watching two mice crossing a sand dune.

A woman—Siduri, I assumed—sat with them, one arm draped over a plump cylindrical cushion. Her bare feet and hands were decorated with henna patterns that shifted and transformed with every breath. Aside from that, she could have been any corporate businesswoman in her deep crimson silken pantsuit. Her hair was loose and decorated with silver trinkets. She, too, puffed on a shisha, cloaking herself in a mauve mist. She pointed to a scattering of pillows. "It's been a while, Rabisu. Take a seat and introduce me to your friend."

"This is Sikander Aziz. He's not bad," said Rabisu. From her, that was a big compliment.

Siduri nodded in acknowledgment. "Ah. I was wondering when I might meet the defender of humanity. Make yourself comfortable, Sikander."

A scaly-skinned goblin brought us a cup of freezing-cold lemon sherbet before disappearing, literally, into the smoke.

"So, what brings you to my humble establishment?" Siduri asked.

"How much do you know about what happened at Tower Bridge last night?" I asked her.

"Assume she knows everything," said Rabisu between slurps of her sherbet.

The pub owner nodded in agreement. "That's right. I've heard it all before. Every hero has the same story. A great evil threatens all that they hold dear, someone needs rescuing, and there's usually an annoying yet surprisingly wise sidekick. But I want to hear your version, Sikander Aziz."

Okay, then. Start with the obvious? "You know Lugal? Well, he has the tablet of destinies. He's planning to do something big with it—what, I don't know. He's kidnapped Belet, Ishtar's daughter, and I need to get her back and stop him. In that order."

Siduri tucked her mouthpiece away. "What makes you think Belet wants to be rescued? Perhaps she's happier now than she was before."

That made no sense at all. "She can't be. Lugal is everything she hates. Do you know where she is?"

"Lugal's easy to predict. He's found a home here that suits him perfectly—a temple of war and madness. Your friend is with him, as are other embittered, lost unfortunates. But he's counting on you to show up, Sikander Aziz.

My advice? Leave Belet to her fate. If you go after her, you'll only suffer."

"You're saying Belet is being used as bait? To trap me? But why? He already has the tablet...."

"Your feelings are a trap. You can't save everyone, Sikander. Some must fall by the wayside. If you don't learn that now, how will you manage your immortality? Year after year, you'll see your loved ones wither and fade. You must harden your heart if you want to survive. Otherwise, there is much pain ahead of you. Too much to bear, perhaps."

"Maybe, but that's a long way off. Right now, I want to know where Belet is, please. Whatever the consequences are, I'll deal with them."

"I tried my best to warn you," said Siduri, shaking her head. "Your answer lies on the path of madness."

I stepped off Urshanabi's rowboat and onto dry land. "What a waste of time!"

Rabisu followed me, nodding her thanks to the ferryman. "Why? Siduri's advice seemed pretty clear to me."

"What? Abandon Belet?"

"Sometimes the truth ain't what you want to hear."

"Of course you agree with her. You don't care what happens to Belet. You hate her."

"This has nothing to do with me, Sik. You heard what

𒀀𒌷𒅁𒀭

Siduri said. Going after Belet will only make things worse. So forget her."

"You're a demon. You wouldn't understand."

"Oh?" said Rabisu, her voice dropping to a dangerous whisper. "Understand what, exactly?"

I know, I know. You're waving your hands, telling me to stop before I say something I might regret. But right then and there, I wasn't interested in doing anything sensible. I couldn't get past the feeling that Rabisu was happy about Belet's disappearance. She was a demon after all. Still, the next part was really stupid. Skip over it if you want.

My words weren't angry, at least not hot angry. They were cold and icy, and that made them worse, because it sounded like I'd been holding on to them for ages and letting them chill in my heart. "Loyalty. That you stand by your friends. That people can be unselfish and help others. Like I said, you wouldn't understand."

I wish she'd attacked me. I wish she'd snarled and given me a solid punch in the gut. But Rabisu didn't do any of those things because, hey, you don't hurt people you care about. Not with fists, and definitely not with cruel words.

She looked at me with tears in her eyes. I was sure they were just irritated from the ferryman's cigarette.

"You'd risk everything for her, wouldn't you?" she asked in a small voice.

Ya Allah. Now I felt truly despicable.

She laughed. "Sikander. The defender of *humanity*. I forgot that doesn't include me."

Thinking back on it now, I can come up with a hundred things I should have said. But at that moment, I just stood there with my mouth clamped shut.

Rabisu gave a small shrug, like nothing mattered. But it looked like she was bending under the weight of my words. "It's lunacy, don't you see that?"

Then she adjusted her kaftan, making sure her tail was tucked in, and walked off. She didn't look back, and I didn't call out for her. If either of us had, things would have turned out differently—better. A lot better.

Other mistakes were made, but this was by far the biggest. Everything went wrong from here on out.

Don't say I didn't warn you.

TWENTY-ONE

I WAS STILL BLAMING RABISU FOR ABANDONING ME IN London. She was only here because of me. Well, also Lady Gaga, but mainly me!

I wandered the streets, not caring that I was getting soaked. I wasn't going to go back for her, and I wasn't going back to the commune. I knew if I saw Mo, I wouldn't get the sympathy I deserved. He'd probably tell me to find Rabisu and apologize, but that wasn't going to happen. She hated Belet and was happy to let her suffer at the hands of Lugal. I was in the right to go and save Belet, by myself if I had to.

That would show Rabisu. That would show them all.

And how dare she call me a lunatic? Now, that was just plain rude. Given what was going on, I was staying incredibly sane.

I'd find Lugal myself. I didn't need ancient pub owners. I

didn't need stunty-horned demons. And I definitely didn't need gods who fought with daffodils.

The problem with Rabisu was she was old-school. But there was a more modern way to find Lugal.

Such as Google fu.

The answer to finding Lugal was out there in internet land. Everything was out there—the good, the bad, and the crazy. I typed *War and London* on my phone and let the hits pour in.

Ya salam.

World War II was a big deal here—the Brits had gone full jihad on that one. This was going to take some trawling. I searched through the most likely suspects.

The Churchill War Rooms. A vast underground complex dedicated to Britain's wartime leader. Now, that would appeal to Lugal, wouldn't it? The word *lugal* meant "warlord," and who was Britain's greatest warlord? Winston Churchill. Definitely put a pin in that.

Next up was HMS *Belfast*, a ship turned museum that was docked...just a few hundred yards from Tower Bridge.

Was that how Lugal had found us so easily? Had we literally driven past his front door? And what's the best way to survive a deluge? Get yourself a boat. The ancient Mesopotamian gods had tried to destroy humanity with a flood, and we'd only survived because the wise man

Utnapishtim had built a boat and filled it with his family and all the animals. Maybe Lugal remembered the tale and had made similar plans?

Pin that one, too.

Suduri had said Lugal would be found in "a temple of war and madness." So maybe I needed to look for something connected to madness. What would be a good place for someone like Lugal? The guy was clearly not well in the head....

A psychiatric hospital.

There was an infamous one in London. Bethlem Hospital, better known as Bedlam, a word now forever associated with uproar and discord. It had been founded over a thousand years ago, and in the nineteenth century, it had been moved from its decaying, crumbling site in Moorfields to a palatial new building in South London. Then, in 1930, the hospital had moved again, and its former building had been converted to a new role—as the Imperial War Museum. And war was its own kind of bedlam.

I'd found Lugal's temple of war and madness.

Closed for refurbishment. How convenient. There was a big anniversary coming up about some country Britain had conquered a few centuries ago, so the museum was getting out the bunting. I peered through the black iron railings at the unlit, monolithic building across the wooded lawn.

Plenty of dark places inside for a renegade god to hide with his captive.

I'd waited till well past midnight, made sure no one was around, then climbed over the railings and, keeping to the trees, made my way toward the main entrance.

Which was guarded by a pair of great big cannons. They were at least fifty feet long, the sort of guns you'd find on a battleship used to destroy towns on another continent. Beyond them stood a large building with a colonnaded portico and a single domed tower with green copper tiling.

How to get in? Maybe a side door? A fire exit was always a good option. Maybe I'd get lucky with a window near the kitchen—those were often left open for ventilation. The café was off to the right.

Then a large shadow moved across the grass. I ducked behind a row of recycling bins and caught a glimpse of a broad, heavy-browed head topped by a pair of curved horns. Not blunt stubs like Rabisu's but real gut-rippers. The ground shook under the creature's heavy footfall. It paused nearby and I held my breath, but I couldn't resist a quick glance.

It stood over ten feet tall and was massively broad. The head and back were covered with a thick black pelt, and the horns glinted in the landscaping lights. The monster snorted as it turned its head to the side.

A kusarikku, a bull-man.

Greeks called it a Minotaur, but this beast had first been created by the chaos goddess, Tiamat, to serve Lugal in his war against the gods. The kusarikku stank, and his hindquarters were encrusted in filth. It looked like his tail had been torn off long ago. His hide was mangy, crisscrossed with old scars, and his eyes were cloudy with cataracts. He hobbled as he walked, as if his bones could no longer support his weight, and leaned against a tree trunk to catch his breath. Instead of making a chest-shaking bellow, he wheezed.

This was the kind of being who had rallied to Lugal's cause—the destitute and downcast. I wondered which hero had given the kusarikku those scars. Was the monster's tail adorning a grand hall somewhere?

I've often found myself trying to see the good in so-called bad guys. Maybe it's because we Muslims are usually portrayed as villains. I don't feel like a bad guy, and the kusarikku probably didn't, either. Had the creature come here because he felt the same way as Lugal? Cast out? Despised? Did he just want peace?

Didn't we all?

There was a breeze—or maybe it was only a breath. Then the creak of a tree bough as something moved along it. I heard only the faintest rustle of cloth, but I turned toward the tiny disturbance.

Someone leaped down from the tree in an ambush. I

was already sliding to the right, far enough to dodge the attack. My assailant was dressed all in black, complete with a face mask, and the steel of their sword, a Japanese katana, glinted in the lawn lights. Its edge looked limb-severingly sharp. They knew what they were doing.

But so did I.

It doesn't matter what you see in the movies or practice in the dojo. If you mess with someone wielding a blade, you will get cut. The best thing, always, is to run. But sometimes that isn't an option. So, as they drew back for another attack, I charged. They sliced, and I winced as the edge burned a fiery wound across my ribs.

I could take it. I locked my arm over the blade, wedging it between my body and arm, then grabbed their collar and twisted.

My throw wasn't all it should have been, but it tossed them to the ground, and they let go of the sword. I flung the weapon far into the bushes. My opponent took that moment to spring back onto their feet and claim their fighting distance. Behind them the bull-man snorted and lowered his head as he pawed the dirt.

The attacker raised their hand. "He's mine."

Wait a minute... "Belet? What have you done to your hair?"

No wonder I hadn't recognized her. She'd shaved it to little more than stubble. Belet frowned as she looked at me but didn't lower her fists. I should have paid more attention to that, but I was so happy to see her I ignored the obvious *wrongness* of the situation. "Belet! You're okay! Alhamdulillah!"

Her eyes narrowed and delivered the finest slow squint this side of Clint Eastwood. "Aziz..."

"A bit formal, but... Yeah, that's me. What's going on?"

It was only then that my inner alarm bells starting ringing. Not loudly enough, unfortunately.

Belet snapped her fingers. "Take him."

The bull-man threw his arms around me, and I might as well have been bound in concrete. He lifted me off my feet and had me dangling like a minnow on a fishing line, arms clamped to my sides, and no amount of wriggling or clever moves was going to get me free. "What are you doing? I came to save you!"

She shook her head. "Take him to my father."

Okay, now I was really confused. "Dumuzi's here?"

"Dumuzi? That fool's not my father." She turned toward one of the side doors. "My father is Lugal."

Yeah, that's exactly what she said.

TWENTY-TWO

BELET WALKED NEXT TO THE KUSARIKKU AS HE CARRIED me inside.

The main hall was several stories high. Fighter planes hung from the ceiling like gigantic mobiles, and there were tanks from earlier wars parked on the floor. How much death and destruction had these things caused? And yet, I'm ashamed to admit, in the sparse light, shrouded with shadows, they were eerily beautiful.

"Look who I found, Father," said Belet.

Why was she calling him that? Why was she helping him? Last night, she'd been trying to kill him, and now all I saw was subservience. Something was horribly wrong.

Lugal stood among the relics of yesterday's battles. There were others with him—a few desperate-looking vagabonds and scorpion-folk. Anzud, in the hybrid form of a human with wings, watched from atop the Spitfire suspended overhead.

"Salaam." Lugal gazed around the gloomy hall. "Welcome to my home, Sikander."

The bull-man dropped me to the floor. But I got up, dusted myself off, and tried to act a lot braver than I felt. "Just let Belet go, and we'll call it quits."

"Why should I give up my one and only daughter?" he asked.

Belet just watched me, her stare as steely as the katana in her hand.

"She's not your daughter," I said.

"Oh, no?" He smirked as he tapped his chest. "Kismet is a fickle thing, isn't it?"

He'd bound the tablet of destinies to his chest with black duct tape.

Of course. I should have known.

It wasn't just her haircut. Belet's demeanor was different. She'd always walked with a dancer's grace, her head and spine straight. Now she stood hunched and brooding. Her gaze wasn't aloof, but predatory. Whereas before she'd been calm, settled with a stillness that could explode into action, she now fidgeted, her nerves on edge.

"You changed her destiny, all of her past. You raised her, not Ishtar."

Lugal nodded. "I found her scavenging among the

rubble of Baghdad. She'd been orphaned at a young age and lived on the streets for years. She'd witnessed... terrible things. Endured many hardships." He turned to address her. "But I saved you, didn't I?"

Belet nodded. "I owe you everything, Father."

But her answer sounded hollow, robotic. Obliged.

So, he'd changed her past. She hadn't been rescued by Ishtar, the goddess of war and love, but found, already broken and feral, and raised by the god of madness. My insides plummeted like the broken stones of Tower Bridge. What had Lugal turned Belet into? Was there anything left of my friend in there?

There had to be. I had to believe that the Belet I knew still existed. The one who stood by her friends and fought on even when all hope seemed lost. The girl who cared for others and was loved by more people than she knew.

I had to win her back. I had to find the part of her heart that knew she deserved better than a father like Lugal. But how could I make a child betray their parent? That went against everything I believed in. Yet it was my only hope.

Lugal approached me and cupped my chin between his thumb and forefinger. This close, I felt the almost overwhelming pressure of his disturbed mind digging into my own. When I'd been near Ishtar, there'd been a sense of love, of being cared for. With Dumuzi, the world bloomed. But Lugal's god surge was all... bedlam.

⌇⌇⌇⌇⌇⌇

"You seem unchanged," he commented. "Why is that? Kismet has been altered, yet you remember the previous strands of fate. . . . Ah, I see it now. There's a conflict inside you. I can feel the personalities fighting for dominance—the warrior versus the deli cook. Which will win, I wonder?"

"I'm still me," I snapped as I pulled myself away. "And so is Belet, deep down."

Lugal's use of the tablet hadn't transformed me, but what *had* he changed? There was more to this than his gaining a daughter. I kept thinking of that river of time and the ripples I'd created in it. Lugal had thrown in another rock, and he had many more boulders lined up on the riverbank, waiting. There was no way to control how those ripples would react with one another, and how much of the past would be affected to accommodate Lugal's plans for the future.

"So, how's your quest for peace coming along?" I asked.

"These things take time, Sik. I'm initiating big changes. But soon enough we'll all know true peace. Nothing will bother us anymore, ever."

I really didn't like the way he said that. There was a dreadful finality to his idea of peace.

"Sure, things can be tough," I said. "But people are inherently good. You just need to give them a chance."

Lugal scoffed. "They've had their chance. Who knows better than I, the one whose blood gave you life? You are wayward, disrespectful children. I remember how my mother railed at the torments the young gods imposed on her. She would drown the world with her tears if she knew what they had created from her bones and flesh."

"Your mother? You mean Tiamat, the chaos goddess?"

"All things come from her, Sikander. And all things will return to her."

I just hoped that would be no time soon. "Are your torments that terrible, Lugal? All those voices screaming in your head? Is this why you're doing this?"

For a second, I thought I'd gone too far. Lugal leaned forward, and the air became thick with the promise of extreme violence.

"You're more than human now, so perhaps you can hear them, too? Listen carefully. Look around you, especially in the dark places."

I scanned the room. There was something pitiful about his followers. They were lost souls—you could see it in their eyes and the way they held themselves, as if standing straight and proud was too onerous. The world had crushed them a long time ago and what remained was only held together by bitterness and misery.

They reminded me of people I'd served free meals to while working at our mosque's "Kebab Kitchen." A soldier back from war. A refugee escaping slaughter. Runaways from abusive families and cruel homes. They'd taken to living on the streets because it was better than what they'd left behind. But these folks? Whatever had tormented them still haunted them now. There was no escape.

I picked up something else, too. I heard soft, pitiful whispers and despairing cries echoing from the chambers beyond. There was even laughter—not of joy, but of hopelessness. In the deep shadows, I caught glimpses of figures dressed in tattered rags, pale and lost. They were there only for an eyeblink, but their wails echoed long after they had disappeared.

Lugal saw the shock on my face. "You heard them?"

"Who are they?"

"The prior residents. Before this building became a shrine to war, it was Bethlem Hospital, better known as Bedlam, the lunatic asylum. Where visitors could watch and laugh at the chained inmates for a tuppence. For a shilling, the warders would make the 'patients' perform. What jolly good fun that must have been. The inmates died within these walls, some not having been out of their cells for entire decades, and here their spirits still linger, captive even in death. Do they not deserve peace? The bliss of oblivion?"

What was he getting at?

How many souls were down here?

He sneered at me. "What's this? A tear?"

I hadn't even noticed, but I wiped my face. I didn't want him to think I was weak, but maybe I was. Who cries for ghosts?

Lugal turned to Belet. "This is what they send against us. Pitiful, isn't it? A weeping boy, feeble-hearted and without the...without the..." Lugal suddenly swayed and turned pale.

Belet took a step toward him as he rocked backward. "Father?"

I felt a flash of anger, the same, brutal pulse I'd felt back at the British Museum. Belet was supposed to be my friend, and yet there she stood, beside my enemy. Didn't that make her my enemy, too? Maybe I'd been wrong about her all along....

No. I knew Belet. She was my friend, and I was hers, no matter what.

The god screamed as he tottered backward into a column, all strength draining out of him.

"Father!"

Belet ran to him, her arms outstretched to catch him before he collapsed. Watching her tenderness toward him made me feel like she'd stabbed me in the gut with Kasusu.

But then Lugal shook himself and, with a single, savage sweep of his arm, knocked her backward off her feet. "Get away!"

◄╣ ╬╣ ╫▷╎ ◄╫

Belet lay on the floor, gazing up at her father even as Lugal loomed over her, snarling. "How dare you? Do you think I am so weak?"

She'd only wanted to help him, out of love. But in that gloomy chamber, I saw that Lugal was far beyond love. He despised Belet in that brief moment, and she saw it. How could any child survive such a look from their parent?

Belet's eyes narrowed as she buried away all her pity. "No, Father. You are not weak. You are the Lugal."

He took a step closer, his fists tense and trembling at his sides. "You would be nothing without me. You understand?"

"Yes, Father."

There are many forms of abuse, I know. I'd seen its effects on victims at school and around the neighborhood. I know what can happen behind the closed doors of "decent" homes. And what happened between Belet and Lugal was pure cruelty. He'd raised Belet to believe she was worthless. She couldn't possibly think otherwise because a child will always believe what their parent says, no matter what.

What can you do? It's not like you can save everyone.

But that doesn't mean you shouldn't try to save some.

I held out my hand. "Let me help you up."

Belet stared, shocked. She didn't slap it away, not quite. She got herself up, straightened herself out, and glanced again at my offered hand as if it were some alien object.

Lugal slowly turned back to me, his rage simmering just beneath the surface. "I can't kill you, but neither can I have you running free around the city, disrupting my plans." He snapped his fingers. "Ah. Bring him along, daughter."

"Where are we taking him?" Belet asked.

"Do as I command, and try my patience no longer."

So, with Lugal and the bull-man leading us, we headed deeper into the museum. Walking next to me was not the Belet I knew—this one had definitely gone over to the dark side—but I couldn't leave her here, where she was subject to the god's brutal whims. I had to try to bring her back.

I waited until Lugal was a fair distance ahead and slipped closer to her. "Did I tell you how you and I first met?"

"I know how we met. It was about an hour ago."

"No, not in this version. In the *real* version."

"There's only one version of life, Aziz. You're living in it." She drummed her fingers on her sword hilt. "Too bad it's not one you like."

I pushed on. Words were the only tool I had. "It was at my parents' deli one night. At the beginning of last fall. I was fighting Nergal and his two demons. You kicked the door in, wielding Kasusu. You must have heard of it, right?"

"Kasusu? Of course. The sword of legend. I . . . I had it? Impossible. It was Gilgamesh's weapon."

⤙⟊⫶⟊⫶⟊⫶⤚

"I've got it now. You dropped it when you were kidnapped by Lugal."

"You're a liar. I wasn't kidnapped, and you're not worthy of such a weapon. You're no warrior."

"Neither is Gilgamesh anymore. He gave up fighting, Belet. To become a gardener."

"That is the most ridiculous thing I've ever heard. Gilgamesh giving up war? He was the greatest warrior who ever lived. Why give up what makes you legendary, what you were born to be?"

"People aren't born to be anything, Belet. They are made into what they are. Sometimes it's good; sometimes it's bad. And sometimes we learn how to change. Gilgamesh knew that his path led nowhere, so he got off it. You can leave this behind, too."

"You know what you sound like? A coward." She stepped up to me, drew her sword, and pressed the flat of the cold blade against my neck.

Belet had always had a darkness in her. How much of it had been kept at bay by Ishtar? Had it totally consumed her now? There was only one way to know.

"You won't hurt me."

"Oh? What makes you so sure?" She smiled and turned the blade slightly so its razor edge rested against my throat. It wouldn't take any pressure at all for her to cut through and open an artery. "Why wouldn't I?"

I was sweating, I'll be honest about that, but I put all my willpower into staying still, remaining calm, and meeting her gaze. "Inflicting pain for its own sake is just cruel. And you're not cruel."

"Life is cruel, Aziz. You can't imagine what it was like growing up alone, in the rubble and ruin. All the things I did to survive, until Lugal found me."

How could I argue with her? I'd never missed a meal in my life. I'd always had a roof over my head, my parents there to tuck me in and brush away my nightmares. It had made me soft, no denying that. I knew I was lucky, privileged in a way so many others across the world weren't. Worst of all, I'd taken it for granted.

I looked into Belet's haunted eyes and glimpsed the darkness in them, but I also saw something else there. A small, flickering, unbelievably weak candle flame of hope.

That's all it takes, isn't it? Hope is what gets you through the dark times. That feeble little flame convincing you that tomorrow will be better. That you'll be better.

I stopped in the corridor, making sure I had Belet's attention. "You're my best friend. Will you help me?"

She knew what I really meant.

Let me help you, Belet.

Belet stopped as we caught up with Lugal and the bull-man. "Is this necessary, Father? We could just lock him up."

Lugal turned around to face her. "What better prison is there than the one I prepared?"

Prison? Where were they taking me?

"But, Father—"

"What's this?" snarled Lugal. "Disobedience? After all I've done for you? Are you that ungrateful?"

It was as hurtful as a slap in the face. Belet lowered her head, ashamed for defying her parent. "No, Father. Forgive me."

"Go see to the perimeter," he growled. "Make sure none of his companions have followed him here."

"As you wish, Father."

She turned to do his bidding like an obedient child, but for a moment, our eyes met. It was fleeting, but I recognized that expression. Pity. Then she was gone.

Lugal's attention shifted to me. "Don't think I don't see how you look at her. But the Belet you knew never existed, thanks to the tablet. Just like you have changed."

"I'm the same as I ever was."

Even as I said those words, I knew they weren't true. The ripples Lugal had created were affecting me, too. Details of my past, my life in Manhattan, were becoming faint, indistinct. I couldn't remember the name of my school anymore, or the restaurant that had been across the street from our deli. Worst of all, images of the deli itself were fading from my memory. We'd decorated the walls, but with what? Framed paintings? Photos? Pressed flowers? But why? I *did* have two destinies fighting each other, and I had to hang on to my true past. The one that included my parents.

Lugal continued along the corridor toward a single door at the end. "You're different than you were, but not enough. Why is that? Once your kismet's been changed, it should be total and complete." He opened the door. "But I don't have time to puzzle over this mystery. Instead, I will lay it to rest."

The bull-man shoved me forward through the door. We were in a large underground chamber. It was an area under construction, with jackhammers, piles of bricks, and steel containers full of tools. The air down here was thick with dust. In the center, a cement mixer turned as two of Lugal's people shoveled mix into it.

There was an open pit in the floor in front of me, about the size of a grave.

"No!" I gasped.

"Yes." Lugal snapped his fingers.

The kusarikku shoved me hard enough to send me flying. I splashed down in the wet cement, spluttered, and fought the weight of it, trying to stand up.

"You can't be killed, but there are worse things than death, boy." Lugal squatted at the edge of the pit, his eyes burning. "How long will you last? Oh, not your body, but

⚒ ⚒ ⚒ ⚒

your mind. A day? A week? How long until your mind shatters? The worst of it is, you won't even be able to scream. It'll all be trapped inside you, forever." He nodded to the pair by the mixer. "Good-bye."

They turned the mixer, poured the cement over me, and I was buried alive.

TWENTY-THREE

I CAN'T BREATHE. I CAN'T MOVE. I CAN'T SEE.

I can't scream.

I can't breathe. I can't move. I can't see.

I can't scream.

I can't breathe. I can't move. I can't see.

I can't scream.

I can't breathe. I can't move. I can't see.

I can't scream.

I can't scream.

I can't scream.

I can't scream.

I can't scream.

I can't scream.

I can't scream.

I can't scream.

TWENTY-FOUR

YES. I *CAN* SCREAM.

It's going on in my head.

I can't stop it.

TWENTY-FIVE

THEY HEAR ME. THEY HEAR MY SCREAMS. JUST LIKE
theirs.

They come for me.

All of them.

The ghosts of Bedlam.

TWENTY-SIX

LIZZY REILLY HAD FITS. SHE WAS EPILEPTIC. HER PARENTS didn't know what was wrong with her, not back in 1845. They brought her here when she was eleven. She lived in a small, windowless cell, chained to the wall, for the next fifty-three years. She tells me she misses her parents. She sings me the few nursery rhymes she can still remember. She gets them jumbled up.

Amanda Clarke had a baby, a beautiful boy. She wasn't married, so they took her son away and locked her up in here. You don't want to know what happened to her baby, but she told me.

Joe Smith can't remember why he ended up in Bedlam. But he remembers how the visitors laughed when he ate the scraps they threw at him. Laughed when he ate on his hands and knees and acted like a dog. I understand all this, even though all he does is bark.

The world is a good place, filled with decent people. There is love and kindness and generosity all around. I have to believe that. I have faith in the goodness of others.

The ghosts laugh. *Now who's insane?*

TWENTY-SEVEN

FAITH. WHEN ALL ELSE IS GONE, YOU HAVE TO HAVE FAITH.

In that declaration, there is something greater than the moment you're in. There is a purpose to your life and, by extension, to all lives.

So I declare my faith.

Ashhadu ana la ilaha illa Allah, wa ashhadu ana Muhammadan rasul Allah.

There is no deity but Allah, and Muhammad, peace be upon him, is His messenger.

It's the Shahaadah, the first of the five pillars of Islam. Simply put, it says I'm a Muslim and this is what I believe.

That's it.

I have witnessed wonders. I've seen with my own eyes the deeds of beings who were called gods and were worshipped for thousands of years. I know there is more to the material world, that the supernatural exists right beside us, even if we don't see or acknowledge it. And I have faith that there is something greater, something that is, above all, merciful.

That when the scales are set, they are unbalanced. That there is more good than evil in the world. That people strive to be good.

If I can't have faith in the essential goodness of humanity, then it's all for nothing. Who would want to live in a world ruled by selfishness and greed?

I desperately cling on to the memory of my parents, even though it's slipping further from my grasp every moment. Baba and Mama would never have made it if not for the kindness of strangers. People put themselves in danger, sometimes risking not just their lives but also their families' lives, for them to have a chance.

My parents never forgot that. Even when they were bone tired, when the day had been hard and things looked hopeless—and there were plenty of times like those—they knew they needed to do good themselves. There's no greater purpose in life. The desire to make the world a better place. That's the ultimate jihad.

And how do you make the world better?

You hold out your hand to someone who needs it.

That's what I have faith in.

A tremor passed through me. Was it my imagination? I couldn't tell anymore.

The ghosts mocked me. *Why do you think you're worth saving? No one has saved us. You're here to stay.*

It was getting hard to resist them. Maybe they were right. None of my friends knew I was here, what had happened to me, and there was no way they'd ever find out.

You'll be here forever and ever. One hundred years from now, maybe two hundred, when this place is demolished—if it's ever demolished, because London is filled with ancient buildings— what will you be when they dig you out? A raving lunatic. You think this is the worst it can get?

The second tremor was stronger. It lasted a few seconds this time.

It was real.

I hear a distant, dull thudding. Over and over again. Hear it... or feel it. My ears are filled with concrete.

The reverberations grew stronger, and steadier. The ghosts around me hesitated.

The blow was deafening. The concrete shattered, and I felt air on my back. Huge, chunky fingers dug me out of the fractured rubble, and I breathed. *I breathed.*

I breathed the first breath of my rebirth.

"Aziz?"

I shook from coughing. My legs buckled, but someone held me up. I rubbed my face. I think my tears helped get the grit out of my eyes.

Belet stood facing me, holding me up. She flicked concrete from my hair. "Say something so I know you're not completely insane."

I coughed hard, trying to empty my throat of dust. It felt like I was spitting broken razor blades. But this physical pain was a million times better than the despair I'd felt in the ground.

She remained the scarred, brutal war orphan. Belet still had her katana tucked through her sash, and she had the monstrous bull-man behind her, wielding a pickax.

I coughed again, trying to clear dust out of my aching lungs. Belet gave me a bottle of water.

"Why?" I asked after I'd chugged it down.

Belet did enigmatic really well. I was good at reading people, but not her. Those black eyes of hers were a total mystery to me, and I thought they always would be. But eventually she relented. "Because what my father did to you was wrong. It was cruel, and that's not me."

It sounded like she was betraying him by showing mercy. But now I knew that the *true* Belet was still there. The one I . . .

I took her hand. She jerked, tensing up as if I was about to flip her. But I didn't let go. "Yes, you're better than that, Belet."

"You don't know me at all."

᚛ ᚚ ᚔ ᚑ

I was practically on my knees, begging her to believe me. "Please, I know what you really, truly are. You have so much compassion, so much to give. I know the way your smile fills the room with light. I know that dancing makes you happy."

She pulled her hand away. "Can you walk?"

"Come with me, Belet. Help us stop Lugal."

"You want me to fight the man who raised me? No. He gave me a life, a purpose."

"He's using you, Belet. Nothing he does is out of love. You deserve more." I gazed back at the hole she and the kusarikku had just dug me out of. "He's not just wrong; he's evil. He's too far gone to be saved."

"That doesn't mean I won't stop trying," she said. "I owe him that."

She believed she could save him. How could she be so oblivious to what a monster Lugal was? But the answer was bitterly clear. Love is blind. Belet gazed up at Lugal with a daughter's eyes.

I gave it one last go. "You freed me. That proves you don't believe in him."

She laughed. "Don't misinterpret my moment of weakness as anything more than it was. Now go before I change my mind."

"Won't he know you did it?"

She shook her head. "We've moved on from here. He

found a place more suited to his rank. No more skulking around in places like this."

I'm sure if I'd had more time to recover I would have thought of some better arguments. But I was so exhausted, right down to my soul. "Please, you have to—"

Belet shook her head firmly. "Don't come looking for me or my father again. Just go home, Aziz. Go and don't get involved. This is too big for you."

"I don't have a choice, do I?" How could I get through to her? "Whatever Lugal's planning, it'll be horrific, on a scale you can't imagine. He's too damaged, Belet. And I don't want him taking you down with him."

"I will not betray him." Belet nodded to the bull-man. "Open the door."

The hinges of the heavy iron door screamed from a hundred years of rust, and I stood there waiting for the noise to summon Lugal and his monsters before I remembered that they had moved on. To where?

Before I could ask, Belet pushed me into a cramped, dark tunnel draped with cobweb curtains. She handed me a small flashlight. "This is one of the old maintenance tunnels. It'll take you to a storeroom out in the lawn. Just get out and away from here. Don't try and take on Lugal, Aziz. You can't win."

"I could if you helped me. Like last time. It was you and me against Nergal, and we beat him."

᱘᱘ ᱷᱷ ᱤᱤᱤ ᱣᱤ

"Maybe, in another life." She shook her head again. "But that one no longer exists, Aziz. You're wasting your time clinging to it."

Was I? Or maybe it was all I had left.

"At least tell me where he is," I pleaded. "He still has the tab—"

The bull-man pushed the maintenance door closed. I was on my own.

Except for the spirits.

Don't leave us.

You're one of us.

The ghosts of Bedlam crowded the shadows, urging me to stay. This was where I belonged, they said. *Why go outside into the dangerous world? You think you can beat Lugal? That's pure insanity! See? You're mad; you belong here with us. Safe inside, screaming at the walls.*

They wore me down, piling on the doubt, reminding me what a failure I was and how great Lugal was. He was the son of the great goddess Tiamat. He'd been there *before* the beginning. He'd seen it all, survived it all. He was a god who'd fought other gods. Who was I? Just a kid who could make a decent shawarma. Lugal would swat me aside like a fly.

I couldn't do anything. I was useless. I wasn't even the son my parents had preferred. Mo—now, *he* was a hero. Belet had been one, too. Rabisu was braver than me, and

Daoud more talented. They were all full of life, with passion and big hearts. Me? How could I ever measure up to them? They'd stayed with me out of pity, not love.

Come on, said the ghosts. *You know it's true. You and Belet? In your dreams, Sik. You don't deserve her; you don't deserve any of them. You hold them back. Think how happy Mo and Daoud would be without you. Remember how devastated Mama and Baba were when they heard about Mo? You honestly think they wouldn't have swapped the two of you in an instant? They can get anyone to make shawarma, but no one could replace Mo. You were mad to even try.*

"That's not true!" I said, my voice cracking. "It's not true."

The ghosts laughed. *Go ahead and believe that. We know better, and deep down, so do you. We're trying to help you, Sik. You aim too high. You're going to fail. Best to not even try. You can't fail if you don't try.*

"What kind of life is that?" I pushed on along the tunnel. I had to get out. Get out before I ended up agreeing, falling to my knees, and just curling up in the dirt. "I never said I was a hero."

But you want to be, don't you? That's what makes you so pathetic, Sik. Face it.

"Shut up. I've listened to you—now you listen to me. I've only got one thing to say."

What could you say that would possibly make—

᯽ ᯫ ᯤ ᯰ

"Assalamu alaikum." I had come to the end, in more ways than one. "You know what that means?"

The ghosts were silent. There was more, much more to life than war and conflict.

I crawled into an old storeroom. It held rusty pieces of gardening equipment draped in cobwebs, and the air was dusty and still. A wheelbarrow contained a starling nest, and mice scurried under a stack of cracked flowerpots. I banged my head on a warped beam when I stood up. The door leading out of the storeroom was rotten all the way through. The wood was almost soggy with moisture, and its frame had been honeycombed by generations of hungry woodworms.

I took a deep breath. "It means 'peace be upon you.'"

I kicked the door hard. Really hard. I had a lot of anger I needed to let out. The door didn't stand a chance.

It was morning. Early morning. The rooftops were painted with the gold of the sunrise, and the breeze still carried the night's chill... or that could have just been my soul. I looked back at the broken doorway and into the darkness beyond. The ghosts weren't following me out. They were too frightened to flee Bedlam. Their prison was the only home they knew.

I had to drag myself across the grounds to the fence, leaving a trail of dusty footprints. I barely had enough strength to climb over, and when I reached the street, I saw a food truck nearby. The woman working inside stared at me as I wobbled past. "You all right, love?"

I shook my head.

She picked up a doughnut and wrapped it in a napkin. "'Ere. On the house."

You have no idea how grateful I was for a little kindness. My hands were trembling as I took it. "Shukran."

She smiled warmly. "Today's gonna be a lovely day now it's stopped raining."

I hadn't even noticed. The sky was a fresh, clear blue. Despite the beautiful morning and the singing birds, I knew the worst was still to come.

I closed my eyes to savor the taste, the warm, sticky dough, the crisp sugar. People were wrong about British food—I'd never had anything so delicious. "What day is it?"

"Thursday, of course."

Thursday? But that meant...

"Are you all right, sweetheart?"

I began shaking all over. I gripped the doughnut with both hands to stop myself dropping it.

I'd been buried in concrete for two days.

TWENTY-EIGHT

I COULDN'T GET RID OF THE SMELL IN MY NOSTRILS. I made it back to the commune—not an easy feat, as half the streets were flooded—and the first thing I did was shower, turning the dial all the way to "volcanic heat." Yet afterward the smell of dust and concrete still clung to every pore. So I bathed, scrubbing again and again. Mo had to stop me from filling the tub with bleach.

Everyone has their breaking point. Being buried alive for two days had been mine.

That smell...

I couldn't sleep. Each time I closed my eyes, I was back there, trapped, suffocating within solid concrete. Fear had gotten under my skin, into my bones. I couldn't stand the dark. It felt too much like being entombed.

The heat outside didn't help. The temperature was rising by the hour, and the air was thick with humidity.

What if Belet hadn't dug me out? I'd still be in the War Museum's floor. Maybe I was. Maybe this was just my mind playing tricks on me. How could I know? Maybe I'd joined the other old inhabitants of Bedlam and found the only safe place there was, in madness.

How do you know if you're insane? How do you know if you're not?

My brother and friends had all been waiting frantically for my return, even Rabisu. Dumuzi had given me food—it had tasted like dust—then put me in his own room. The sheets were pure Egyptian cotton, but lying on them felt as though I was enrobed in gravel.

I dug my fingers into my skull until they ached. Rubbed my skin until it bled. There was a Brillo pad in the kitchen. Maybe the steel wool would finally get the concrete dust out of my skin. . . .

"Sik?" Mo tapped at the bedroom door for the third time that morning. "Come and have something to eat."

"I'm not hungry. I don't feel well. Go away."

"You've been in there almost three days now. Please, talk to me."

"There's nothing to say. I'll be all right. I just need to rest."

"You're not resting; you're hiding. This is no good, Sik. I'm coming in."

He didn't wait for me to answer, just shoved the door open, paused to take it all in—and there was a lot to take in—and marched over to the window and slid it fully open. "It's boiling in here. You must be smothering."

I drew my sheet over my head and curled into a tight ball. "Go away, Mo."

"Not happening, Yakhi. You've got to talk to me. Everyone's worried about you. Especially Rabisu. She even made you a pie."

"Made of what?"

"I don't even want to guess, but it's the thought that counts." I heard a wooden crate scraping across the floorboards and a creak as he sat down on it. Mo wasn't leaving. Fine. I could ignore him just as I was.

"What happened?" Mo asked.

"It doesn't matter."

"This isn't like you, Sik."

"How would you know? Maybe this is the most 'me' ever. Me, Sikander Aziz. Just a fourteen-year-old kid from Manhattan. I want to go home, Mo. Don't you get that?"

"What about Lugal? We need to stop him."

"Go right ahead. You don't need me. You never did. Anyway, he hasn't acted on his threats. Maybe if we leave him alone, he'll leave us alone. Did you ever think about that?"

𒀀 𒈾 𒁹 𒋡

"You know that's not how it works, Sik. If we don't take a stand, who will?"

"Literally *anyone* else," I snapped. "Why does it have to be us? I didn't choose this, Mo. This isn't clearing a field and planting a few trees out in the desert. It can't be fixed with a packet of seeds and a watering can. We are way out of our depth. We can't beat Lugal. He'll destroy us if we try."

"And what will he do if we don't? You think he'll just go away? You know he won't. Without us opposing him, his evil will continue to grow. We've got to remove the weeds before they choke the life out of the whole field."

"Wow, that's a pretty extreme analogy. I'm talking about the god of madness, firstborn son of the queen of chaos, and you're talking about gardening."

There was a furious banging on the door. "Is he decent?"

"No!" I yelled.

Rabisu ignored my protest, flung the door wide, and barged in, holding aloft a pie. "Freshly made just for you!"

She sat on the mattress and extended her dish. "Go on. Try a slice."

I gazed at it suspiciously. "Why is it making a noise?"

"That'll be the pigeon," she said matter-of-factly.

"It's still alive?"

"Can't get fresher than that, can you?"

Daoud popped his head around the door. "Is he up yet?"

"Oh, why don't you all come in and make yourselves comfortable? Here." I threw a pillow at Daoud. "Sit on that!"

Rabisu scooted over, still holding that stupid pigeon pie (which I later learned is a real British dish) while Daoud balanced himself on the corner of the bed. "There's no smell more unique than 'teen boy bedroom.' What happened to that deodorant I got you? It was Extra Extreme Strength!"

With Rabisu, the pie, and Daoud on the bed, I was being pushed to the edge, literally and figuratively. "Is this an intervention? Seriously? I'm in my underwear! Get out!"

Mo gently but firmly turned my head so we were nose-to-nose. "Only if you promise to help save the world."

"That's not my job! And I've done it already! Twice!"

Rabisu snorted. "Oh, please. It was me who held back the elemental forces of annihilation that last time. You were at the rear, waving that shovel."

"You were the one who summoned them!"

"Po-tay-toe, po-tah-toe. You're quibbling over minor details."

"And that shovel is the greatest magical weapon in the world! Gilgamesh himself gave it to me."

"And where is it now?" said Rabisu. "A real hero always has their weapon handy. They anticipate danger."

"I was anticipating fish and chips on this vacation! That's all!"

"What's wrong?" Mo asked me. "Tell us and we'll fix it."

"How do you know you can, Mo? Some things are beyond fixing. They're completely broken, and no amount of hugs and pigeon pies will make anything better."

I was terrified of Lugal. He wasn't playing by the rules. There was no depth he wouldn't sink to, no horror he wouldn't inflict on us. Imagine a cage with a rabid, blood-thirsty dog in it. I wasn't going anywhere near that cage again. But Mo and the others were talking about entering it and trying to put a muzzle on the dog without getting torn to pieces. Guess what? I wasn't about to join in. Why? Because I was scared? Yup. And because I knew I was going to *fail*.

"What are you all looking at?" I peered around at the trio surrounding my bed. "What do you expect of me?"

Rabisu leaned forward. "A plan. For how we'll stop Lugal and save that girl, whatshername—"

"Her name is Belet, and you know it," I said.

Mo and Daoud looked at each other, bemused. Then Mo turned to me. "Belet? That's a cool name. Mesopotamian for . . . 'lady'? Am I right?"

"This isn't a time to be funny, Mo. She's being held pris-oner by Lugal. She thinks he's her father now."

Mo's frown deepened. "When did this all happen?"

"On Tower Bridge! You were there, taking photos of Daoud. Here, give me your phone."

The moment he took it out, I snatched it from him and began flipping through his gallery. There were a lot of photos of Daoud. A *lot*. "Wait, there have to be some..."

I moved to videos to find what I was looking for—the day he and Belet had danced in the breakfast room. Daoud had recorded it. But I scrolled and scrolled and saw nothing. "Did you delete it?"

"Delete what?" asked Mo.

"You dancing with Belet. You were all there. Why don't you remember?"

"They're mortals," Rabisu said. "Their senses are limited to the here and now."

I kept on scrolling, desperate for a single glimpse of her, but there wasn't even a shadow. "But I remember Belet."

"For now. Probably because you're a little more than mortal. But soon"—she snapped her claws—"that past will be all gone."

"No, it can't.... Belet helped me save New York! We fought Nergal and defeated all his demons—"

Rabisu shot me a dark look.

"Except one. Then she was here, in London. She came with all of us to the Fitzroys', and she fought on Tower Bridge. She's my best friend!"

"Then you have very low standards," Rabisu snorted.

"Ya Allah! Not now, Rabisu! I am not going to forget her just like"—I snapped my fingers—"that. This is my life, too. I'm not going to forget Mama, Baba, and the deli we have on Fifteenth and ..."

Daoud shook his head. "Deli? Since when did you have a deli?"

"Since *forever*, Daoud. You worked there! It's on Fifteenth and ..."

For the life of me, I couldn't remember.

TWENTY-NINE

MO LITERALLY DRAGGED ME OUT OF BED WHILE DAOUD
picked out my clothes. I managed to stop Daoud from
arranging my hair, but soon enough I was ready to face
the world again and, whether I liked it or not, get down
to work.

Where was Lugal?

I scanned the internet, checked the news, and googled
all the things I thought might relate to him. But how could
I trust my own memory now? What if I'd forgotten that
I'd forgotten? I didn't know what I was searching for anymore. And everything I found was depressing: more fires
in the US and more flooding in the UK. Apparently, the
repair of the Webb Space Telescope hadn't worked: It was
losing sight of more and more stars.

But there was one thing I knew I needed to fix—myself.
I'd done wrong by Rabisu and had to make it right.

I found her up on the roof after dinner, trying to catch a breeze to escape the stifling heat. She didn't even look around as I climbed up, just picked at the flakes of piecrust scattered all over her lap. "I didn't save you *any*."

"How did you know it was me?"

She snorted. It takes some skill to put that amount of disdain in what's basically a nose blow. "What do you want?"

"I brought you something." I came up beside her and put down the compost bucket. "It's full to the brim. Enjoy."

"I'm already stuffed."

"There are eggshells. Plenty of banana skins. And oh, look—moldy bread. Yummy."

"How . . . moldy?" she asked, trying hard not to look at the bucket overflowing with culinary delights.

"Practically green."

"Fine. Pass it over," said Rabisu oh-so-reluctantly. Then she snatched the bucket out of my hand and held it up to the moonlight. "Hmm. More gray than green. It'll have to do."

She rolled it into a ball, and it vanished with a single gulp. She reached for another rotten slice, then stopped herself. "Why are you doing this?"

"I'm trying to say I'm sorry. I shouldn't have said those things to you after we left Siduri's. I was upset, but that's no excuse. I was wrong."

"You're apologizing?" Rabisu sat up straight. "By Ea,

no one's ever done that to me before. We demons don't, as a rule. We tend to go for inventive and cruel punishments instead."

"Are we okay, then?"

She sat there, pondering. "Is that it? Now what do I do?"

"You accept my apology, and we go back to how things were before I upset you."

"You, a mere mortal, upset *me*? You think waaay too much of yourself. Do you know I was on a first-name basis with Genghis Khan? Or Jerry K, as I called him." Then she sighed loudly. "Fine. Apology accepted. Here." She slid the compost bucket over. "Help yourself."

"Ah, no. You enjoy it."

"You always complain I never share anything, and here I am, letting you have half of my bucket, and you don't want any? Are you my friend or not?"

I peered into the compost. The smell was...putrid. Some of the vegetables had been left to stew. I picked out an apple core. I could handle an apple core. I hoped.

Rabisu watched me expectantly. "Well?"

I nibbled at it, closing my eyes and trying not to think about what else it had been soaking in. I could definitely taste mushy onion and week-old cabbage.

"How is it?" she asked.

I gave her a double thumbs-up. I didn't dare open my

mouth in case I hurled. I reminded myself that I couldn't die of food poisoning.

"You like it?" Rabisu asked cheerily. Then she started fishing out another bit of fruit. "Here's a mango stone. It's only been lightly chewed—there's still plenty of flesh on it. You have it." She dropped it in my palm with a squelch.

"Shukran. I love mangoes."

A deep, sorrowful sob behind us saved me from having to eat any more garbage. Dumuzi appeared at the top of the roof ladder. He looked awful. His face was gaunt, and his once-luxurious hair was stringy and dull. The light in his eyes was dim. Even his clothes looked faded. His god surge wasn't so much surging as dribbling out.

"Hey, guys, room for one more?" he asked, sniffing loudly.

How could we say no? He was on the verge of tears.

"No," said Rabisu. "Get lost."

I patted the space between us, ignoring Rabisu's dramatic sigh. "What's going on? You look terrible."

He flopped down and folded his legs in the lotus position. Closing his eyes, he sagged in utter defeat. "It's no good, Sikander. I can't align my chakras. My aura is in turmoil."

"Have you tried crystals?"

He shook his head. "It's no use. All the positivity's been

𐎀𐎐 𐎌𐎗 𐎗𐎋𐎐 𐎐

sucked out of them, and everything else. There's bad, bad karma ahead."

As if I didn't know that already. But we immortals were the only ones who had a chance of stopping Lugal. "We'll find Belet. I promise."

"How, man? I promised Ishtar I'd keep an eye on Belet, to make sure nothing bad ever happened to her. But I never thought anything would actually happen!"

"So, you weren't ever intending to watch out for her?"

"In spirit, not in actual...actual." He sighed again. "Parenthood's a bummer, man."

I was losing patience with this dude. "Then what's the point of you, Dumuzi?" I blurted. "You've just drifted through history. What have you actually *done*?"

He pointed at his T-shirt. "This. It was my idea."

"Woodstock? Oh, Alhamdulillah! You created a music festival!" Now I was spitting mad. Someone needed to take charge, and between the three of us, surprise, surprise, it was coming down to me. "Listen, both of you. We're going to find Belet. We're going to save her. We're going to deal with Lugal and get destiny back on track. Got it?"

They both nodded, staring at me with wide eyes. Dumuzi adjusted his hairband. "So, what's the plan?"

I turned to Rabisu. "Any ideas?"

She nodded enthusiastically. "We find Lugal, charge him all at once, and tear him to pieces. Easy-peasy."

"That's light on the details," I said.

"Oh. Well, that's the only plan you get out of a demon. We're pretty straightforward, to be honest. If we can't tear it to shreds with our claws, we tend to flounder."

"Where do we even start looking for Lugal?" Dumuzi whined.

"Maybe we could ask that apkallu friend of yours," I suggested. "If they aren't mad that you didn't meet them at the airport the other night."

Dumuzi shook his head. "They're long gone by now."

Rabisu drummed her claws on the bucket. "Lugal must have given you a clue of some kind, Sik. Villains often reveal their plans when they have the hero in their clutches and are subjecting them to elaborate and drawn-out death traps."

I tried to rewind my memory to our conversation.

"He said something about his mom."

Rabisu nodded thoughtfully. "Ah, yes. Many villains have unresolved issues with their mothers. There was this one guy in Thebes, who . . ."

Dumuzi and I both looked at her. Maybe it's an Arab thing, but you do not speak ill of anyone's mom, villain or otherwise. Mothers are sacred.

"What?" asked Rabisu. "Just what did Lugal say about his mom?"

"He said she would drown the world with her tears.

That and something about how we all came from her and we'd all return to her."

"Huh. That's not gonna happen," said Rabisu. "Did he say anything else? Plans for world conquest? Villains are big on ruling the world. Just seems like a big headache if you ask me."

She was trying, in her own way. I turned to the god of flowers. "What about you, Dumuzi? Any ideas?"

He sat, arms wrapped around his knees, gazing up at the night sky. "I come up here when I feel lonely. I come up just to look at her, talk a little."

I tried to follow his gaze. "Who?"

"You call her Venus now. But, of course, she's Ishtar. The brightest of the planets. She's right..." He frowned. "Where is she?"

"There's too much light coming from the city to see much."

I saw fear spreading over Dumuzi's face. "Where's Urgula? Pabil's gone, too. And I can't find Girtab. He should be right there, in the second quadrant. Right there!"

I stood up and peered harder at the stars. It was a clear night.... Surely more should have been visible? "Did you hear about the Webb telescope? It's losing sight of the stars."

"So?" asked Rabisu.

What had I read online? "They say it's as if...they are disappearing."

Dumuzi turned around, frantic. "They're gone, Sikander! The constellations are gone!"

There were all these disasters happening, and I hadn't realized they were all related. "The drought in Iraq. The Tigris and Euphrates have dried up, remember? And there've been earthquakes in the Zagros Mountains. It's like the whole country's breaking apart."

"I guess she's not crying anymore," said Rabisu.

I turned back to our demon. "Who?"

"Tiamat. The waters of the Euphrates and Tigris flow from her eyes. Everyone knows that!"

Dumuzi and I looked at each other, and I said, "The Enuma Elish."

Bit by bit, the pieces of the jigsaw puzzle were falling into place. I just needed to rearrange a few more of them, and I'd see the whole picture. The trouble is, I wasn't sure I wanted to.

"Could you tell me your version of the story?" It was one of the Mesopotamian myths I was familiar with, but Dumuzi had been there when it had happened.

He cleared his throat. "I just want to say I wasn't the ringleader. I was just starting out, a seedling. Nothing like the rowdy Enki and the rest. They were young and liked to party—you can't blame them. But Tiamat grew tired of the racket; she was not hip to our scene. That's why she declared war on us. Very uncool, if you ask me. She raised a massive host of monsters and put Lugal in charge. We were all terrified, but Marduk stepped up, grabbed as many weapons as he could, and rode off on his chariot to face her." Dumuzi acted out a fight. "She manifested as a great dragon, the size of a continent, with wings covering the skies. There was an epic battle with thunderbolts and lightning, all very, very frightening, but in the end, Marduk won. He slew Tiamat and then created the universe from her body. The tears from her eyes became the springs of the two rivers. Her bones were used to create the mountains. Her scales were put up in the black sky to create the stars, the dwelling places of the gods."

"And now the stars are going out?" said Rabisu.

"That's bad," I said. "Real bad."

Rabisu slapped her hand against her forehead. "Not just bad—terrible! They'll all come down here! They'll be wanting ziggurats on every street corner, like you have for your white-faced god!"

"What white-faced god?" asked Dumuzi before I could stop him.

"He of the fiery hair! His temples are everywhere, and during spring break, they're more popular than Ishtar's!"

⸸⸷⸸⸷⸸

I had to end this before the conversation detoured off a cliff. "Ronald McDonald is not a god, Rabisu."

She snorted, unconvinced.

"Can we please focus?" I said. "The rivers have dried up. The stars are going out. The mountains are breaking apart. We have the seas rising here, and her brood on the loose, sinking fleets. It's all unraveling."

Rabisu frowned. "What's unraveling?"

I stood up and walked to the edge of the roof. "Everything. All of creation."

Dumuzi gasped.

Rabisu was pale with fear. "But that's not..."

Lugal's plan was finally evident. This would bring peace for sure. It would also bring extinction on a cosmic scale. "He's resurrecting Tiamat."

⬧ ⬧ ⬧ ⬧ ⬧

THIRTY

IT WASN'T JUST THE END OF THE WORLD. IT WAS THE end of *everything*. The lights of the universe were already going out. Galaxies were disappearing. One by one the constellations were fading.

And what was I supposed to do about it?

Nothing. Exactly nothing. This was waaay above my pay grade. "We need to contact the heavy hitters. Find Gilgamesh. Message Marduk. Get some proper heroes involved."

Dumuzi sank his head down even lower. "They're gone."

"Then get them back, right here, right now!"

But the god just shook his head. "Lugal would have anticipated it. He's used the tablet to erase them from existence. I can feel how the god surge has waned. It's as if he's drawing it all into himself."

"But you're still here."

"What am I, dude? The god of flowers. I'm no threat to anyone."

"Then it's time to level up, Dumuzi! This is the chance you've been waiting for! Hit him with a tulip! I mean, really hard!"

Yeah, I was desperate. Who wouldn't be? "There has to be a way to fight destiny! Think of something! I know the story—you went to Kurnugi and got Ishtar back. We need her. Do that again. How hard can it be?"

He looked straight at me. His sunglasses were off, but the starlight of his gaze was fading fast. Once, it would have been filled with the light of the cosmos; now it was just the vast emptiness of the void. "Ishtar may not be here, but she provided the next best thing," he said. "One of her children."

Yeah, and I really wished Belet were here, too. The good version. Could I somehow make her remember that Ishtar had raised her, in her own haphazard way, not Lugal? If I could get Belet back in the game, then maybe we would stand a chance. We needed a true hero. But to do that I needed to know where she was, where Lugal was.

Dumuzi got to his feet and shuffled off. Apparently, he'd given up already.

Rabisu finished off the last of her bucket and we went back inside. The demon rummaged around her corner of the attic. A moment later, she brought out a large nail file and held it out. "Could you?"

"Could I what?"

"File down my horns? They need tidying up."

"Really? At a time like this?"

"Hey, if we're fighting Tiamat, I want to look my best!"

When would I learn there is no point arguing logic with a demon? I snatched the file from her. "Fine. Anyway, you might be wrong. Maybe there'll be no fight. Dumuzi might get everyone to hug it out over some herbal tea. Or something."

She snorted. "Oh, believe me, there'll be fighting. You can bet— Ow! Not like that!"

"Like what? You told me to file them!"

"Long, smooth strokes! Not like a dog scratching its fleas! Long, smooth strokes!"

Who knew filing demon horns was so tricky? "Okay. Long, smooth strokes. Like this?"

"That's better. Anyway, where were we? Oh, yeah, the fighting. There'll be a big battle, just like there was the last time he was here."

That was news to me. "Lugal came to England before? When?"

"In 1066, of course. Sailed over with Duke William. Back then there weren't stars fading out of the night—there was one blazing in the sky for weeks. So bright you could see it in the daytime."

"Halley's Comet? It's always been a sign of disaster."

Rabisu snorted. "Gods aren't known for their subtlety."

The Battle of Hastings. It wasn't really my period, but you couldn't be a fan of knights without knowing about the day England fell to the Normans. "You were there, I suppose?"

"Among the archers. I got in a lucky hit that day, I'll tell you." She smiled at the memory.

"Why didn't the rest of the population rise up against William? The invasion force wasn't that large."

"A bit more off the left," Rabisu instructed. "He stamped his authority on it right away. Marched his boys to London, built a great big castle smack in the center of it. I suggested a ziggurat, but the builders just couldn't get the design right."

"What about Lugal?" I asked. "What did he do after the battle?"

"Lugal's there for the death of kingdoms, not for the making of them. He hung around for a while, helped to build the castle and make sure all resistance was well and truly crushed, and then he was off. I admit I stayed well out of his way. I knew the guy was trouble."

"Lugal built the Tower of London? It's on the top of our must-see list. Daoud is desperate to see the Crown Jewels."

𒀀 𒄿 𒌋 𒋼

"The Handsome One should be adorned in gold and diamonds. But I wouldn't visit the Tower right now. Not with the ravens gone."

"The ravens again. What is it about the ravens? Is it a dietary thing?"

She scowled at me. "The ravens of the Tower are the protectors of the kingdom, Sik. Everyone knows that. And everyone knows that if they leave, the kingdom's doomed."

I dropped the file as the last piece fell right into the middle of the jigsaw puzzle.

Where had Lugal gone after leaving Bedlam?

To a place he knew, somewhere that symbolized conquest and the death of kingdoms.

Like Rabisu had said, gods weren't known for their subtlety.

THIRTY-ONE

WE'D FOUND LUGAL. HE WAS IN THE TOWER OF LONDON, preparing for the rebirth of Tiamat.

We just needed someone to stop him.

What?

Not us, no way. I'd already done the whole a-bunch-of-ordinary-plucky-teens-get-caught-up-in-events-beyond-their-imaginings-and-save-the-day trope and hadn't enjoyed it at all. Now it was someone else's turn.

The heat wave broke at dawn. More than broke—it shattered. Gigantic, ominous thunderclouds loomed overhead, the sky flared with lightning, and the city was bombarded by torrential rain. The walls shook with each thunderclap, and each gust of wind swept off more roof tiles.

Dumuzi stood at the window, staring at the deluge that was turning his garden into a swamp. "It was like this when the gods tried to wipe out humanity last time. Only Ishtar was against the plan, and she told Utnapishtim to build a big boat. It was my job to help gather the animals."

"Two by two, right?" I said.

We were all in the kitchen, the nerve center of any house. Mo was trying to get through to the authorities while Daoud was scanning social media on his laptop for the latest news. "The Thames has burst its banks. Everything along the waterfront is underwater, all the way from the coast to the city, and beyond. The royal family has been helicoptered out. The government is evacuating, and the price of dinghies has quadrupled in the last hour." Daoud held up his smartphone, showing us a clip of people wading waist-deep through murky green water and cars floating along streets now transformed into rivers. "That's the Mall."

"Any luck with the police?" I asked Mo.

He sighed as he put down the phone. "The police don't believe me. I tried telling them that someone had broken into the Tower and was planning to summon a dragon, but they thought it was just some prank. Threatened to arrest me for wasting their time."

"What about getting in touch with the press? Someone might act if we get hashtag EndoftheWorld trending."

"It's trending already," said Daoud. "They've canceled *Stranger Things*. People are taking it badly."

"Here we go again," I muttered. I'd hoped I'd left all this behind in New York. Defeating one god should have been enough for anyone's résumé.

Daoud turned up the volume on his computer. "It's the prime minister. He's giving a live address to the nation from the Houses of Parliament. Take a look."

Reception wasn't great and the screen was small, but I could just about make out a very disheveled-looking old guy standing on a pile of crates as water swirled around him. In the background, cops were giving the politicians piggybacks through the water while waves crashed against the stained-glass windows.

Daoud shook his head. "I can't understand a word he's saying."

I listened more carefully. "It's Latin. He's saying that we should not be afraid of 'the rabbits at our doors.'"

Daoud frowned. "Rabbits?"

"I think he means wolves—*lupus* in Latin. The word for rabbit is *lepus*," I said. "Even stupid things sound smart if you say them in Latin."

Rabisu leaned over my shoulder to get a better look at the screen. "What's that at the window?"

We all leaned closer.

Daoud zoomed in. "What *is* that? It looks like a giant gold disc. It can't be the sun. It's—"

I watched, and a dense ball of dread began growing in

𒀀𒐲𒄑𒌋𒀪

my guts. "Getting closer. Someone needs to tell him to get outta there."

Daoud winced as the gold disc came right up to the stained-glass windows. "You can't interrupt the prime minister."

"He's about to get very interrupted unless he leaves asap."

The disc had to be fifteen feet in diameter, at least. And then it...blinked.

The basmu serpent was back. Its glowing reptilian eye peered through the windows, filling the chamber with a fierce golden light. The walls shook, and cracks opened in the ancient stone.

The prime minster turned slowly toward the blazing eye. "Oh, cake."

The claws tore through the walls as if they were made of tissue paper, and the screen went blank. A moment later, it was replaced with *We are experiencing technical difficulties. Please stand by.*

Daoud looked at me. "His last words were 'Oh, cake'?"

"I think that was more bad Latin."

Dumuzi sniffed loudly. "Can we take a moment to reflect on what just happened? The leader of this nation was squashed by a sea serpent. I think a minute of respectful silence would be—"

Rabisu giggled. She clapped her hand over her mouth,

but it was too late. We all looked at her, and she stared back defiantly. "Come on. It's funny when you think about it."

Dumuzi glared at her. "Aren't you upset?"

She made a long, sad face. It was very unconvincing. "I was, but I'm over it now. So, what's for breakfast?"

Dumuzi looked at me pleadingly, but what could I do? Rabisu was Rabisu. She was either the most twisted person I knew, or the perfect person to have by your side in a disaster because she could always see something positive in the situation, no matter how bizarre.

I started handing out breakfast—croissants and bowls of organic yogurt with figs and honey. It seemed the natural thing to do. "What about the US Embassy?"

Mo shook his head. "Went straight to voice mail. Office hours are from nine till three."

"It'll be too late by then," I said.

Mo and Daoud, sitting side by side, eating off the same plate, Dumuzi with a wilted daisy chain in his hands, and Rabisu, sharpening her claws across the stone countertop. They were all looking at me. I tightened my hands into fists to keep them steady. It wasn't fair, but that's the way it was. I couldn't let them down. "So, who wants to go visit the Tower of London?"

* * *

Kasusu stood, sheathed, in the corner of my bedroom. Water dripped through a hole in the ceiling, forming a puddle on the warped floorboards.

Everyone was getting ready. Outside, Dumuzi honked the van's horn. I picked up the sword and withdrew it from its scabbard.

I wrapped my fingers around the worn leather binding of its hilt, letting the weight of it settle. It was ancient—I knew it was the first sword ever forged, and it contained all swords that followed. Though it was a scimitar now, at other times it had been a Japanese katana or a Saxon broadsword—the weapon of rogues, kings, and legends. According to Kasusu, King Arthur had fought with it. And now, somehow, it was mine.

It was heavy, but there was a way of holding it *just so* that felt comfortable. I won't lie—a chill ran up my spine. A thrill chill.

The blade shimmered with rainbow hues and hummed softly. "You ready for this, Private Clown?"

The nickname reminded me that I had trained with Kasusu once. Very badly. "Like I have a choice."

"Heroes rarely do. It's all about stepping up when it matters. You can hit a home run a million times on the practice field, but can you do it when the World Series is at stake? When it's all or nothing and you're buckling under the weight of a nation's hopes and dreams? That

﹏

takes another level of strength, of courage. You won't know whether you've got it in you until the moment comes."

"You don't have any tips for me?"

"Remember what it is you're fighting for. Forget about yourself. Think about others. It's love that'll get you through war. Ishtar understood that."

"The contradiction of her being the goddess of love and war?"

"There isn't any contradiction if you dwell on it long enough," said Kasusu. "I guess we *should* do some exercises. You will be going up against Belet after all."

"Belet?" I asked. Why did that name seem familiar?

"You remember Belet, don't you? The two of you defeated Nergal last year. Come on, Private Clown! Think!"

It was like trying to remember a dream. It was so real when you were asleep, but when you're awake, it's almost impossible to hang on to. How had I beaten Nergal? I remember flying on a chariot drawn by lamassus. I remembered Daoud, but anyone else? Then, through the mind fog, I glimpsed a girl doing a pirouette. "Belet."

She was my friend. I think....

Kasusu hummed softly in my grasp. "You forgot her, didn't you?"

I closed my eyes to try to draw up all the memories I had. Like the first time I met her. She'd saved my life when I was attacked by Nergal and two of his demons.

ᚐᛁ ᚷᚻᚻᛁ ᚎᛁᚦᛁ ᚻᛁᚷ

The fight had taken place in a deli. What had I been doing there? Maybe it was my regular place; maybe I knew the owners. That wasn't important. I needed to hang on to my recollections of her. "I'll save her. Make her remember who she really is."

"She's Lugal's daughter now." Kasusu briefly glowed a deep and bloody red. "She'll come at you without mercy. Her style will be simple, brutal. She won't back down, and she won't hesitate. Her aim will be to kill you, so we need to use that to your advantage."

"I'll handle Belet."

"We need to discuss tactics, Private! Make a plan!"

"I have one!" I snapped. "I'm not going to fight her." I turned the blade in my hand. It felt worryingly *right*. "You just said I need to remember what I'm fighting for, and who."

"I don't believe it. You're in love with Belet! But you're only fourteen—you don't know what love is. What you have are hormones on overdrive. Take a cold shower, and get ready to kill her."

I shoved Kasusu back into his sheath.

What did he know? The sword only had one purpose, and it wasn't mine. Not everything had to end in a fight.

I rested my head against the wall. I just needed a moment of peace to get my thoughts in order.

⩗ ⧣ ⍰ ⊣

Who was I kidding? This was headed one way, and it was the complete opposite of peaceful. What part about a sea serpent tearing down the Houses of Parliament didn't I get?

There was a creak from outside the door.

"Come in, Mo."

"You knew it was me?" he said as he opened the door. "The others are waiting in the van, but I thought you and I should talk now. About things. Just in case we don't get a chance to later."

"What's that supposed to mean?"

Mo looked around the room as if he was searching for something to make this easier. But there wasn't anything. We were going to have this conversation. "We need to get the tablet and return things to how they were," he said. "That's it."

"Not really."

"C'mon, Sik. There's a giant sea serpent out there!"

"We'll deal with it." I buckled on the sword belt. "Kasusu has slain plenty of them in his time."

"Do you even know what you're doing?"

Wow. He was angry. That didn't happen much with Mo. "I know better than you, Yakhi. This isn't my first jihad."

"Please, Sik. I don't want us to argue."

I turned on him. "You so desperate to be a shaheed? A

martyr? Dying once wasn't enough for you? Forget it, Mo! If we reset things to how they were before I got the tablet, I lose you, again! That is not going to happen."

"There's more at stake than just what you want."

Wow. First angry, now surly.

The horn sounded again.

You got a sibling? Or maybe a best friend who you've gone through everything with? How is it that the people you love can make you so insanely furious? I wanted to shake Mo, to yell at him, scream at him. He looked like he wanted to do the same to me.

But he was right. I'd had no training as a fighter. I couldn't do flashy spinning hook kicks. Not to mention hip throws, wrist locks, leg sweeps, and flying armbars. I hadn't spent a summer in Paris learning savate, or a Christmas vacation in Bangkok training in Muay Thai. I couldn't pick up, say, that candlestick by the door and use it to incapacitate a person in three moves. Four if they were left-handed.

They say it takes ten thousand hours to become an expert in something. Get a calculator and figure out how many evenings that would be in your life. Call it four hours a day and that would still take seven years. What sort of parent would start their kid on a four-hour martial art training regime at age seven? There'd be no time to learn Latin, too, that's for sure.

⚞⚟ ⚞⚟ ⚞⚟ ⚞⚟

Or was it?

But I knew Latin, and I'd handled myself pretty well when I'd been forced into combat on this trip. I shook my head to clear it. There were two Sikander Azizes pushing and shoving against each other—the deli cook and the refugee—and now I couldn't remember which was which. Both couldn't be true, but both were *me*.

The window shattered as a rock flew straight through it. Rain swept in as glass tinkled out of the frame. Rabisu stood in the driveway, a second rock in her hand. "Get down here! We need to save the cosmos right now!"

Yeah, we did, didn't we?

THIRTY-TWO

WHEN TROPICAL STORM ELSA HIT NEW YORK AND turned the Bronx into a swimming pool, I'd thought, *Here we go again. What ancient Mesopotamian monster got up on the wrong side of the tomb this time and decided to get all catastrophic on us?* As it turned out, that had just been a regular natural, rather than supernatural, disaster. But now, as we drove through water-clogged streets and drains that had turned into fountains of filth, it really was *Here we go again.* There was nothing natural about this disaster as military helicopters buzzed overhead in search of the sea serpent that had just flattened the prime minister.

I watched the helicopters do another fruitless sweep overhead. "How hard can it be to find the basmu serpent? It's sixty leagues long."

Dumuzi looked out the van window. "It's outta sight, man."

"The Age of Aquarius ended a long time ago. Could you please drop the hip lingo, daddio?"

Dumuzi almost scowled at me. "I just did. The serpent has not fully established itself in this reality. It's blinking in and out of existence, and right now, it's outta sight. You dig?"

I blushed with embarrassment. "Yeah, I dig."

The van rocked as it was buffeted by a wave. We were still a mile from the Tower, but it wasn't just that the Thames had burst its banks. Underground canals and sewers were all rising from the drains and maintenance holes and washing away the foundations of the streets and buildings. Huge sinkholes lay hidden under the water, and we passed a double-decker bus that was all but submerged.

We were off to save the cosmos—a botanist, a supermodel, a demon, a god of flowers, and an increasingly confused fourteen-year-old—with a single magic sword between us.

Not exactly the Avengers.

But all I needed to do was stop Lugal and regain the tablet of destinies. Put like that, it seemed simple, right?

We plowed onward.

It was unreal. Mo kept glancing over at me. He smiled, wanting to be supportive, wanting me to know he believed in me, and once that would have been more than enough.

Despite his terror, Daoud did look amazing, even

soaked through, his hair bedraggled with rain. He looked like he'd emerged from the ocean as some gender-swapped Aphrodite rather than a guy who'd gotten drenched because the side window of the VW wouldn't close.

And Rabisu was taking it all in. She gazed at Daoud with the longing of a lovesick teen, despite being over four thousand years old. But even she was nervous, I could tell. She constantly clicked her claws, inspecting them over and over again, working them with her file and testing their sharpness by engraving hearts on the interior paneling. She whistled tunelessly, trying hard—too hard—to act casual. More than any of us, the demon knew what we were up against. She pulled out a smushed sandwich with a filling that included a pink wormlike tail, stared at it, and tossed it out the window. Rabisu had lost her appetite. The situation was *that* bad.

Dumuzi's hands tightly gripped the steering wheel as he forced his vehicle along in the ever-deepening murk. The engine coughed and spluttered but battled on. What was he thinking? I was glad we had an actual Mesopotamian god on our side, but his plan, as far as I could tell, was for everyone to gather in a healing circle and hug it out. Still, he was nervous. Flowers were sprouting everywhere within the van's interior. The dashboard was sprinkled with poppies, and there were roses climbing over the seats.

A sunflower had sprouted in the empty cigarette tray and was forcing itself out of the sunroof.

I sat wedged between Mo and Rabisu with Kasusu across my knees. I drew the sword halfway out of the scabbard.

"Any advice?" I asked it.

Kasusu sighed. Or at least it made a sound like a knife being dragged across china, which set everyone's teeth on edge. "Your heart's not in it. You're brave enough to fight—I've seen you in action—but you won't, because you think there's a better way."

"Isn't there?"

"Not against monsters there isn't."

"Why is the world like this?" I asked.

"You could say it's because humans were made with the blood of Lugal. There has always been a madness in you all, a darkness you can't let go of because you love it too much. But I don't philosophize about it, and neither should you. Concentrate on the job ahead."

Mo nudged me hard. "Look."

We'd reached the Thames. We'd passed through the abandoned city, detouring down the less waterlogged streets, past unguarded police barriers and looted stores, and reached Parliament Square, or what was left of it. The great clock tower, Big Ben, was now Little Ben, as the top half had been bitten off. The Houses of Parliament were little more than rubble, and Westminster Cathedral had a massive hole in its roof. Helicopters droned back and forth overhead, their searchlights rolling over the Thames, still fishing for giant serpents.

Dumuzi turned a sharp right onto the Embankment, the long, broad avenue that ran along the river. Great waves pounded the bank, throwing giant sheets of water over the street, bringing pebbles, mud, and the smashed remains of a barge. The huge oak trees lining the edge had been ripped out by their roots and were being carried by the current, crashing against one another and piling up against the supports of Waterloo Bridge.

That wasn't the only thing crashing.

Tour buses were parked along the Embankment. All had disgorged their passengers and sat empty. . . . All that is, but one.

Maybe these tourists had thought they could sit it out. Everyone knew it rained a lot in England. Maybe they hadn't noticed it go from downpour to state-of-emergency flooding until it was too late. Now they were trapped.

We watched as the wall between the street and the river was washed away. We saw the trees get uprooted, taking soil, concrete, and streetlights with them as they tumbled into the churning water. The asphalt crumbled like dry flour. The coach tilted as the weight of the water began to drag it toward the river with what looked like malicious intent.

Some passengers had made it through the door and were paddling away for all they were worth, but too many remained inside, banging frantically at the windows, their faces stark with terror and mouths open in unheard screams.

I flung open the van's side door and splashed through knee-deep water to reach the bus. I grabbed one of the passengers who'd managed to escape, an older guy in soaked-through tweed. "Get across the street and to one of the upper floors! Now!"

Ya Allah, the bus's back wheels were hanging over the edge. One big wave and the whole thing would get knocked in.

"Let me help." Rabisu was right beside me, dancing through the floodwater.

"Shukran." Maybe I was wrong about her. Maybe not all demons are bad.

Rabisu gestured with her arms, waving them up and down. "If we both rock it from the front, we'll build up enough momentum to tip it right into the river. It'll make a huge splash!"

Maybe...not? "We're trying to save them, Rabisu."

⚒⚒⚒⚒⚒

"Er . . . you sure you don't want to see them beating their fists against the windows as they sink under the waves? It'll be hysterical!"

"Just grab the bumper and hold it *down*." Mo and Daoud were now stumbling toward us. I met my brother's gaze, and he nodded.

The door to the bus was open, but it took me a jump and pull to grab hold of the step and clamber on board. The bus rocked, but my friends were holding the front bumper and hanging on for everyone's dear life. I turned to the passengers. "Pay attention, everyone! We're gonna get you all out, but we have to start unloading from the rear. That means that you—yes, you with the purple hair—have to sit down and wait your turn. Just don't panic."

And you know what they did?

They panicked.

Everyone scrabbled over the seats, over other passengers. It was total chaos, with one granny pulling another woman's wig off just to get a few inches ahead. They clawed at one another, biting and snarling in their animal desperation to survive. And that doomed them all.

The bus rocked, and the rear hit the water. The current grabbed hold, and water began pouring in as the vehicle tilted backward into the Thames.

⫸⫷⫸⫷⫸⫷

THIRTY-THREE

I GET IT. THEY WERE AFRAID. I DON'T BLAME THEM...
much. Still, with one hand I grabbed the closest guy and
with the other I held on to the doorframe as the bus leaned
back to almost vertical. The rest of the passengers tumbled
down the central aisle or were jammed into their seats by
gravity. Any second now the current would sweep us away
and that would be it.

Any second...

What was happening?

Leaves rustled and the windows cracked as branches
wrapped around the bus, holding it steady. Metal groaned
as a tree lashed its roots to the axles.

Rabisu climbed on board, completely nonchalant. She
looked at the terrified faces staring at her in dread silence.
"Why is that old woman holding a scalp?"

"It's a wig," I said.

"Oh. That's a shame." Her disappointment that scalping wasn't a thing didn't last long, and she clapped to get everyone's attention. "So, we having fun yet?"

The bus gently rocked forward. The roots latched on to the chassis and dragged it away from the river's edge.

"Yallah! Yallah!" I shouted, hauling the passengers out as quickly as I dared.

The coach settled back onto the street, and Mo and Daoud helped everyone clamber out, directing them to the buildings opposite, where they could shelter until... whenever.

"Dumuzi saved us." I needed to apologize to him. I thought he was just about making daisy chains and flower arranging, but this thing with the tree was inspired! I looked around, but there was no sign of him. "Where is he?"

"Right there," said Rabisu, pointing at a huge tree.

It had sprouted in seconds. The trunk was vast, as thick as an ancient redwood but twisted and gnarly like an oak. The tree looked, if you let your imagination do the heavy lifting, like a man crouching with his arms spread out. His hair was made up of long fronds, and his appendages were covered with silver and golden blossoms. A haze of sparkling pollen surrounded the tree like a mist.

"God surge. He must have been saving it all up for one

big miracle," I muttered, gazing in awe at Dumuzi's transformation. "What sort of tree is it?"

Rabisu picked up a petal as it floated by. "It's the huluppu, the tree of wisdom. Or a version of it."

The tree of knowledge. The bodhi tree. Yggdrasil. It was part of so many cultures and beliefs. What had Dumuzi said? All those branches spreading out from a single tree trunk.

The water covering the street bubbled and frothed as more plants broke up through the asphalt. The trees that had fallen lifted themselves back into place. In the public garden across the street, all the flower beds and trees were swelling in size and exploding in riotous, kaleidoscopic colors—enough greens, blues, reds, and yellows to make my eyes ache.

The sparkling pollen defied the rainfall as it swirled around the huluppu and spread silver clouds over the Embankment, over us. I was drawn to the tree and started walking toward it.

Rabisu put her claw on my arm. "Careful, Sik. It's the tree of wisdom. Sometimes there are things you don't want to know."

"I could do with some wisdom right now, Rabisu. Anything that might give us a chance. You understand?"

Then she slipped her claw into my hand and squeezed.

⁂

She didn't say anything, and if I hadn't known her better, I would have said there were tears running down her cheeks, not raindrops. Then she let me go.

I stood in a cloud of pollen. It settled on my eyelashes and on my skin, creating silver patterns, even cuneiform words. I closed my eyes and breathed it in. Deep, then deeper, then deeper still.

There was a fog in my mind, around the point where my two destinies clashed. I'd had a feeling that there was a reason for it, that the fog had been put there to protect me, to prevent me from going insane. But now I needed to see clearly.

Who am I?

A warm breeze caressed my face. Sunlight shone down on me. The rain and floodwaters vanished. I felt rich, soft soil between my toes. The air was scented with perfume, of lemons warmed in the sun. I opened my eyes.

The huluppu stood in the heart of a magnificent wild garden. A pink flamingo waded through a small sparkling stream to my left, and in the distance rose a ziggurat clad in brilliant lapis lazuli, shimmering in the high, bright sun. Kingfishers and brightly plumed parrots darted among the branches.

A growl rumbled from the shadowed canopy of the huluppu, and I met the amber gaze of a lion. Silver pollen fell from its mane as it gave its head a shake before settling on the grass like a lazy house cat. But the lion wasn't the only one in the shade of the tree of wisdom.

"Assalamu alaikum, Sikander."

Ishtar sat beside the lion, stroking its shaggy head. She smiled the way she always did, as if I was the only person in the world.

"What is this? Am I hallucinating?"

"It's Dumuzi's last gift." She sounded sad and wistful, then shook her head and rose to her feet and joined me. "It's good to see you, my child."

She wore a linen kirtle with a golden hem that trailed behind her. Her hair was unbound, shiny black and wavy all the way down to her waist. Her shirt of gold scales sparkled and chimed as she moved. She was the goddess of love and war after all.

The lion opened one eye as I knelt beside her, then closed it, grunting with satisfaction. "I don't know what to do. How do I stop Lugal?"

She put her palm against my cheek, and all my fear just fell away. "His blood runs through your veins, Sikander. You share so much."

"The only thing he shares is his madness. When he opens his mind, I feel like I'm falling into a whirlpool and being pulled apart. It's just chaos in there."

"Use that, use that opening, but show him there is much more to you than what he sees. And that there's more beyond his pain and anguish. He's built a high wall in his mind. He built it to protect himself, but all it did was trap him in his own thoughts. Every now and then the wall cracks and his emotions spill through. But as he lets the darkness out, you must find a way to let the light in."

"That'll destroy him?" I asked.

"It'll do so much more, Sikander. So much more."

I wanted her to take over, to come and make it all better for me. Like a mother would. That's how it is—moms are the place of safety. You go to her when you've hurt your knee falling off a bike, or when you've had your heart broken, or when your grades aren't going to get you into Yale like you'd hoped.

Paradise lies at the feet of mothers.

"What about Belet? How do I save her?"

Ishtar stroked my cheek. "Believe in her. That's all she's ever wanted, from anyone."

"But she's Lugal's child now."

"So?"

Her eyes shone with the starlight of distant galaxies. There was eternity in them, the light of creation and also the darkness of the end.

Ishtar leaned close and whispered, "Go write your own kismet."

She kissed my forehead. Like a mother would.

The fog lifted.

𒀸𒀸𒁹𒊓

The warmth of the garden faded, but the feeling of her kiss lingered. The rain pelted me, and cold water sloshed around my knees.

Rabisu was staring at me, waving her claws in front of my face. "Where did you go?"

What makes you...you?

The place you were born? The people who raised you?

Is it the clothes you wear, the TV shows you watch? Your favorite band? Your friends?

Aren't we all a hundred distinct people? All at once? Different with our parents than we are with our buddies. Treating our teachers one way, our relatives another. We might show one side of us to our brother, another to our sister.

But beneath all that there is a true, unalterable core. The part that is really, always *you*. The part that's always going to be the same no matter where you were born or who raised you.

"I saw Ishtar," I said to Rabisu. "My mother."

𒀸 𒈨 𒂖 𒋼

THIRTY-FOUR

I AM SIKANDER AZIZ. I AM FOURTEEN. AND THAT'S AS much as I know for sure.

I was born and raised in Manhattan. My mama is Fatima, and my baba's name is Nadeem. We have a deli on the corner of Fifteenth and Siegel. It's called Mo's after my older brother. He died three years ago in a motorcycle accident in Iraq. But before that happened, he mailed me a cutting from the flower of immortality. I planted it in our community garden and in doing so unknowingly absorbed some of its sap. It made me immortal, which came in handy when Nergal, the god of plagues, hit New York last year.

But there is another me. One who took a different path, who lived another destiny...

I was born and raised in Markazi refugee camp in the Al Anbar province. My mama and baba died when I was little. They got sick—diseases spread quickly in refugee camps—and never got better. That should have been the end of the story, but Mo and I were adopted. Our new mother was very beautiful, very wealthy, and perfect in all ways. She was like a goddess come down from the stars to rescue two poor orphans. She took us in and raised us to be like her.

Her name was Ishtar.

She was delighted when Mo took an interest in fashion and the finer things in life. Because he had stronger memories of what it was like to be a refugee, to be without, he appreciated the finer things in life more than I did. He was eternally grateful for having food to eat, a place to sleep, and a mother to tuck him into bed and brush away his nightmares.

As for me, Ishtar supported my interest in ballet. I was light-footed, flexible yet powerful, and had perfect balance and great muscle memory. It was the ideal foundation to build on. So, while she taught Mo the difference between Egyptian cotton and American cotton, Ishtar taught me how to fight.

Right now, talking to Rabisu under the huluppu tree, I relaxed my grasp on Kasusu. Ishtar had trained me to hold a weapon firmly but not tightly. To find that point of balance so you're not struggling with it, to make the weapon an extension of yourself. I turned my wrist in slow, steady circles, adjusting the grip so it was just right.

Kasusu shimmered. "Who taught you how to do that?"

"Mother." Even as I said it out loud, acknowledging that this was the path my life had taken in this destiny, the lessons came flooding back. How had I found time for them? Ishtar had made them fun, that's how. I'd learned speed, grace, and deadly reaction from playing with her cats. In the ballet classes, I'd learned poise and how to go from utter stillness to explosive action. And that was all before Ishtar took me to the armories and explained how to use each weapon. She'd shown me everything from how to make a fist to how to pirouette when delivering a hook kick to the head. On my eleventh birthday, she'd handed me Kasusu.

Destiny had changed. So, while Lugal had taken Belet and raised her as his own, Ishtar had taken *us*. Dumuzi had said that Ishtar had provided one of her children for this righteous struggle, this jihad. I just hadn't realized he meant me.

Did I feel different now that I knew? No. I was still Sik. That fundamental *me*, whether working in his parents' deli or raised by the goddess of love and war, was exactly the same. So, did that mean that ...

"Belet ..."

Rabisu frowned. "What about her?"

"Some things never change," I said. "The best things." It was a gamble, a huge one, and I wasn't going to explain it right now. We were still a mile from the Tower, and the VW van was long gone, swept away by the Thames.

Mo and Daoud joined us, Daoud's gaze lingering on the tree that was once Dumuzi. Mo and Rabisu looked at me expectantly, like I was the one with the plan and somehow I was going to save the day.

"Come on," I said. "Dumuzi gave us our chance to escape, so let's not waste it."

We walked. We waded. We swam and almost drowned twice as underground tremors generated sudden waves that surged down the streets. We linked arms to stay together, kept our heads down, and plowed forward. The raindrops struck like lead pellets and the noise of the waves became a roar. This wasn't how I'd expected to tour London.

All the buildings along the waterfront had been abandoned. We spotted a small armada of rowboats evacuating a nearby hotel, the last of the residents still in their pajamas and bathrobes. The rain fell in *sheets*. You couldn't see more than a few yards before everything became obscured behind a curtain of wet. And the debris! There were cars floating by, and I felt bad for whoever would wake up after the deluge and find their 1962 Ferrari 250 GTO no longer parked outside their home. Maybe they'd be able to fish it out of the river one day? Ishtar had always preferred Jaguars, of course. Trees, torn out of the soil, came thundering along, and they were dangerous, but so were the benches, mannequins swept from storefronts, and even a neat line of twin beds, drifting along like so many ducks paddling one behind the other.

We were more than soaked through. We'd gone waaay past drenched into a whole new realm of wet. And wading was exhausting. In the end, Mo and I were being pulled by Rabisu and Daoud. The demon had offered to carry me on her back, but I felt we weren't quite at that point in our relationship.

And then it was right in front of us.

The Tower of London. Not just a fortress, but also a legend. A palace, a prison, a place of execution and horror, and the mark of tyranny. It was a double-walled military base made up of dozens of buildings, churches, and towers, all gathered around the grim, monolithic White Tower, William the Conqueror's original keep. Where, we hoped, we'd find Lugal.

The Thames had invaded the Tower of London, turning it into a bleak island of stone and dark weeds connected to the bank by a crumbling strip of road. Tower Wharf had fallen into the river, and the moat surrounding the outer walls had flooded once more. The walls themselves were cracked from tremors that were increasing in frequency and power. Cradle Tower had collapsed entirely, leaving a stub of ancient stone just visible over the waves, like a broken tooth in an old man's gums.

We approached the main gates of Middle Tower, which had once borne the heads of traitors and rebels. Its immense walls radiated despair.

Abandon all hope, ye who enter.

"That's another one off my bucket list," I said. "I've always wanted to assault a castle."

I searched the long battlements for signs of life. There were none.

Daoud shook the rain from his long locks. "Maybe everyone's gone? Evacuated like every other place along the bank."

Mo didn't think so. "There'll be a reception waiting for us, one way or the other."

So, we needed to be sneaky.

The walls looked to be about fifty feet high, and the stones were smooth. But the place was a thousand years old, so there might be enough cracks in the mortar to get our fingers in. Not easy, but doable. Once, the version of me that was happiest mixing sauces and building classic shawarmas would have quaked at the idea. Knees might have even trembled. Now all I felt was a hot thrill. "The walls are an option."

"Get a load of you," said Mo. "A genuine ninja!"

Daoud raised his hand. "How about—"

"Just a sec, cuz." I surveyed the layout. "There's scaffolding beside Legge's Mount along the eastern wall. It's just the first twenty feet, but it'll save us a lot of effort."

Rabisu snapped her fingers. "There's always Traitors' Gate. We could try to swim under that."

"Has that ever worked?"

"There's always a first time," she replied.

Daoud waved his hand. "I have an—"

"Not now, Daoud. The badasses are talking," I said. What did he think this was, a trip to a nightclub? We weren't going to be able to go to the front door and tell the guards that our names were on the list. No jumping-the-line tactics would work here—this was going to be old-school.

Over the walls, or under Traitors' Gate? The Tower was a big place, where would Lugal be lurking? "We should—"

Daoud clapped his hand over my mouth and pointed to the main gates of Middle Tower. "Notice anything strange about them?"

Iron-bound oak. Twenty feet wide and as high. Each door would be a few tons. It would take hours to smash through them with a battering ram, except for one small weakness.... "They're open?"

"Good catch."

I adjusted Kasusu, and the blade hummed with

suppressed laughter. "Obviously I knew that," I said. "I just didn't mention it because it was so clearly a trap. Might as well have a massive sign hanging over it saying *Trap this way!*"

Rabisu swept her arms around Daoud and gave him a spine-adjusting hug. "O Handsome One, you are so clever."

"So, we're going through the main entrance?" said Mo.

"So, we're going through the main entrance," I replied.

"We can't." Rabisu pointed at the display board. "It says we need a ticket for a timed entrance."

"*Now* you worry about the rules?"

She smiled smugly. "See? Isn't it fun being bad sometimes? Since we're here, how about having a look at those jewels?"

"We are not stealing the Crown Jewels." Honestly, why were we even discussing this?

"I just want to try on a crown! It'll only take a minute! I need a photo for my Instagram account."

"Since when do you have an Instagram account?" This from someone who thought using soap was pushing the limits of technology. "And how many followers do you have?"

"One-point-five—"

"You can't have point five of a—"

"—million. I only had three people until Lady Gaga

started following me, then loads more came on board. I'm an influencer now."

You know reality is truly broken when a third-class Mesopotamian demon starts trending. "Just use your powers for good."

"As if," replied Rabisu with a dismissive snort. "I intend to use my power for personal gain and glory and as a weapon to destroy my enemies."

"That, too. Shall we? Somehow, I feel we're against the clock. If time even has meaning anymore."

The fortress was waterlogged; torrents poured from the nesting gargoyles, and streams ran over the cobblestones. We passed through the doors and under the raised portcullis into the kill zone between the first set of walls and the second, taller, inner defenses. Any army getting over the first walls would have been trapped here, and it was easy to imagine the second row of battlements being lined with crossbowmen, all shooting down at the trapped invaders until the passage was clogged with bodies. Where were the Beefeaters? Every entrance should have been guarded by them and their halberds. Yet there was no sign of them, or anyone else. It was the perfect place for an ambush, but we passed through unopposed and waded along the aptly named Water Lane and under the arch of the Bloody Tower into the heart of the fortress.

Tower Green was a quagmire. Torrents of water flooded

down from the Inner Ward. The lower floors were already submerged. Another tremor hit, and a great crack opened up along the chapel wall, its roof buckling in on itself. The Tower of London had dominated the city for a thousand years, but now it seemed as if it would sink under the waves within minutes.

There were dozens of buildings—armories, accommodations for the guards, treasure rooms.... Lugal might be in any one of them.

"We need to Scooby-Doo this," I said. "Split up in pairs."

Rabisu grabbed Daoud's hand. "Me and the Handsome One. You can go with your brother. We'll start...over there? Waterloo Barracks?"

"You mean where the Crown Jewels are kept?" Daoud asked.

Rabisu tried, and failed, to look surprised. "Are they? What an amazing coincidence."

Mo turned to Daoud. "You'll be careful, won't you?"

He wanted to say so much more—they both did, I could tell. Destiny had taken them along such different paths, and yet they'd ended up together again anyway. Mo took Daoud's hand and squeezed it. My brother tried to smile, but this time his easy joy was nowhere near.

"I'll keep him safe," said Rabisu, and she really meant it. Then she tugged him along. "If you get in trouble, Sik, just scream very loudly. Yalla bye!"

⩜ ⸾⩘ ⫸⫝ ⤙⟊

"Just look after Daoud! And do not touch anything!"
Then I turned to Mo. "He'll be a lot safer with her than
with us. Don't worry about him."

But Mo was watching them fade into the rain. "Do you
think we have a choice? That love's something we can control? Or is it already decided for us and there's no point
fighting it? I should have told him how I feel."

"You can tell him later. When this is all over and the
sun is shining."

"Inshallah." He sighed. "You really believe we can win?"

I put my arm around my brother. We were almost the
same height now. So much had changed in the past three
years, but the important stuff, all the things that mattered,
that was exactly the same. "The two of us together, like
in the old days? We've already won. It's just everyone else
who needs to know it."

And then he laughed. Like the Mo I knew.

He ruffled my hair, like a big brother. "Where to,
sultan?"

"If you were an ancient warlord, where would you
make your home?"

"Easy." He thumbed over his shoulder. "There."

I gazed up at the rainswept walls, wondering whose
eyes might be peering down at us through the arrow slits.
"The White Tower?"

It was a squat block of a building with turrets on each

of its four corners. There was nothing clever or flamboyant about its design. Its elegance was its brutal simplicity. Just the sort of place Lugal would pick. "Good choice."

I led us up the creaking wooden steps into the White Tower.

We pushed open the heavy doors and stepped into the entrance hall. We were out of the rain *at last*. I shook off the worst, gave myself a moment to drip, and then kicked off my boots. The stone floor was freezing under my feet, but it was better than sloshing around in those worn and ill-fitting foot buckets from the commune.

I unsheathed Kasusu and threw the scabbard away. I wasn't going to need it. "Stay behind me, Yakhi."

We entered the first hall and ahead were ranks of unmoving armored figures, even horsemen with lances tipped to strike. Rain fell through a crack in the outer wall, and the gray glow of the morning illuminated swords, medieval halberds, and other ornaments of ancient warfare. Metal rattled as the tower shook from another tremor. Ancient blocks ground against themselves as dust fell from above. We crept under a creaking stone archway.

"What is this place?" whispered Mo.

"The Line of Kings." I tapped the nearest horse and was rewarded with a wooden echo. "They're just displays."

The life-size mannequins looked ready to move, the horses about to stomp and snort, and the knights poised to

⟨⟨ ⟩⟩ ⟨⟩ ⟩⟨

swing their terrible weapons. Each suit of armor had been polished to mirror brightness. Minute versions had been crafted for young nobles and kings in waiting, and there were suits built for giants with swords long enough to slice a horse lengthways. Henry VIII—he of the six wives—towered over us in a suit embossed in gold.

There was just our breath, the splatter of rain on the ancient stone, and . . .

The soft sound of a hand tightening around a haft. The rustle of cloth against muscle. The scraping of a boot on bare stone.

Mo peered into the darkness. He wasn't scared yet, but he was getting there. "What's going on, Sik?"

"Didn't you wonder where the Beefeaters had gone?"

"You found them?"

Light glinted on cold, sharp steel. Feverish eyes glowered from the darkness. A growl echoed from the shadows. Figures, very much living ones, moved through the Line of Kings.

The Beefeaters emerged from hiding one by one, their black uniforms ragged and stained, weapons tight in their fists and insanity bright in their eyes.

"Pretty much," I replied.

⩗⫣⫭⫬⫯

THIRTY-FIVE

THE BEEFEATERS STOOD SHOULDER TO SHOULDER, blocking any way forward. Their old-school weapons— axes, swords, halberds, and maces taken from the displays around us—looked brutal, with edges and spikes still sharp enough to ruin my day, immortal or not.

"Come on, guys," I said, beckoning them closer. "You want to try one at a time, or all at once?"

"You'd better know what you're doing," murmured Kasusu.

You know how it goes—you've seen it a million times in the movies. The lone hero against a horde of stuntmen. They attack neatly, one at a time and a little slowly to give the actor a chance to react and make it look good. Each goes down with a single hit, usually falling out of the way so no one trips over them in the sequence.

This was nothing like that.

They charged as a single mob. I feinted, jabbing toward the first guy's eyes. I was too far away to touch him, but blades near eyeballs will make anyone flinch. He tried to parry but ended up swatting his companion across the face. Another swung wild and wide, shearing off the head of an adjacent mannequin.

Numbers aren't everything. Just ask Leonidas.

I blocked the first thrust, ducked under the second sweep, and kicked the legs out from under the third. (What? Who says you can't kick in a sword fight?) Suddenly I was in the middle of the throng. I could strike in any direction and hit someone, but they had to be careful not to slice one another. They got their halberds tangled up, and one man cried out as I slammed Kasusu's pommel into his kneecap. I spun low, swept high, and caught the middle of a halberd clean on Kasusu's edge. The sword went straight through the three-inch oak shaft as if it were a hay stalk.

I chopped off the front legs of one of the fake horses and let gravity do the rest. Both horse and armored rider came tumbling down on two of my opponents, clanging like a riot in a saucepan factory.

Time doesn't slow; your thoughts speed up. You see patterns and moves before your opponent's even thought of them. You unleash long-practiced combinations when there's that one-minute opening that seems as wide as a barn door. How could I not slam my fist into that exposed belly? It would be rude not to. My fist went deep into his gut. The Beefeater's eyes widened even as his face turned red. He crumpled, gasping.

I wasn't here to kill anyone. That wasn't my way. These guys were being controlled by Lugal, and they didn't deserve to die. That didn't mean I was going to go easy on them, though.

The dudes were big—Beefeaters tend to be on the large side thanks to their high-protein diets. They were veterans, too. They'd spent decades in the armed forces and seen battle. They knew how to fight and could take a hit.

But when was the last time the British army had used these weapons in combat? The sixteenth century? These were modern soldiers, trained in using firearms. I was a warrior trained in the old ways—the oldest.

I jabbed my sword tip an inch into a Beefeater's thigh. It was enough to make him wobble and stumble so I could ram his head into the wall with my foot. That was another one down.

The next was the danger. His friends were no longer in his way, and after seeing me in action, he was wary. He stepped forward, using the length of his halberd to keep me back. He was going to box me against the wall so he and his pals could finish me off.

One thing you never do is throw away your weapon.

Yet I threw Kasusu.

The pommel hit the Beefeater right between the eyes. Kasusu bounced off the guy's face and flipped through the air to land, hilt first, straight back in my hand. The Beefeater's eyes rolled in their sockets as he swayed on his heels and finally fell with a hard, heavy thud.

Yeah, totally planned that.

That rebound was so outrageous, the other guards stopped and took a few steps back. Somewhere in their befuddled minds they wanted to come up with a new approach because what they were doing wasn't working. Five were down already, two having been taken out by their own side. The remaining seven began to spread out, keeping the mannequins between me and them.

"You okay, Yakhi?" I said over my shoulder.

"Safely hiding behind Henry the Eighth," Mo replied. "Mother would be proud, by the way."

Seven opponents left. Maybe not a magnificent number but still pretty impressive.

Then a sensation came from the depths, like an earthquake in the ocean. So deep that it wasn't even a sound—not yet—but a soul tremor. An echo from the very beginning of time, maybe even before. The walls cracked, dust and mortar fell from the ceiling, and the wooden posts holding up the ceiling bowed and splintered.

"She's coming," said Kasusu. "You need to wrap this up."

᚛ ⱶⱶ ⱷⱶ ⱶⱶⱶ

No need to even say her name. There was only one *she* who mattered.

From outside I heard thunder, but it wasn't the mere sound of colliding air pockets—it was colliding realities. Existence was breaking apart as a colossal weight pushed against the barrier between this universe and another.

One of the main stone support columns had cracked right down the center. The wooden ceiling above was riven with wide cracks as the entire structure began to buckle.

What would it take to end this? I tightened both hands around the sword hilt. "You boasted that you were called Excalibur once."

"That was no boast. What of it?"

"You were the sword in the stone?" I slid sideways, and the Beefeaters did the same. "How did you get into the stone in the first place?"

"What are you talking about?"

"It must have been hard to pull you out, but I bet it was even harder putting you in." I took a wide step back toward the door. *C'mon, take the bait.*

The guards thought I was scared and on the verge of fleeing. Each wanted to be the one who finished me off, so they began pushing against one another to get closer, to get ahead.

I took another step back. They took one forward. Right beside the cracked column.

⚔ ✦ 𐤃 ⊱⊰

I put my all into it. I gave a massive shout and took a huge swing, right from the soles of my bare feet, through the legs, and into the hips. My torso and shoulders twisted so my arms whipped across me with all my energy focused into a few inches of sword edge. If this didn't work, I'd break my wrists.

The edge took the ancient column straight and clean. Nothing had the sharpness of Kasusu, a god-weapon. Metal sheared through the stone, and sparks tore along the blade, unleashing a brilliant glare that revealed the blood-crazed faces of the Beefeaters.

A second cavernous sound, a roar from below, did the rest. True, I'm pretty sure my cut through *ten inches of solid stone with a four-thousand-year-old sword* did most of the important work, but hey, I'm trying to be modest here. The column collapsed and the ceiling along with it.

"Mo!" I yelled as I dived for the archway. He didn't need to be told twice, and the two of us curled up against the arch, the strongest structure in the whole chamber. It shook, cracked, and showered us with dust, but it held. Which was more than could be said for the rest of the chamber. The wooden ceiling came tumbling down.

By the time the dust and splintered debris had settled, all that was left was a pile of Beefeaters, battered and bleeding but still alive.

⟐⟐⟐⟐⟐

Mo helped me back up. "Whoa. I mean, Mashallah, Sik. *Mashallah.*"

"So much for the minions." I wiped Kasusu clean. "Let's head up to the boss level."

THIRTY-SIX

WE CLAMBERED UP THROUGH WHAT REMAINED OF THE Tower as the structure shook and groaned. The Tower had all but sheared away from the main keep, and the interior was a gaping drop. We clung to the edges of the spiral stairs as internal supports gave way and wooden floorboards snapped.

I wanted Mo to leave this to me, but after one look at him, I knew there was no point in even asking. He'd grabbed one of the halberds, but he'd never handled anything more deadly than a shovel. Which is why he'd already come close to slicing off my ear as we'd wound our way up the spiral stairs.

"How are you doing?" I asked.

"No place I'd rather be."

"You're a poor liar, Mo." Then I winked. "Love you, Yakhi."

"That's the only reason I'm here. Shall we?"

I nodded, then pushed open the door at the top.

The roof of the White Tower was the size of a football field. Rainswept battlements formed the boundary on four sides and were lined by a walkway of slick granite. The center was covered by a double-pitched roof of lead panels affixed to an elaborate steel frame, already twisted from the Tower's seismic upheavals. Huge raindrops pummeled the metal, creating a cacophony of war.

We'd come out of the doorway of the northeastern turret. In the opposite corner stood Lugal, gazing out at the raging river.

He watched the river expectantly, his face alive with awesome joy. Water ran through his matted hair, over his bare, scarred torso, and down his tattered pants. The seams of his shoes had split open, and his bare toes poked out of the ragged, creased leather. The tablet was fixed to his chest by yards of black duct tape. How could someone be so monstrous and terrifying and yet still pitiful?

We could reach him by running around the walkway, or straight across the roof. But that presented another obstacle.

Belet.

She was waiting in the middle, cradling a twelfth-century Crusader sword she must have grabbed from downstairs. It gave me a sick feeling in my gut to see her

𒀀𒈾𒊏𒋼

with a sword like that—it was a bad guy's weapon. She watched me through hooded eyelids, her gaze as dark and unreadable as a shark's. Despite the freezing rain, she only wore black combat pants and a T-shirt. Her feet were bare, like mine.

Was there any of my friend Belet still left? Any goodness? She didn't believe she had any. Lugal had worked hard to break her, to leave her bitter and pitiless, like him.

I had to believe she was the same deep down. Just like I was, despite my two different destinies. The best of her was hidden away, buried deep underneath a lifetime of abuse and brutality. I just had to find a way to reach it.

Mo chuckled. "There is something special about her, isn't there? I mean, beyond the whole angel-of-destruction vibe."

"What do you mean?"

"What do you think I mean?" He wiggled his eyebrows.

Ya salam! I admit it! I had . . . strong feelings for Belet. Strong and *very* complicated.

Lugal had his back to us. He wasn't worried—he had Belet protecting him.

"It doesn't have to be this way!" I yelled at him. "You can still stop all this!"

He replied without even looking at us. "You haven't seen the true nature of it all, Sikander. Your view is that of a child—innocent and naive. I know better. You were created out of pain. It's not for nothing that a baby's first sound is a scream."

I really needed to word this next part carefully. I was trying to talk him off the ledge, literally. One wrong word and—

The door behind me crashed open as Rabisu charged in. "Have we started fighting yet? I was worried I'd missed it!"

"Ya Allah, Rabisu! Can you just let me deal with— What's that on your head?"

Rabisu put her claws over it protectively. "I found it."

"You did not! You stole Queen Elizabeth's crown? Really? Now?"

"It's not the queen's crown! I'd never do that!" She tapped the big diamond in the middle. "It's the queen *mother's*."

"Oh, *just* the queen mother's. That's fine, then." I had to remind myself that Rabisu hadn't learned to recognize the subtleties of human conversation. "That was me being sarcastic."

"Where's Daoud?" asked Mo. "Is he okay?"

"I locked the Handsome One in the treasury. He wanted to come, but I didn't want him getting his hair hurt," said Rabisu. She stretched herself out. "At last. The three days are up."

"What three days?" I asked, trying not to get too distracted by the crown.

She scraped her claws together. "Three days have long

since passed. The Bedu laws of hospitality no longer apply. I'm here to kill Belet."

"After all that's happened? The universe is about to end, Rabisu!"

"But not before I kill her!"

Why was it that every time I talked to Rabisu I got a headache? "How can that...? Wait a minute. What did you just say?"

Rabisu looked confused. "I'm going to kill Belet?"

"No, before that. The Bedu rules."

Could Rabisu have found the answer?

"Ya Allah, that's it!" I said. "I think I know how to stop Lugal!"

"Er...good? After I kill Belet, okay?"

Islam may have been planted in the cities, but it had flowered in the desert, among the Bedouin tribes of Arabia. They inhabited a harsh, pitiless world in which food was scarce and water even more so. But if a stranger turned up at their tent, he or she would be fed, cared for, and protected for three days. The courtesies would be given freely; the stranger would owe nothing in return.

But why? Why share when you have barely enough for yourself?

Because in the eyes of that stranger you see yourself. You see that you and they are one and the same.

𒀸𒐊 𒐊𒐊 𒀭𒁺 𒄴𒇹

Empathy. Compassion. Mercy. These are the greatest qualities of the desert dwellers—have been since time immemorial—and of people anywhere. They bond us all. They are what make us human.

"I've got this," I said. "We need to split up."

"I'll go across the roof," volunteered Rabisu.

Much like gods, demons are not known for their subtlety. "No, I'll deal with Belet."

"Then who am I going fight?" complained Rabisu.

"Oh, how about him?" I said, pointing over our heads.

We'd almost missed Anzud, and he'd been counting on that. He'd been circling above, battling the wind and rain, hoping to swoop down and tear through us before we even knew he was there. He was Lugal's backup plan.

"Anzud," said Rabisu. "I suppose he'll do."

Anzud settled himself on a nearby crenellation. He'd come ready for trouble, carrying a long spear and wearing an old leather breastplate strapped across his thin chest.

"You reckon you can handle him, Rabisu?"

"Oh, please." She started across the walkway.

"Bon appétit!" I called after her.

Mo tightened his grip on his halberd. "What about me?"

"You go right, but leave Lugal to *me*. I have an idea that—"

We stumbled as the Tower shook to its foundations, the

structure rumbling with its last breath. The city around us became indistinct, as though the rain were washing it all away.

Lugal laughed. It was big, chesty, and sincere. He beat his fists on the battlements until the stone cracked. He leaned over them and yelled into the winds, "Welcome back, Mother! Welcome back!"

The Thames surged . . . and transformed. Instead of looking murky brown and green and surging with huge waves, it became deeper and darker—bottomless. Lights shone from the infinite depths—not stars, but entire galaxies.

She rose from the depths of another, empty universe. Her claws tore the barrier between realities. She opened her vast maw and began to devour . . . everything.

She'd been destroyed at the beginning of time, and her remains had been used to create all that we knew. But now she was back.

With a sky-shattering roar, Tiamat, the goddess of chaos, returned to our world.

THIRTY-SEVEN

A COSMIC-LEVEL EXTINCTION EVENT.

That's what Tiamat was. The lights were going out.

She was something too big to take in, to describe as a whole. Tiamat was pure chaos, beyond understanding. It was like looking through a kaleidoscope and seeing the world fractured into countless pieces.

She was a dragon—or I imagined she was, because that was all I could comprehend and still stay sane. Were those scales on her body, or stars snatched from galaxies? Her wings were rainbow-painted thunderclouds whose feathered strands stretched to the horizon. Her eyes held the sun and the moon, her teeth were flashing lightning bolts, and the maw beyond them was an all-consuming black hole. She continued to claw apart the dimensions, fading in and out but growing more real, more solid, with every passing moment. We didn't have long. Once Tiamat was fully formed, she would devour existence.

But first there was Belet.

The castle was cracking apart, and yet she didn't move even as the panels under her were torn out of their frames. Any second now she'd go plummeting a hundred feet down through the Tower. Why didn't she move?

Because she wanted to prove herself to Lugal. She wanted his approval, even if it killed her.

The things we do for love.

I stepped gingerly onto the roof. The flimsy lead panels creaked under my weight. With each tremor the frame twisted a little bit more, but I couldn't rush this. This was about saving Belet from Lugal . . . and from herself.

She waited, perfectly balanced on the framework, watching me shuffle slowly toward her. "I don't know if you're very foolish, or very brave."

"You don't have to throw your life away like this, Belet. Lugal doesn't care for you, and nothing you do will change that. Come off the roof."

She tightened her grip on her sword, anger seething in those dark eyes of hers. "I owe Father my life. He saved me from the ruins, sheltered me, fed me. He taught me everything I know."

"Yeah? What exactly did he teach you?"

"That life is cruel," she replied.

᯾

The entire frame buckled, and the panels on either side of me fell away. The drop would break me into a hundred pieces, immortal or not. "Has it ever crossed your mind that he might have been wrong? That he's only ever allowed himself to see the dark side of life? If that's all there is, how did humanity make it this far?"

"You never grew up in a war zone. You don't know what life's really like. You've been sheltered and pampered, and you're weak as a result. Happiness is an illusion, something to keep the sheep focused on the grass and not the slaughterhouse. But that's where we're all headed in the end."

That perspective was extremely glass half-empty. Still, I was getting closer to her, just beyond sword reach. I tried to ignore the deafening roar of the emerging chaos goddess, the world fading around us. Belet was all that mattered right now.

"But you don't really believe that," I said. "And I can prove it."

Now she was glaring. *That* was a look I knew very well. "My father taught me—"

"*Whatever*, Belet." I held up Kasusu. I felt power and anticipation radiate through him and into me. The sensation was—I'm ashamed to admit—thrilling. It would have been the most natural, logical thing for me to give over to it, to fight Belet and prove Lugal *right*. That's what Belet was expecting because that's all she knew. Everything was conflict, everything was war, and everything was destruction. "We could fight..."

She lifted her Crusader sword in a two-handed grip.

As for me? I threw Kasusu away. It slid across the roof and clattered against the battlement wall on the far side. I couldn't risk being tempted.

"What are you doing?" Belet cried.

I held out my hand. "Or we could dance."

I stood before her, my arms outspread, defenseless. And guess what happened next?

Yup. She attacked me.

THIRTY-EIGHT

"FIGHT!" YELLED BELET AS SHE SWUNG THE SWORD.

"No!" I ducked below it, barely. I twisted aside as she jabbed. I caught a nick across the cheek, just enough to draw a thin line of blood and sting a little.

"Fight, you coward!"

Belet kept coming, jumping along the framework even as it began to buckle. I retreated, trying not to fall through any of the gaping holes in the roof.

She cried in frustration as she stabbed forward. The sword tip took off a few of my buttons and scored another bloody line across my chest.

Each of her blows was harder than the last, more earnest, wanting to cause damage. Belet swiped horizontally and I blocked with both my forearms, but she anticipated the move and dragged the blade back sharply, slicing my arm from elbow to wrist. Blood glistened at the open wound, then began to run freely. The cut didn't hurt instantly; it was that sharp, but soon my arm felt like it was on fire.

But...that shouldn't have happened.

I put my hand against my cheek. It was *still* bleeding.

Why wasn't I healing? That gash should have closed within seconds. Blood dripped down my shirt, too—the wound on my chest was still open.

Belet paused. "*Now* will you fight?"

My left arm was going numb. I could barely feel my fingers.

Belet gestured toward Lugal as he climbed up on the battlements to be closer to the emerging Tiamat. "Father used the tablet to change your fate again. What difference can one more alteration really make?"

"I'm no longer immortal?"

She nodded. "Go pick up your sword, and let's finish this properly."

No longer immortal. Fine. Neither of us had a way out now. "No."

She swung her blade, and the tip passed an inch from my throat. "Why won't you defend yourself?"

"I don't fight my friends."

"Friends are for the weak, those who cannot stand up by themselves." She swung again. Half an inch away this time. "Fight, or I'll kill you where you stand."

"You won't."

𒀀𒆠𒀭𒉽

The next swing just, *just*, cut the skin over my Adam's apple. "Why? Why are you so sure?"

I shrugged, or at least I tried to. My left arm hung limply by my side. "Years of customer service. You get an instinct about people. The good ones, anyway."

Did she just twitch? Did Belet have a moment of doubt? No one had ever believed in her in this destiny, so the fact that I did must have come as a shock. Especially as I was staking my life on it.

Unfortunately, I'd momentarily forgotten about something. Lugal.

"Belet!" he bellowed over the din of thunder and dragon roar. "Kill him! Now!"

She tightened her grip on the sword. "Please, please try to defend yourself."

A dark, heavy throbbing was building in my head. And not just mine—Belet gritted her teeth against the pain.

"Kill him, daughter! Do as I command!"

The mind pulse beat harder and harder, the urge for violence ever increasing. If Kasusu had been nearer I might, just might, have tried to grab it. But then I would have lost and Lugal would have won. Even though the metal panel beneath me creaked and wobbled, I stayed right where I was, facing Belet.

The pain brought tears to her eyes. "But, Father, he's defenseless."

My head felt like it was cracking apart as it filled with raging crimson visions. But however bad it was for me, Belet was being overwhelmed. Lugal was flooding her mind with his madness, driving her to lash out. She couldn't resist for much longer, I knew.

I reached out for her. "Belet..."

She screamed even as she lifted the sword over her head. She held it aloft, her eyes burning with bloodlust.

I'd lost. She was Lugal's child after all.

The floor beneath me bowed. The rivets snapped free in a series of loud, sharp pops. The metal panels gave way entirely. There was a moment of weightlessness, and I was falling, falling the hundred feet down to the ancient cobblestones.

And then...I wasn't.

I hung in the air, dangling by my useless left arm. But I was too surprised to notice the pain.

Belet locked her hand around my wrist, dropping her sword to do it. The blade tumbled past and clattered far, far below.

Instinct. It's that part of you that never changes. And Belet's instinct was to save me.

"You're heavier than you look," she said as she began hauling me up.

"You've got muscles." I managed to swing my right arm over the steel framework. "Use them."

She sank down to her knees beside me as I lay there, steadily dripping blood. She whipped off her belt and tied it high on my bicep. "Dancing? Really? That was your plan?"

"It's the only thing that makes you happy, Belet."

She looked at me and smirked. "Perhaps not the *only* thing, Sik."

"Hey, did you just call me Sik?"

"Get over yourself." She pulled me up onto my feet. "We'd better get off this roof before it collapses entirely. And I need to have a word with...Father."

I'd lost a lot of blood, so standing up straight wasn't easy. Or was the world tilting at an odd angle? It was hard to tell as reality warped all around us. Thankfully Lugal's rage was no longer filling my mind.

Belet helped me to the walkway and propped me up against the wall near where Kasusu had landed. Then she went to face Lugal.

I picked up Kasusu. The blade flashed red as it cried, "You threw me! Like I was a disposable knife! How dare—"

"Another time, Kasusu, another time." I felt some strength returning as I gripped the hilt. My left arm wasn't any good, but at least I could stand without swaying.

Rabisu scurried over. She looked battered but happy, and there were feathers decorating her crown. *Magpie* feathers.

𒀀 𒇷 𒁲 𒀖

"Where's Anzud?" I asked. "Did you—"

Rabisu burped. Loudly.

"I guess you did. You ready for more fighting?"

She looked me up and down. "Are you?"

I watched Belet climb onto the battlement where Lugal was standing. Would she be able to talk some sense into him?

My question was answered when he swatted her aside as if she was nothing. Belet tumbled down to the walkway.

I charged. The stones were perilously slick, but I went straight at him, Rabisu at my side, screaming.

I tried to slice Lugal's calf with my sword, but it was like hitting marble. The impact traveled up through Kasusu and made my teeth rattle. Kasusu was a god-weapon—it should have cut him. How much power was Lugal gathering from Tiamat? I ducked as he tried to slam my head between his palms. The shock wave caused by his clap sent me sliding away ten feet. Rabisu slashed with her claws, but Lugal grabbed her by the arm and tossed her away. She flew, tail over horns, and crashed into the wall opposite.

Belet stumbled back into the fray, determined to save us all, including Lugal. "Father, please! You have to stop!"

I helped Rabisu to her feet. Somehow her crown was still on, but flatter than before.

"This isn't working," I said. Belet cartwheeled over

Lugal as he tried to squash her with a giant fist. Instead, he knocked off one of the Tower's crenellations.

Rabisu snarled as she flexed her claws. "Demons don't do tactics."

"You do now. Get close and distract him. Keep him busy. And don't let him hit you."

"And what about you? What are you going to do?"

"Something sneaky."

Belet stumbled back a few paces beside us. I turned to her. "Get away from here. You can't take him."

"I'm not abandoning the fight," she snarled.

Of course she wasn't. Why had I even asked? "Fine. But let me go first. You look for an opening."

"What opening?"

"You'll know it when you see it."

Lugal roared as Rabisu and I attacked like gnats against an elephant. We couldn't hurt him, but each blow we landed was a blow to his pride.

So he didn't notice Belet coming up behind him. Why should he care about her? She couldn't hurt him. But I kept on attacking—cutting here, slicing there. Over and over across his limbs, his head, his chest. The duct tape hung off him in tatters.

"Now!" I yelled.

Belet jumped onto his back. He turned to grab her, but

she hung off his arm and swung to the front. Pure balletic grace. Ishtar would have been proud.

Belet grabbed the tablet and pulled.

Lugal may have taught her everything she knew, but it was not everything *he* knew. I should have realized that. He swung around and slammed her into the wall. She tried to hang on, but it was no use. She dropped to the wet ground, empty-handed and unconscious.

Lugal whipped around to look at me, a smile slowly spreading over his face. "Is that all you have, Sikander?"

"Not all," said Mo.

Lugal turned just as Mo slashed with the halberd. The blade tore through the last of the duct tape, and the tablet fell away. It spun across the slippery flagstones until I trapped the prize under my heel.

Rabisu limped to my side, hurt but happy. "Admit it— that was pure luck."

We'd done it.

All I needed now was—

Mo screamed.

No, no, no.

Lugal held Mo aloft by his neck with one hand. The other hand gripped Mo's arm, and my brother screamed again as Lugal pulled it. "Give me the tablet, Sikander, or I will tear him to pieces. Now!"

⸗⸗⸗

I had it. I could fix everything now that I had the tablet. I just needed a few seconds—

"Now!" Lugal roared. He began pulling, slowly, with the power of a locomotive. I could hear Mo's joints popping. . . .

"Go get it, then." I threw the tablet over the battlements.

Lugal dropped Mo onto the roof and dived for the tablet, stretching for it. Then both the god and the clay slab disappeared over the side and into the churning maelstrom below.

THIRTY-NINE

IMMENSE IS TOO PITIFUL A WORD FOR TIAMAT. SHE WAS A gravitational force, pulling everything into her. The trees along the riverfront tore out of the earth as she beat her wings. Lightning crackled across her scales, and the air rippled with heat as streams of lava dripped from her jaws, incinerating everything in her path. She slammed one colossal foot on Wakefield Tower, and it collapsed like a sandcastle.

Tiamat continued to emerge into our reality, and reality couldn't take much more.

"We just going to admire the view, or actually fight?" said Belet as she limped up beside me, using Mo's halberd to support her.

Rabisu joined us. "Well?"

"It looks like it's the three of us against Tiamat," I said.

"Four," said Mo, cradling his injured arm.

Rabisu laughed. "Tiamat doesn't stand a chance."

"Does she even notice us?" I asked.

"We'll make her," said Belet. "And we need to deal with Lugal once and for all. Where is he?"

"Up there." Rabisu pointed her claw at the top of Tiamat. "Waaay up there."

He was on top of the dragon's head, in full, glorious god surge, glowing in an ethereal light, flooded with all the power he'd lost so many millennia ago.

I sighed. "Nothing's easy, is it?"

Rabisu gazed at the great dragon. "It won't be long now before things come to an end." Then she smiled at me, a little awkwardly truth be told. "Despite everything, I've had a great time, Sik. I never thought you mortals could be . . . well . . ."

This time I knew it was tears in her eyes, not raindrops.

Belet turned to the demon. "I'm sorry I killed your friends."

"I found better ones," said Rabisu.

"We'll see one another again," I said. "Inshallah."

There was nothing I could think to say to Mo. He just put his arm around me and kissed my forehead.

We climbed the dragon, each taking a separate path toward Lugal. I tried to keep my attention locked on him and not get distracted by the dissolving universe.

Lugal had transformed into what he must have been once, when he commanded Tiamat's armies and was beyond even the power of the gods. Fifty feet tall and shining in the lightning that struck him harmlessly. He wore a crown with four horns, the symbol of ancient divinity, and embedded in his chest was the tablet, equally expanded. The words on it were melting even as I watched.

Destiny was ending.

The scales I clambered over shone with the starlight of galaxies. Tiamat's spines were mountain ranges with storms swirling around their peaks. Great rivers poured from ruptures in her flesh. It was as if the world had been laid flat and I was standing in the heart of it.

I clambered onto a large boulder that had rolled off the nearby mountain. "Lugal! Lugal! You need to stop it!"

Somehow, he heard me. He smiled. "This is the end, Sikander. It comes to us all. There is nothing to be afraid of."

"You have no right to decide for everyone!"

"Do I not? I am your father, little mortal. I have the right to decide the fate of my children."

"But you've never known us. Not who we really are."

"You think I don't know humanity?" he sneered.

"How can you? You've never been part of it. You judge us without understanding us even in the slightest. Let me show you what we are; then you can decide."

"Decide what, mortal? What could you possibly say that

would make any difference now? What fresh idea do you have that I have not already pondered for centuries?"

"You only see the world through your eyes, Lugal. But if you could see the world the way I do, the way mortals do, you'd feel different."

"Such things are impossible. I am what I am."

I pointed at the tablet. "Nothing is impossible. Be a mortal, just for a moment. Feel what we feel."

"And what is that?" asked Lugal.

"Find out for yourself."

"You are a strange one, Sikander Aziz."

"You are not the first person to think that." Mo staggered up beside me and draped his arm over my shoulder even as he addressed the god. "He's always been like this."

Rabisu stood on the bones of a gigantic ancient beast to my right. "That's our Sik. I've given up trying to understand him."

And then came Belet, light-footed and as intense as always. "This has to end, Father."

Lugal laughed. "You know the story of the fisherman and the genie, of course?"

"Of course," I said. "Who hasn't read *The Arabian Nights*? The fisherman frees the genie from his bottle. The genie is huge and terrifying and intends to kill the fisherman. But the fisherman tricks the genie into going back in the bottle and seals it up again."

Lugal slapped his chest. "You want me to use the tablet to turn myself into a mortal, and then you and your companions will launch yourselves at me and rip the tablet from my hands while I'm vulnerable. I am not a fool."

"We won't," I answered. "You have my word."

I was gambling everything, I mean *everything*, on Lugal just sharing a moment with us.

"Well?" I asked him. "What are you afraid of?"

Lugal turned his gaze toward me. I felt the pulse in my mind building, but this time it was not a tidal wave of raw, uncontrollable emotions, but an opening, allowing himself to see and feel what I did.

The radiance dimmed as Lugal shrunk down to our scale. He gazed, at first suspiciously, at each of us. But I'd promised this was no trick, and the others knew this was the only chance we had.

Lugal put his palm upon the tablet. "Very well. Show me what it is to be human."

Mo's leaving tonight. Off to Iraq for six months to help rebuild the country, one farm and field at a time.

He's so excited.

I'm not.

We've closed the deli early so we can all have this last meal together. Mama has laid out small pots of hummus, tzatziki, the homemade spicy sauces. The Baghdad is making my eyes water from across the deli.

Baba drops the freshly made pitas into a basket in the center of the table. "Yallah, while they're still hot."

Mo and Daoud sit next to each other. They steal glances, and we pretend not to notice.

Did I know this was going to be the last time we saw him? Did I have a premonition? Was that why I was upset?

The deli's lit by candles—Daoud's idea. The rest of the light spills through the windows facing Fifteenth and Siegel. Streetlamps, the headlights of a passing car, even the glow from someone's phone as they pass. This is Manhattan— light is always present. I wouldn't want it any other way. Why would anyone want to leave a place like this?

Why does Mo have to go so far from us?

Mama adjusts her hijab and casts an expert eye over the tabletop, making sure everything's exactly right. She smiles and gives a little nod. We're good to go.

But Mo's not. He's gazing at the door. "Someone's there."

"I'll get rid of him," I say, and head for the door. I don't want anyone spoiling tonight.

I open the door a crack, just enough to get my face through. "Sorry, but we're closed. Private event. Come back tomor— Wait... do I know you?"

"We've met," he says.

He's a big man—taller than the doorway, and just as wide. He'd be terrifying if he wasn't so...pitiful. His shoes are held together with duct tape, and his suit is torn, patched, and shiny with age. His beard is straggly and his hair tangled into rat tails.

Baba's at my shoulder. "What's keeping you, Sik? We don't want Mo to miss his..." He catches sight of the big man. "Salaam, brother."

The man merely grunts in response.

Then Baba draws the door wide open. "Come in, please. Join us."

I feel ashamed for almost turning away a stranger. It's not our way.

Mo grabs another chair and puts it at the head of the table. It creaks as the big man sits down and gazes at the food, then at each of us. What does he see?

Mo's excitement? The dreams he has, even when he's awake, of how he'll make Iraq beautiful again? When I think of Iraq, all I envision are ruins and desert. Mo imagines fields and orchards abundant with fruit. His love transforms war zones into gardens.

Can the big man see all the heart Mama and Baba have poured into this place? Into making a new home? And all the people who helped them along the way without asking for anything in return? Does the man know that's why he's sitting here? Love creates ripples across time and space, and even beyond. I've been to the netherworld, the place souls go at the end of life, and I saw love there, too.

What does the stranger make of Daoud? Is he captivated by his flawless beauty? Or does he see that Daoud is so much more, with his unshakable loyalty and endless generosity? That his greatest joy is to make those around him happy?

The big man turns to me.

What does he see in me? Not much. I'm nothing special.

Baba looks around the table. "Shall we?"

Heads lowered, palms cupped in front of us, we recite the du'a and give thanks for what we have.

"Bismillahi wa'alaa barakatil laah."

We're about to start in, when Daoud suddenly springs up. "Wait a sec," he says, drawing his phone out of his pocket. "We need a picture of this for the wall."

The wall, of course. One corner of the deli is filled with photos. There's some of Mo and me as little kids, like when we dressed up as Gilgamesh and Enkidu for Halloween, and many images from Mo's previous visit to Iraq to help his people. The wall's crowded, but there's always room for one more.

The big man starts to get up, to remove himself from the shot, but Baba stops him. "Sit, please."

𒀀𒈨𒂗𒁷𒀀

The man frowns but sits back down as Daoud angles his phone on the counter to make sure the camera can capture us all. "Ready?"

Timer pressed, Daoud darts back to the table, and we all squeeze together. One flash later, it's finally time to eat. I pick up the basket of warm pitas and offer it to the big man first. That's all I can do, isn't it? That's all any of us can do. Share what we have, share who we are. That's basic humanity.

The man hesitates, then takes a slice. He holds the pita in his massive palm, staring at it like he's never eaten one before. He looks at me and nods. "Shukran."

As the vision faded and I returned to the present, I still felt a pulse in my head. But it was slower, calmer now. We all stood around Lugal as he lowered his palm from the tablet still strapped to his chest. "That is how you chose to spend your final moments of life."

But his tone was not sneering this time. Instead it was full of . . . wonder.

"You shared a meal with me, a stranger."

"It's what we do," I said.

"I . . . I have never been welcomed to a table before."

I knew how lucky I'd been in life. I'd always had Mama and Baba to protect me. They'd lived through war and survived—more than survived, they had prospered. They hadn't let the dark times define them. My parents were proof that even the bleakest moments come to an end, and things can get better. They'd had each other to keep hopelessness at bay, and they'd gotten help from their community. They'd taught me that no one is totally lost. Not even Lugal. All he needed was someone to offer him a hand.

That's what you learn from refugees.

Lugal pulled off the tablet and held it out to me. It was that simple. Though the guest owes the host nothing, he'd decided he wanted to give me something in exchange for the meal he had shared back at our deli. I accepted it, and for a brief moment, our fingers touched.

There was no great surge, no sudden shock wave of power. I just felt... a quiet. The maelstrom that had raged within Lugal for millennia had stilled like the sea after a great storm. All his power remained, and the depths were as dark and as dangerous as ever, but calmness now spread across its endless surface.

Lugal glanced down at the tablet, perhaps wondering if he might change destiny one more time, but he shook his head and let go. "Salaam, Sikander Aziz," he said, nodding at the finality of it all. He said it not as a greeting, but as a statement. His achievement, at last.

And then he faded away into the darkness.

I raised my hand. I didn't know if any essence of him still lingered, whether he might be able to hear me, but I called out anyway. "Salaam."

Peace.

FORTY

LUGAL WAS GONE, BUT THAT LEFT ONE BIG PROBLEM—
the biggest. Tiamat herself, still absorbing everything
around her. I realized with a shock that Rabisu was
nowhere to be seen. And Daoud...he must have disappeared along with the Tower of London.

Belet, too, was fading.

"No, no, no!" I dropped the tablet to try to hold on to
her with my one good hand, but my fingers passed straight
through her. "Hang on. I'll change everything back to how
it was."

She shook her head. "Anything you do will only cause
fresh ripples."

"I'll just get rid of Tiamat!"

"No!" Belet cried. "She's the source of creation, Sik! You
get rid of her and nothing, *nothing*, ever existed."

She was barely visible now. "What do I do, Belet?"

⚔ ⚒ 𒀭 ⊱

This was even worse than losing Mo. He'd been thousands of miles away when it happened and gone before we knew it. Belet was standing right in front of me. "Don't cry, Sik," she said. "It doesn't suit you."

Those were her last words.

A part of me went with her, leaving an emptiness in the center of my chest. Only now did I realize how much Belet had become part of me.

Now it was just Mo and me left.

"I don't understand why this is still happening!" Reality was imploding all around us. "I thought everything would return to how it was before."

"There's one thing that definitely doesn't belong here," said Mo as he picked up the tablet. "Me."

I stared at him. "Stop talking like that."

"This all began when you brought me back. That's where you need to reset it all. It's the only way, and you know it. You can't save everyone, Sik."

There wasn't much left aside from Tiamat. She dominated the starless black sky, finally getting revenge on her wayward children, the gods who had conspired to slay her countless eons ago. The stars were their homes, and she'd devoured them whole. Within her immense maw I could see constellations sparkling like diamond dust.

"The tablet is the key. This is all happening because we messed with destiny. A path was plotted for us on this clay, and we strayed from it." I picked up Kasusu. Maybe it had some ideas. "Any suggestions?"

"It's a knotty problem for sure," said the sword. "But my answer is always to attack with maximum effort."

"That's not gonna . . . Wait a minute. What did you say?"

"Maximum effort?"

"No, about it being a knotty problem." Something stirred in the dark corners of my memory. Kasusu was legendary, as it was *constantly* reminding me. It had been wielded by some of the greatest heroes in history, Alexander the Great being one of the, er, greatest. "You cut the Gordian knot, didn't you?"

"I did. So?"

Could that be the answer? "What if we destroy the tablet? If there's no fate, we can't deviate from it, right? Destiny will become whatever path we choose."

"You sure?" asked Mo.

"Nope. But, given this is the end of the universe, it's not like we can make things any worse."

Mo turned the tablet over in his hand. The cuneiform moved through the clay. Destiny was in turmoil; chaos reigned. The stars above, the few that remained, began exploding. Stunning kaleidoscopic supernovas lit up the darkness. The death of the cosmos would be beautiful.

"I can't be sorry," continued Mo. "Not many people get a second chance."

𒀸 𒀸 𒀸 𒀸

"It's not over yet, Mo."

"You never give up, do you?" he said, shaking his head. "Have you ever felt hopeless?"

"Only once."

He smiled sadly. "But life continued, right? You had other people to love."

"I've got you. That's all I need."

"Don't make this harder than it already is," said my brother.

I should have paid closer attention. "Make what harder?"

He ran, the tablet tucked into his jacket. He climbed over the pitted scales of the dragon, dashed through the forest of spines and jagged ridges. Up and up he ran, toward the vast, all-consuming mouth of Tiamat.

I'd been so stupid! Why was Mo so determined to be a shaheed? Some guys just have to be heroes, even if it kills them—*especially* if it kills them! Why? Don't they want to be around for the sequel?

"Come back, Mo!" I yelled as I climbed after him. The closer we got to the vortex of annihilation, the harder it got. Time and space were being devoured, and that has a tendency to make things weird. Countless dimensions were collapsing in on themselves, not just in our universe, but in the others, too. Tiamat was hungry for it *all*.

Mo reached the cavernous opening. He stood there,

gazing hypnotically into the abyss. The winds roared as the landscape was sucked in—cities, mountains, seas, and more. He looked back at me. There was a trace of a smile—*I'm your older brother. I'll take care of it. Everything is going to be okay.*

I wasn't going to reach him in time.

He held the tablet against his chest and closed his eyes. His lips moved over the Shahaadah. And then he jumped into the void.

I froze. For a moment, it felt just like last time, that moment of dizzying bewilderment when it felt as if there was no gravity and I was free-falling down into a pit of despair.

But that moment passed and something new, something raging, filled the hole. I wasn't going to let it be like last time.

I shook the tears away. "It's not over yet. I'm not losing him again."

Kasusu hummed gently. "He's already gone."

I continued to climb, hand over hand, my eyes blurred with tears, toward the dragon's maw.

"Er...what do you think you're doing?" the sword asked.

I reached Tiamat's jaws. Lava still gushed between her mountainous fangs. Ahead was a swirling vortex, a whirlpool that led to an infinity of nothingness. "This time I'm getting him back."

"You are not going to—"

"I absolutely am." I tightened my hold on Kasusu and leaped in after my brother.

FORTY-ONE

I TUMBLED THROUGH THE INFINITE VOID. I HAD NO IDEA of how long or how far. Time and space had either not started yet or had come to an end. There were galaxies in here, all jammed together, vibrating with unmeasurable energies, trying to explode apart and fill an empty black universe.

But there were also...us. All of us. Living our daily lives—grabbing a cup of coffee on the way to work, rushing out the door to make a class, being with the people who mattered most. It all seemed so insignificant compared to the forces that commanded the cosmos, yet it was all that mattered. Out of that vastness around me I was determined to find just one person, and I was determined never *ever* to lose him again.

Life may push you hard in one direction, but that doesn't mean you can't push back.

He'd been there my whole life. Not just as my hero,

Gilgamesh to my Enkidu, but the guy I'd aspired to be and envied because it felt like Mo was always leading—trailblazing—with me scurrying behind, shouting for him to wait. I wasn't going to let him leave me behind, not this time. I'd been told that love was one of the two things that defied time and space. I was counting on it.

"Sik! What are you doing here?"

Here? It took me a moment to realize I'd stopped falling. I had arrived . . . somewhere. A place made of shards. Fractured pieces of time and space had been jammed together haphazardly, and they ground and groaned as they kept shifting in a vain attempt to fit. And through the cracks? Who knew what lurked there?

I rushed over to Mo and grabbed him. "You're okay?"

"You shouldn't have come, Sik. I really wish you hadn't."

"You can't ditch your younger brother that easily."

"The stubbornness of siblings. Where would we be without it?" Mo replied, grinning. "So, what's your cunning plan?"

"We're in the belly of the dragon goddess. You can't plan for situations like this. We're writing the manual from scratch. Which reminds me—you still got the tablet?"

He pulled it from his jacket. "Look. The letters are fading. That's bad, isn't it?"

"No idea. We're well past anything making sense." I gave Kasusu a shake. "Heads up. We have work to do."

Tiamat's brood came slithering toward us through the cracks in the universe, twisted nightmares the dragon goddess had made real. Hybrid monstrosities that were part serpent, part spider. Others with leathery wings and claws, some humanoid with dozens of arms and heads growing from their bellies, their jaws open wide and dripping with acidic juices. They were as tall as skyscrapers, as wide as the Hudson River, and they blazed with the fires of creation.

"You want to fight all of them? At the same time?" asked Kasusu. "Overcompensating much?"

I tightened my grip with my one good hand. "I thought you were the greatest weapon in the world. How many heroes have wielded you?"

"All the ones who count."

"Any of them back down from a fight? No matter the odds?"

"Fighting against insurmountable odds is what I do best," snarled the sword. "Start with the giant spider."

"What about me?" said Mo. "Let me help."

I wanted to protect him, make him leave the rough stuff to me, but hey, he'd always been Gilgamesh in our games. I couldn't prevent him from being a hero this one last time. "You'll need a weapon, Mo."

"But I gave the halberd to—"

"Hold on." I cut the first two legs from the spider so

it smacked down on its face. Then I sliced off its head. The remaining six legs thrashed madly, sending its body spinning into the other monsters before it realized it was dead and stopped. I wedged my foot into its mouth and extracted a two-foot-long fang. "How 'bout this?"

Mo picked up the venom-soaked tooth. "Perfect."

Side by side, like Gilgamesh and Enkidu, as in the old days. Still clutching the tablet in one hand, Mo raised the fang as the horde surrounded us. "Allahu Akbar!"

I held Kasusu high. "Allahu Akbar!"

And then we charged.

God surge flowed through Kasusu, feeding me with preternatural strength and speed. With every slice, every stab, monsters fell like scythed hay. I parried the stingers of colossal scorpion-folk and snipped off their pincers with a flick of my wrist. But still more spewed from the writhing belly of Tiamat. Serpents bit me with their venomed fangs, lion-men slashed me with their claws, and grotesque vultures with the wingspan of a jumbo jet tore at me with their beaks and talons. Yet the same creator goddess who was giving them strength was also multiplying my own.

Even so, I knew Mo and I couldn't last much longer. Darkness surrounded us as the cracks in the space became wider and wider.

"The letters!" yelled Mo. "They're fading away!"

We were running out of time. The tablet would soon

return to its original form—mud dragged from the primordial sea.

No fate at all...

I rammed Kasusu through the heart of a twelve-headed snake. It thrashed and spat fiery venom as it died, its tail shuddering in its death throes. "Mo! The tablet can save us!"

"What? How?"

I waded through the gore of dismembered monsters and looked at the tablet. The words had all but disappeared. "It's a clean slate. If we stay in here, it'll melt away, but if we take it out, it will set solid."

"But there'll be nothing on it."

"Yeah, and that's how it should be. With no one's future decided and laid out before them. It will be up to us to make our own destinies, not have one dictated to us by a lump of clay."

"But how exactly are we going to do this? We can't just crawl back out the way we came."

"Leave that to me," said Kasusu. "Marduk didn't take me with him that first time, when he slew Tiamat. He had plenty of other god-weapons in his armory. I've always regretted not being there for the Big One. Not going to let another opportunity pass me by. Take the tablet, boy."

I did, shoving it into my shirt. "Yes, sir."

The blade shimmered. "And cut like you mean it."

⚔ ⚔ ⚔ ⚔ ⚔

"Yes, sir!"

"Louder, boy! I can't hear you! Louder!"

"YES, SIR!"

The first slash allowed in a thin streak of light. The second created a tear, inches wide, that wind howled through. I spun around with Kasusu, ripping a pattern of illuminating cuts, slicing the darkness apart, piece by piece.

Tiamat's brood screamed and fought each other to escape. The darkness that had given birth to them was disappearing, leaving them nowhere to hide. A tremor shook through the chaos dragon. She couldn't escape because I was inside her, so she tore herself open to try to reach me, too filled with rage and pain to realize she was destroying her own body.

Tiamat dragged herself through a crack, clad in her mythic form: winged, ivory-clawed, and iron-scaled. Still titanic, eyes blazing with primordial fury, terrible to behold.

Kasusu screamed with bloodthirsty joy. The blade itself blazed with devastating brightness. I continued to cut, each slice leaving a dazzling wound across Tiamat, tearing her open and letting in more and more light. . . .

Tiamat thrashed, trying to escape the net of light that was surrounding her and slicing her to ribbons. Each bisected piece would writhe in blind rage before dissolving away. Soon enough the cavern at the heart of it all was littered with pulsating maggot-like fragments of the dragon goddess. Mo finished them off with furious stabs of his venomed fang.

Finally, I knew it would only take one more blow. A single piece of slithering darkness was all that remained of Tiamat. I flicked the serpentine shadow with Kasusu, and it curled in on itself, hissing and spitting with hate. It was so full of fury that it attacked the only thing in striking distance—its tail. It bit, and the more pain it felt, the more it attacked, tearing and ripping itself apart until it dissolved in the light.

One great brightness lay ahead of me—but what was it? The end? Or the beginning?

Mo stood beside me, shading his eyes from the light. Then he took my hand, tightening his grip, filling me with his strength. "It'll be okay, Sik."

Whatever lay ahead, we'd face it together.

As brothers should.

FORTY-TWO

SUNLIGHT SLIPPED THROUGH MY FINGERTIPS. WARM summer air blew against my cheeks. The river gently rippled along its bank at low tide.

The floodwaters had receded, but London lay in ruins. The Tower was now just rubble. Buildings had collapsed, and chunks of the Embankment had washed away. The Thames was choked with floating debris, ranging from trees to cars to houses to half-submerged sections of castle wall. Tiamat was no more, but she'd left her stamp all over the city.

I looked up and down the riverbank. It seemed I was the only person here. There was no traffic noise to be heard, not a person to be seen. Was I the sole survivor?

Not quite.

A raven perched on a tree trunk that was half-buried in mud. Wings rustled overhead as more ravens swooped down from the clear sky and settled on the stripped branches. Six in total, watching me watch them.

They were back, the guardians of the kingdom.

I flexed my left arm. The wound had vanished, not even leaving a mark. Was I immortal again? Was I back to being the deli-cook version of me?

Yes and no. Some memories of my upbringing as Ishtar's child must have lingered because, as I looked at the world around me, returned to normal, all I could think of was a Latin phrase: Audentes fortuna iuvat.

Fortune favors the bold.

I glanced down at what was left of the tablet in my hand. The clay was more of a shard than a rectangle and all but blank. It wouldn't be long before it hardened, so I needed to act quickly.

I snapped a twig off a fallen branch. The ravens watched, bobbing their heads as if they knew what I was planning and approved.

Using the end of the twig, I wrote a single sentence on the tablet. It didn't take long, but I'd barely managed to finish the last cuneiform symbol before the tablet solidified. That was it—no more changes, ever.

But would it be enough?

There was no answer. Only silence, broken by the occasional flapping of wings.

The tablet hadn't worked. I'd lost everything. I tightened

my grip on the useless lump of clay. Time to hurl it into the Thames and let it sink into the mud. I'd throw it as far as I—

"Help!"

I turned at the sound of splashing. Someone was struggling in the river.

"I'm coming!" I yelled as I waded toward the thrashing swimmer.

I got waist-deep before his head rose again, spitting river water. "Don't just stand there gawking! Give me a hand, Yakhi!"

What else could I do? He was my brother.

FORTY-THREE

"HABIBI? COME HERE AND GIVE ME A HUG!"

Mama didn't wait for me to react before wrapping me in her arms. There's nothing better than a big squeeze from your mom after you've been away.

She smelled of detergent, fried onions, and ripe lemons. She smelled of hand cream and a dash of rose-scented perfume.

The Essence of Mama. Nothing else in the world makes you feel like you're home.

Home. Yeah. I was back, standing on the corner of Fifteenth and Siegel with the morning sun reflecting off the deli's big windows and my backpack dangling from one shoulder.

Mama directed my attention to the wall. "We put up some of the photos you sent us. Next time, we'll come with you. Inshallah."

There were so many photos they were beginning to overlap. I spotted the one with Rabisu wearing the queen mother's crown. That had gotten almost a million likes on her Instagram account. Then there was an old one of Mo and Daoud gardening together. But my gaze stopped at the one of our family sitting around the table the night Mo left, along with...

Lugal.

The big man was in the center, surrounded by the rest of us as we'd pressed together to fit into the shot. His smile was stiff, but he looked...content.

Baba came out from the kitchen, wiping his hands and grinning. "You should have called. We would have picked you up at the airport."

"We thought it best that this happen here," I said.

"We? Rabisu? Or have you brought Daoud back with you?" Baba grinned wider. "Or that friend of yours, Belet?"

"She's a nice girl," said Mama. "A little intense, but that's modern girls for you."

"Not Daoud, and Rabisu sends her love. She went off with Lady Gaga. I think Berlin is her next stop."

My friends and I had spent the last few days in London resting up and saying our good-byes. Daoud had wanted to come home with me, but he'd gotten a callback on the spy gig. Apparently, it was down to him and one other actor. I can't tell you which role it was for—the producers want to keep it top secret until they announce it officially—but I can tell you that Daoud spent two days at Savile Row getting measured for a tuxedo and posing with a Walther PPK.

But that didn't mean I'd traveled home alone.

He'd gotten out of the cab a few blocks back, wanting to feel home through his soles. He wasn't far behind.

Should I have warned my parents? Called ahead of time to prepare them? The two of us had talked about it right up to the moment we landed.

"What's wrong, son? You look distracted," said Baba.

"It's been a long trip."

"Did you bring us anything?" he asked.

"He's back home, safe and sound," said Mama. "What else matters?"

I raised my hand. "As a matter of fact, I did bring a gift."

The bell over the door rang as it opened, and he came home after three years, and a lifetime.

"Assalamu alaikum," said Mo.

My parents just stood there, stunned. Baba had his mouth wide open, and I swear I could hear their heartbeats pounding so hard they threatened to burst. I saw sadness literally rise off them. I hadn't realized how heavily it had weighed them down, how it had aged them. It was a magical transformation.

We live in a world where amazement is the exception. No one wants to stand, mouth agape, and marvel at something—it might make us seem naive or uncool. We know so much that everything feels second nature. We don't stop and gaze in awe at the ocean because we've already seen the bluest of waves on National Geographic.

Genuine wonder is truly rare.

I saw it in how Mama's eyes grew wider and wider. I saw it in how Baba was halfway between reaching out and not believing, as if Mo might be a mirage that would disappear if he touched him. I saw it in how Baba's lips trembled when he asked, "Mohammed?"

Mo nodded. "It's me, Baba."

And that was all that mattered.

I left them hugging, crying, and laughing together. They still couldn't really believe it, but they'd get over that soon enough. I flipped the sign on the door to CLOSED and stepped out onto the street. They needed their privacy. There was too much emotion pouring out. Today was going to be tears and cheers and time spent hearing Mo's laughter echo around the deli once again.

Let Mama and Baba have Mo to themselves for a while. He'd always be there when I needed him. One has to share, after all. Share those people who make the world a brighter place, who tell you, *Hey, it's going to be okay.*

If you have one person like that in your life, then you're doing better than most.

But if you have two?

Belet waited across the street, watching from one of the outside tables of Mr. Georgiou's pizzeria. She finished off her Frappuccino just as I sat down next to her. "Now, that's a happy ending."

"The story's not over yet," I said.

She arched her elegant eyebrow. The old Belet was back, for good. "You getting a taste for heroics, are you?"

"Me? I'm just the sidekick, remember? There for the comic relief."

She peered across at the deli. "How did you manage it?"

I know what you're thinking. Why hadn't the two of us talked about this before? Maybe because, until this very moment, neither of us had dared to believe everything was truly *fixed*.

I reached into my pocket and pulled out a piece of clay. The cuneiform on it was barely visible. "Here. Read it."

Belet held it out in the sunlight. She decoded my scribbled markings, then looked up at me. "'My brother lives,'" she said, handing it back.

Then Belet did something so un-Belet-like, I thought destiny hadn't returned to normal after all. She put her hand in mine. "I'm sorry I wasn't there for you when it mattered most. When Lugal..."

"I know what Lugal did. But despite everything, you

stood up to him, and you were on the right side for the final fight. *That's* when it mattered most. I knew you would come around."

"Ah, am I that predictable?" she asked, smirking. "So much for me being all dark and mysterious."

"So, what's next?" I was acutely aware she was still holding my hand. Mr. Georgiou winked at me as he passed by to collect her empty cup.

"You owe me a dance, remember?" She stood up and pulled me out of my chair.

I looked around at the tables cluttering the sidewalk. "Sorry, would love to, but er, there's no room."

She pointed across the street. "Plenty of space over there."

"In front of the deli?" Now I was horrified, but it was too late. Belet dragged me over there. Why wasn't there a demonic invasion happening right now? I'd rather fight Tiamat all over again.

But Belet wasn't going to make it that easy. "You promised, Sik."

"But I don't know how. That Sik's gone. This is the delicook version, and he doesn't know—"

"Everyone knows how to dance. Just don't overthink it."

"Me?" I said with exaggerated innocence. "Overthinking's never been my problem."

Belet laughed, took me in her arms, and we danced. We danced on the sidewalk in front of the deli.

Mo's Deli.

ᴬ⟨ ⭍⟨ ⚏𝇅⟩ ⊣⊬⟨

ACKNOWLEDGMENTS

There wasn't supposed to be a sequel to *City of the Plague God*. It was a classic "one and done." So what you're holding in your hands isn't because of me—it's because of you! To all the readers, teachers, librarians, booksellers, parents, and other people who picked up a book about a boy who battled an unstoppable disease and somehow stopped it, thank you. Many of you asked me what happened next, and now you know.

And to readers who picked up this book first, a mighty huzzah and welcome to the world of Sikander Aziz!

After this? All I know is that it's up to you, again. Spread the word, chums.

No one spreads the word quite like Rick Riordan. I've already mentioned many times how grateful I am that he has supported me from the start, and how his enthusiasm for world mythology never flags—quite the opposite; it only gets stronger. I'll never get tired of thanking Rick. I hope he doesn't get too embarrassed by it!

Next to Rick stands the mighty Stephanie Lurie. I'm honored to have had her eagle-eyed criticism and generosity influence so many of my books and take them to another level entirely. Editors never get enough thanks.

Steph is the matriarch of the mighty team at Rick Riordan Presents. So many amazing people. Special mention to Dina Sherman in marketing, the best of the best with a fine taste in eighties music. She was there when I launched my first book and embarked on my career in the wide and confusing (and thrilling) world of publishing. Glad she's still around to point me in the right direction.

It all began with my literary agent, Sarah Davies, who is less a matriarch and more a fairy godmother. She has sprinkled her magic dust over all my work and transformed a humble engineer into if not quite a prince, certainly a squire of publishing! All you need is one person to believe in you, and the rest will follow.

Speaking of faith, I'd like to thank fellow Muslim writers Saadia Faruqi and Moe Shalabi for their support and advice on my own perception of Islam. There are several billion of us, and Islam is more varied than most suspect or have been led to believe. Sik has many questions about his faith, as do I. Perhaps not quite the same as his . . .

Mesopotamian mythology rocks! It rocks harder when

you have help from the likes of Digital Hammurabi, namely Megan Lewis and Dr. Joshua Brown. Once again they supplied the cuneiform clue* in the book.

Fury of the Dragon Goddess was inspired by Stephanie Dalley's *Myths from Mesopotamia*. I am grateful she gave me permission to use a quote from it for the opening of my own version of the Enuma Elish. The foundations of both *City of the Plague God* and *Fury of the Dragon Goddess* were built upon her work. Any errors and misinterpretations are entirely my own.

Not quite finally, I must thank the staff of Central North West London Mental Health Trust. I have been involved with the trust for many years and felt the issue of mental health worth exploring, much like the subject of disease in *City of the Plague God*. Sadly, Bedlam did exist, and among many people, attitudes about mental health are still based on an unfortunate, outdated stigma. I hope, in my small, clumsy way, I showed that Lugal was to be pitied, and victory did not come from strength of arms, but from understanding. We celebrate the warriors but rarely the caregivers.

I am very, very fortunate to have the best of caregivers. My wife and daughters have been there for me from the very beginning of this adventure, showing love and

---

*My brother lives.

patience through all the dramas of working in this most mercurial of professions. That I'm still writing, a dozen years and books later, is all due to them. I love them, admire them, and try to live up to the example they set for me, day after day.

What's next? I really don't know what destiny has in store for me. I hope our paths will cross, somehow, somewhere, someday, so we can talk about all the good things. Till then,

Peace be upon you.

Sarwat

GLOSSARY

I THOUGHT A GLOSSARY MIGHT BE HELPFUL, GIVEN THAT this story includes a wide variety of terms that may be unfamiliar, some taken from languages that haven't been spoken for thousands of years. Each term is either Arabic (A), Islamic (I), or Mesopotamian (M). While all Islamic terms are Arabic, not all Arabic terms are Islamic. I hope that's clear!

Abubu	M	Supernatural weapon
Alhamdulillah	I	God be praised
Allah	A	Arabic word for God
Allahu Akbar	I	God is greater
Apkallu	M	One of the legendary sages who brought civilization to humanity
Assalamu alaikum	I	A greeting. *Peace be upon you.*
Baba	A	Father

Basmu	M	Gigantic serpent said to be sixty leagues long. Offspring of Tiamat.
Bismillah	I	In the name of God, often used before taking action, commonly said before mealtimes
Djinn	I	Supernatural spirits. Commonly referred to as genies. Some are righteous, many are tricksters.
Du'a	I	A prayer
Halal	I	Permitted
Haram	I	Forbidden
Inshallah	I	God willing
Jahannam	I	Hell
Jihad	I	A righteous struggle
Kasusu	M	Supernatural weapon
Kismet	A	Fate
Kurnugi	M	The netherworld, ruled by Erishkigal and Nergal
Kusarikku	M	Bull-man. Similar to the Minotaur. Offspring of Tiamat.
La	A	No
Lamassu	M	Winged bull or lion. Guardians against evil.
Mabrook	A	Congratulations
Mama	A	Mother
Mashallah	I	God has willed it. Often used as "well done."

Masjid	I	Islamic place of worship. Also called a mosque.
Shaytan	I	A devil
Shaheed	I	A martyr
Shukran	A	Thanks
Ya Allah!	A	Oh God!
Ya salam!	A	Wow!
Yakhi	A	My brother
Yallah	A	Hurry up, get a move on

Other Rick Riordan Presents Books You May Enjoy

Aru Shah and the End of Time by Roshani Chokshi

The Spirit Glass by Roshani Chokshi

The Storm Runner by J. C. Cervantes

Dragon Pearl by Yoon Ha Lee

Sal and Gabi Break the Universe by Carlos Hernandez

Tristan Strong Punches a Hole in the Sky by Kwame Mbalia

Race to the Sun by Rebecca Roanhorse

The Last Fallen Star by Graci Kim

Paola Santiago and the River of Tears by Tehlor Kay Mejia

Pahua and the Soul Stealer by Lori M. Lee

Outlaw Saints: Ballad & Dagger by Daniel José Older

Serwa Boateng's Guide to Vampire Hunting by Roseanne A. Brown

Winston Chu vs. the Whimsies by Stacey Lee